THE DRESS

A Jennings Township Romance

ER Cullen

ISBN-13: 9798393569310

Cover design by: Art Painter
Library of Congress Control Number: 2018675309
Printed in the United States of America

CONTENTS

To Martin for your unerring love and support, for the inspiration behind this book, and for actually reading your first and only romance novel. You have my heart. Always

For all those whose love of everything wedding gowns knows no bounds—this book is for you. May your days be filled with lace, tulle, and satin.

CHAPTER ONE

Charlotte

"Please don't tell me you bought another one."

Charlotte winced. This wasn't exactly the welcome she'd hoped for as she opened the house door. Although, given what she was carrying, she couldn't fault her roommate for protesting. Lisa may have known what she was getting into when she agreed to rent the house together, but knowing an issue and living with it are two different animals.

"I wish I was the sort of person who snuck new purchases into the house," Charlotte muttered, closing the door before turning to face her roommate. "Hi Lisa," she said, injecting as much cheerfulness into her voice as possible. Maybe she could distract her with an enthusiastic welcome. Logically, knowing her friend wouldn't be angry didn't stop the all-too-familiar anxiety from squeezing Charlotte's chest.

Lisa cocked an eyebrow, the picture of skepticism. Her short-cropped hair framed her face and hazel eyes perfectly. Those same eyes stared at Charlotte pointedly. Lisa had a knack for getting to the heart of a matter—no drama, just honesty. It was one of the things Charlotte always admired about her friend... until she was on the other side of that look. Thankfully, Lisa wasn't much taller than her own 5' 4" height. She couldn't imagine if Lisa was six feet tall and had that stare. It would be a lethal combination.

"I thought you were going out for happy hour with some coworkers."

Leaning on the kitchen doorway, Lisa crossed her arms. "I still am, actually. Not many people wanted to go, so Rachel and

I decided to have drinks here." She moved off the wall and took a few steps toward Charlotte. "I was in the kitchen making another pitcher of sangria when I caught you pulling that out of the backseat of your car. Another one, Lottie? Really?"

It was a positive sign Lisa used her nickname. If she was truly upset, she would have called her "Charlotte" using her signature tone. It was a shame Charlotte couldn't replicate that tone. It would be damn handy at work. Why was it certain people had a tone or look that immediately put people on notice? Did they teach a class somewhere on how to do that?

In case she was reading Lisa's mood incorrectly, she said, "Don't be mad. I know my workroom is a little full, but I promise I'm working on whittling down the collection. I just couldn't pass this one up. But I swear, no more buying—at least not until I find homes for some of the current inventory."

Shaking her head and laughing, Lisa turned back to the kitchen. "I'm not mad. I'm just yanking your chain. Sort of. Do you want to join us and have some sangria?" she called over her shoulder.

The tightness in Charlotte's chest fell away as Lisa's acceptance washed over her. "I'd love to. Let me put this upstairs, and I'll be right down." Charlotte dropped her purse on the small table near the door and deposited her keys in the bowl. She navigated the stairs as best she could, but the large plastic bag in her arms made it difficult to maneuver. Reaching the first landing, she readjusted to get a better grip. Tripping now would put a serious damper on her excitement about her latest rescue.

Moving up the final stairs, she heard the familiar creak of the fifth step. The sound had driven her nuts when they'd first moved in, but over time, she'd come to depend on it. It was another sure sign of how much she loved this house. It still surprised her she'd ended up back in her hometown five years ago. Funny how life sometimes took unusual turns that ended up being the right ones.

Now that she'd lived in Jennings Township for a few years, the happy memories were the strongest. When they first moved in, she couldn't help but dwell on some of the more painful shadows of her past. Mostly her father, as he'd had passed away while she was in high school. Although thoughts of him still came with a pang of sadness and loss, as time passed, she could move past the gripping pain. It was surprising, the little things around town that would remind her of how much she missed him. She could still hear his large, lively laugh, and would give anything to feel one of his all-encompassing bear hugs that solved even the worst problems.

A few years after her father's death, her mother had decided she was done with Connecticut winters and moved to South Carolina. Truthfully, it mattered little if her mother was near or far—their relationship had been strained for years.

Careful not to trip over the bag, she walked up the last of the steps, managing to climb the rest without tripping. Both she and Lisa worked in downtown Hartford, but when they decided to rent a house, they agreed they wanted to live in a town that afforded them some space and provided a short commute to the city. As it turned out, Jennings was in a perfect location. Situated near the center of the state, it was a respectable size town —population around 35,000, and it had everything they were looking for.

Having lived together during college, the two girls knew they were compatible roommates and great friends to boot. They just needed the right house. For Lisa, she wanted space to cook and to have a few gardens. Charlotte wanted something homey with character.

Little wonder the house search seemed to take forever. Although, in the end, it felt surprisingly easy. After touring several houses, Charlotte knew this was the one as soon as she had walked in. It was a quirky cape style home not too far from the center of town. A nice, fenced backyard provided Lisa with a superb back deck and room to garden. Charlotte could picture herself sipping a coffee and reading out there. But its crowning glory was a dormer which made the three upstairs bedrooms huge, more than enough space for everything Charlotte could imagine.

Moving down the hall, she opened the door to her room. The afternoon sun bounced off the pale-yellow walls, making them seem to glow in the fading light. Dropping the bag on the unmade bed, she continued into her closet.

In general, she considered her room fairly neat, although her mother wouldn't agree with that statement. Charlotte called it "casual clean," and it worked for her. The bookcases along the side wall were loosely categorized. She tried to lump all her fabric and sewing books together to make research easier. Even her nightstand had a stack of books on it; while some were for pleasure reading, most were books on sewing techniques. In the far corner of the room, a dress mannequin was draped with various fabrics and lace materials.

In the closet, she retrieved a wrapped white package, tearing through the plastic, as she walked back toward the bed. Shaking out the white storage bag, she laid it down before removing the store plastic bag from her purchase. Grasping it with both hands, Charlotte held up her latest find. Or as she liked to call it, rescue.

A wistful sigh escaped her as she took it in. The wedding dress had a high-neck lace bodice that tapered into a brilliantly beaded waist. Running her fingers over the delicate lace pattern, her heart hurt for the beauty of the craftsmanship.

The skirt was soft petal layers of chiffon that moved gracefully as Charlotte shifted the dress to admire it from different angles. It reminded her of a dress her cousin Alex had tried on a few months ago. Shopping with Alex for a wedding gown had been like a trip to the candy store for Charlotte. She'd soaked in every moment, looking and dissecting the latest designs and talking fabrics and lace with the bridal consultants.

Inspecting the dress, she could see a few tears in the full lace sleeves and some stains dotting the skirt. Overall, it wasn't in terrible shape, but from any viewpoint, it was about fifteen years out-of-date, something you might wear as a Halloween costume.

To Charlotte, it was full of possibilities that filled her with excitement. Her head overflowed with design thoughts about how she would transform it. First thing would be to remove the high neckline. Small straps to hold the long lace sleeves would look attractive. If the stains on the skirt wouldn't come out, then she could remove those layers or perhaps hide them with lace overlays.

Grabbing a spare hanger, she hung the gown and placed it carefully in the garment bag, ensuring no fabric got caught in the zipper. Bag in hand, she left her room and followed the hallway toward the back of the house, entering her workshop. As always, walking into the space filled her with a sense of peace. There was so much beauty contained in this room it made her euphoric. This was truly her happy place.

When they'd moved into the house, she and Lisa had struck a deal. Lisa would have the master bedroom—complete with a master bath. Charlotte would take the smaller front room, but she could set up her workroom in the third bedroom. Thankfully, they didn't need a third roommate to make the rent. They were more than happy to pay extra to make that happen.

Tall, metal rolling racks were stationed throughout the room, all stuffed with the same white storage bag she carried with her now. Between the racks, dress mannequins stood guard, each displaying a different wedding gown. Along the front wall, a large desk and shelving units took up every spare inch. A sewing machine surrounded by various piles of fabric pieces dominated the desktop.

Her mother would certainly object to the room's neatness, or more precisely, the lack thereof. It was messy, even chaotic. For Charlotte, it was just an unfortunate part of the creative process. Boxes and bins lined the shelves, and fabric tumbled out of holders onto the floor. There never seemed to be enough time to organize.

At the heart of the room was a dress form with a grand white wedding gown on it—the present project. It had a solid square neckline with tiny cap sleeves, and the bodice was dotted with lace and other embellishments. The train was pooled close to the dress form so as not to be a tripping hazard, but it was clear that it, too, was decorated with lace.

Moving to one of the rolling racks, she shoved the other dress bags back with one hand and struggled to maneuver the new bag onto the bar. Perhaps Lisa had a point—it was getting tight in here. Even Charlotte had to admit her gown rescues had increased since she and Todd broke up. Her retail therapy was catching up with her.

The problem was what to do with a dress once she'd rescued it. Not all the gowns needed major overhauls. Some just needed a little love and the right person, someone who was willing to give it a second chance. Well, to be honest, she had put little work into finding those people. She didn't share her gowns with many. One day she'd have enough experience to sell her gowns, but for now, it was just a hobby.

Just thinking of her rescues like that made her cringe. Her mother's words echoed yet again. "Charlotte, you're talking about getting a degree in something that leaves you with few, if any, marketable skills. Do you know how many people make it in the fashion industry? Where they can support themselves and make decent money? It's one-in-a-million. Do you really think you can win against odds like that? There are thousands of talented kids slaving away, waiting for their big break. Do you think you're better than them? That somehow you have what it takes when they don't? These outfits you make for yourself are fine. But it's just a nice little hobby. That's all it is."

A nice little hobby. Those words had dogged her ever since. Her mother had meant well, simply wanting her daughter to have a career in something logical and practical, but her words haunted Charlotte long after the argument faded. In the end, Charlotte had relented and majored in graphic design, once a counselor had assured her mother of its viability as a career option.

Leaving the racks, she walked over to the dress on the center mannequin, running her hands gently over the lace bodice. She sighed as her fingertips danced across the intricate pattern of the lace, tracing the swirls and patterns of the thread.

Even knowing that a career in bridal design was out of her reach didn't stop Charlotte from dreaming. And it was a vision Charlotte obsessed over constantly, the yearning for it tugging at her even now. Her own shop where brides came to have a dress custom made—a Charlotte Original. Her one-of-a-kind vintage creations would be the centerpiece. She couldn't help but smile, picturing the space.

It wouldn't have to be big, just large enough for her gowns and a section to act as her workroom. It could be a cozy little slice of heaven decked out in lace and satin. She'd have a little seating area where she could sit with brides while they talked. Maybe a table off to the side where she could work on her design sketches. Something by a window so the natural light would filter through and dapple the area in light and shadows. Best of all would be the sign in the front window. Charlotte Baker, Wedding Gown Designs. She'd finally be a real wedding gown designer.

Dropping her hands down, she stepped back from the mannequin. Who was she kidding? She wasn't a trained professional. Maybe if she'd gotten her design degree, that little shop would already be a reality. With something as important as a wedding gown, she'd need experience and a professional pedigree to be taken seriously enough to sell.

With one last look at the dress, she moved toward the door. Perhaps she'd be able to spend some time in the workshop tomorrow. Professional or not, it's where she was happiest. And it'd been a few days since she'd been able to focus on her current project. The only thing on the weekend to-do list so far was to pick up a gown from the dry cleaners. There was nothing like seeing the dress cleaned and pressed. It was by far one of her favorite things to do.

The prospect of being elbow-deep in satin and lace for hours stretched a smile across her face as she went to join Lisa and Rachel on the deck. It was time for some sangria.

Stepping outside, she was reminded again that their instincts were right when she and Lisa first looked at the home; the deck was a major plus. It ran almost the entire length of the house with more than enough space for a grill and a large table and chairs. Lisa had even fit two lounge chairs in the far corner. It was a lovely place to read and an even better location for an afternoon nap.

Walking toward the table, Charlotte guessed that the lovely women with shoulder-length blonde hair must be Rachel, Lisa's co-worker. She looked to be in her early 30s, right around the same age as Lisa and herself. The other woman greeted Charlotte with an enormous smile.

"Lisa's told me so much about you, Charlotte. It's wonderful to meet you finally."

"It's very nice to meet you, too. Please, call me Lottie." Moving past Lisa, Charlotte sat down at the wooden table and poured herself a glass of sangria.

"Lottie is an unusual nickname," Rachel said.

Charlotte took a sip of sangria before answering. "I was named after my grandmother. Gram decided Charlotte was far too formal for the energetic toddler I was, so she started calling me Lottie. It stuck." Looking out over the small but well-maintained yard, Charlotte smiled. "She would have loved this yard. Just enough grass to have green in your eye and trees and flowers to dress up the pretty. That's how she described her yard to me."

"Where does your grandmother live?" Rachel asked.

A shaft of grief pulsed through her, making her chest tighten. She missed her grandmother every day, the pain of that loss left a large hole. Her grandmother had meant the world to her, and they'd shared a very close bond. "She passed a few years ago."

"I'm sorry. I didn't mean to bring up a sad subject."

"No, that's okay," Charlotte responded softly, smiling at Rachel. "I miss her. Reminiscing about her helps me remember all the good times we had together."

"Isn't she the one who started you on this wedding dress

obsession?" Lisa asked slyly. "I seem to remember a story about you playing dress up one day in one of her gowns. To hear your mother tell it, from that moment forward, it was all about the dress for you." Lisa shook her head again and laughed. Pouring them each some more sangria, she said, "You should tell Rachel the story."

Rachel looked between the two women, her eyes finally resting on Charlotte. "Dare I ask?"

Sighing, Charlotte laughed and rolled her eyes. "What can I say? I have an unusual pastime." Knowing she wouldn't be able to drop the subject now, she explained, "My passion—"

"Obsession," Lisa interjected.

"Shut it!" Charlotte swatted at Lisa. "My interest in wedding gowns did start with my grandmother. She had this amazing attic, and when I visited, I loved going up there. It had an infinite number of neat things, and I was never sure what I'd find. Gram had a story for everything. I'm not sure which was better—the objects or listening to the stories behind them.

"One day—I must have been around eight or so—Gram showed me a large trunk tucked into the attic eaves. I helped her pull it out into the center of the room. When she opened it, all I could see was cream-colored material, then she started peeling back the layers of protective fabric. It was her wedding gown. But it wasn't just her wedding gown. The trunk also held gowns from other women in our family. There must have been four or five in there.

"They were all wrinkled and creased, but that couldn't diminish how beautiful they were. Gram let me try on every one of them. As I swished back and forth across the attic floor and tried to twirl without killing myself, Gram told me the story of each dress." Taking another sip of sangria, Charlotte savored the memory of that afternoon. She could still smell the musty air of the attic along with the slight lavender scent from the fabric. Even now, she used lavender satchels in her own clothing drawers, the fragrance forever tied up with the warmth of her grandmother.

“What an excellent way to learn about all your different relatives,” Rachel said, leaning forward. “Like an oral history of your family tree.”

“Well, that was some of it,” Charlotte agreed. “The story of how each dress was created fascinated me most. That was the part Gram focused on. Each gown had its own journey, which reflected on the bride.” Seeing Rachel’s bewildered look, Charlotte put down her glass and leaned her arms on the table. “Take Gram’s dress, for example. She and her mother made it by hand. They spent nights working on it together at home. What was unusual was that, for the longest time, Gram’s own grandmother wasn’t there helping. Since my great-grandmother, Stella, was a fabulous seamstress, her absence was a big deal.

“As it turns out, there had been a disagreement, a fairly heated argument, about Gram’s fiancé, and it caused a rift between Gram’s parents and grandparents. I guess the root of the issue was that Grampy was a tobacco farm worker. He moved around a lot from farm to farm. There was plenty of work, but Gram’s grandparents didn’t think he was good enough for her, that he wouldn’t be able to provide her with a suitable life. The argument affected the whole family, but Gram said the pain was worst on the nights they worked on the dress without Stella.

“Not only was Gram disappointed with Stella’s absence, but it was clear how upsetting it was for her mother. One day, Gram up and confronted her grandparents.” Charlotte smiled. “Gram was a spitfire even back then. She had a way of handling people that wasn’t confrontational or threatening, but still challenged what they were saying. It was like she had a spine of steel wrapped in cotton.”

“She sounds amazing,” Rachel interrupted.

“She really was,” Charlotte responded, reflecting on just how remarkable her grandmother had been. With a sigh, she continued, “She managed to convince her grandparents to at least have a family meeting and talk through things one more time. In the end, it worked. Gram said there was a good amount of pie eaten and bourbon drunk, but as a family, they talked things out.

"Gram could see that the argument was simply her grandparents being nervous for her. They loved her so much and didn't want to see her make a mistake by marrying someone not suited to her. When Gram's parents supported the match, it sparked an argument. From there, it had turned into hurt feelings and bruised egos, but they got past it."

"Pie and bourbon," Lisa said with a laugh. "If that doesn't fix everything in your life, I'm not sure what will."

"It sounds like the perfect prescription, doesn't it," Charlotte replied. "Gram said she learned a lot that night. It was the first time she felt like an adult. She also learned the value of family and of fighting for what you love. Once they'd cleared the air, Grammy Stella began coming over to help with the dress. Gram said those times with the three of them sewing and talking were some of her best memories. To make up for the rift and show her support of the marriage, Grammy Stella used lace from her own wedding dress to embellish Gram's gown."

"Turns out, Gram really did put her trust in the right guy. Grampy worked long days for years in the tobacco fields, and he eventually saved enough money to buy his own farm. Gram said she spent many wonderful years on that farm and couldn't imagine her life any other way."

"Oh, that is so lovely," Rachel sighed, hand clasped to her heart. "You're right. That's an amazing story."

Charlotte nodded. She wished she had an ounce of her grandmother's spirit. She envied her the ability to stand up for what she believed in. "Gram was an amazing lady. As we pulled out the other dresses from that trunk, she told me the story about each one and the bride who wore it. I was hooked. From that moment on, I've been fascinated with wedding gowns. These days, when I'm wandering through antique or thrift stores, I can't help but gravitate to any wedding gown for sale. I imagine the story behind the gown and get wrapped up in its history. Now I ask you—how could I possibly walk away from that dress and abandon it? They look so lonely in the store. Forgotten even. So, I buy them."

"You don't want the dresses' story to end there," Rachel said with a smile.

"Exactly," she replied, pausing. Normally she didn't discuss her passion for gowns in this much detail, but something about Rachel made her feel like sharing. "It's hard to see such exquisite workmanship and history tossed away. It's also about capturing the magic of a wedding and passing that along to another bride."

Rachel raised her eyebrows in question, so Charlotte continued. "I like to think that the well wishes, prayers, and love that surround the gown during a wedding leave an imprint on the fabric. Much like Grammy Stella stitching in goodwill on my grandmother's gown, the emotional energy lives on long past the wedding day. Rescuing dresses means I can capture that upswell of love and bring that to a new bride."

"Oh, Charlotte," Rachel murmured. "That's the most beautiful thing I've ever heard."

"Thank you," she replied, feeling her face flush. It was both embarrassing and heartwarming to hear the other woman's praise. "Well, now you know why I end up buying all the damaged, stained, and forgotten gowns."

"Then you fix them up," Lisa chimed in. "You should see some of her finished gowns, Rachel. They're beautiful. She manages to update them with a modern look while retaining their vintage uniqueness."

Lisa's praise warmed her. It was marvelous to hear, and she appreciated her friend's support. "As Lisa can attest," she added with a nod and a laugh. "It's something that takes up space. I've had to establish some rules to limit the number of gowns that come home with me. Nothing too modern, or nothing in too decent a shape that someone couldn't buy and wear tomorrow."

"Also, no gown that costs more than $25, right?" Lisa offered.

"Exactly. I can't be spending all my money on wedding gowns. I get the bottom of the barrel dresses. Really, I rescue them. They're old. Many of them have stains or tears. People can't see that, with work, they could be breathtaking."

Charlotte took a drink. That was always the hardest part for her. How people couldn't see past the flaws. Dresses made with such obvious skill and talent tossed aside broke her heart. It made her question why she was interested in designing wedding gowns in the first place. Maybe her mother was right. She didn't stand a chance of making it if talented designers ended up on clearance racks at thrift stores.

Mentally giving herself a shake, Charlotte retreated to her mantra. Just because something wasn't perfect didn't mean it wasn't worth time and effort; everything deserved a second chance.

Rachel leaned forward, clearly fascinated. "What do you do with the gowns you've updated? Where do you sell them?"

Lisa threw her head back and laughed. "Therein lies the problem. She doesn't sell them. Hence, her workroom is overflowing with gowns."

"They're not good enough to sell," Charlotte replied, scowling at Lisa.

"You're wrong," Lisa shot back.

"I'm not sure I understand," Rachel interjected.

Charlotte exhaled. "Designing gowns is not a simple sewing project. It requires a lot of specialized skills and knowledge. If I had experience, or official training, or even a degree in clothing design, that would be different. Selling wedding gown designs is best left to the professionals."

"See what I'm up against, Rachel," Lisa said, waving a hand toward Charlotte. "She doesn't realize her skill level and designs are first-class. Degree or training be damned," Lisa speared Charlotte with a hard look before allowing the corners of her mouth to turn upward. "Well, I haven't been successful in convincing her of that yet, but I'm sure I'll succeed soon. I have gown volume on my side," she laughed.

Standing up from the table, Charlotte grabbed the near-empty pitcher of sangria. "I'm ignoring her for now, Rachel. She's a broken record. Please tell me you'll stay for dinner. There's plenty of food, and, on such a beautiful night, we'll eat out here."

"I'd love to. And maybe I could look at your gowns after dinner?" she asked tentatively. "I'd love to see them."

Charlotte forced a smile, her stomach doing a slow flip. Sharing her designs with close friends made her tense. The idea of showing them to strangers made her nauseous. "Ummm. Sure, I guess. But don't let me bore you to tears with all of my wedding gown chatter. I'll grab some more sangria and get started on dinner. If you're still interested after we eat, I can show you my rescue collection."

Charlotte pushed down the familiar twinge of panic as she walked back into the house. While she brushed aside Lisa's comments, her friend wasn't wrong. She didn't think her work was of a high enough quality, and the thought of letting someone see it made her mouth go dry and her heart race.

Maybe Lisa was right. It was time to get past her fear. But making herself vulnerable like that was something she studiously avoided at all costs. What if people didn't like her work? Could she handle that sort of rejection again? As long as she avoided rejection, the dream could stay alive. But then it would only ever be that—a dream.

CHAPTER TWO

Charlotte

Leaning back from the sewing machine, Charlotte stretched her back to work out a cramp. Attaching that final bit of lace was tricky, but she was pleased to see the finished result looked lovely. Charlotte glanced at her watch. Already three o'clock. This day was flying by; granted she'd gotten a late start.

After a splendid dinner the previous night, the girls had stayed up late talking. Thankfully, Rachel hadn't brought up looking at the gowns again, so Charlotte had been able to relax and enjoy the evening. It had been such a pleasant time and was so worth her oversleeping today. To Lisa, sleeping in on the weekend was a requirement. Normally Charlotte wasn't one to jump out of bed super early on the weekend either, but she'd wanted to make some good progress on her current project.

She was happy with how it was coming along now. Although given the time, she needed to call it a day. She still had to swing by the cleaners and pick up the new gown.

Charlotte powered down the sewing machine and put things away, mentally noting the next steps for the project. Dashing down the stairs and into the kitchen, she was shocked to see Lisa kneeling on the counter, neck deep in a tall cabinet.

"Lisa?" Charlotte raised an eyebrow at the chaos. Every counter in the kitchen was covered with jars, cans, and packages of food. "Dare I ask what you're doing, other than making a big mess?"

Lisa craned her head out of the cabinet, smiling slightly. "I know it looks bad, but it's for a good cause. I was in the mood to grill out tonight and wanted to make something different. It dominoed from there."

"Is that what happened in here? Dominoes?" Charlotte laughed.

"I was looking in the cabinets to see if we had anything interesting, and I found an expired can of beans. That made me look at all the cans, and then I thought we should have all this better organized." Looking at the surrounding counters, Lisa shrugged. "And that's how we ended up here. It looks worse than it really is." Lisa stuck her head back inside the cabinet, yelling out, "I'll have it all back to normal—but better—in an hour."

"I have complete faith in you. While you're doing that, I'm going to go pick up that gown from the dry cleaners. Do you need me to pick up anything while I'm out? Or did you find what you're looking for somewhere in this jumble?"

"Oh." Lisa's head shot back out from the cabinet. "What I truly want is something chocolate and scrumptious for dessert. I have dinner covered, but all this work has me craving something decadent. Can you stop at the bakery while you're out?"

Charlotte's mouth started watering on principle alone. Pie in the Sky Bakery had the best desserts, and Lisa was right; tonight would be fantastic for something decadent and delicious. "Consider it done," she called as she grabbed her bag. "I might chat a bit with Mrs. Mac, but I shouldn't be too long." Lisa's reply was muffled, but Charlotte was fairly positive she'd said, "Okay."

Stepping outside, Charlotte took a deep breath, letting the fragrant air fill her lungs. There was nothing better than the smell of spring. It was a combination of flowers, grass, and soil that promised sunnier days ahead. When she got back, maybe she'd grab a book, her favorite Duplin wine, and read out on the back deck in the late afternoon sun. She'd still have time to help with the meal.

Thankfully, Lisa handled most of the cooking and grocery shopping. That left dishes and clean-up for Charlotte to do, which suited them both perfectly. Charlotte wasn't the best cook in the world, while Lisa loved creating new recipes. The closest

Charlotte came to the kitchen was to create the few go-to baking recipes or simple dinners she excelled at, but that was about it.

Driving into town, even though it wasn't the most efficient route, she left MacDonald's Dry Cleaners at the end of the errand list. It would be nice to spend a few minutes with Mrs. Mac, the owner. Besides, she wanted to secure an amazing dessert before they were all gone.

Although she'd grown up in Jennings, Charlotte had only started going to MacDonald's Cleaners when she'd moved back. As it turned out, it was one of her better decisions. She'd taken a few dresses in to be cleaned before Mrs. MacDonald asked about the gowns. When Charlotte explained what she was doing, Mrs. Mac was kind enough to give her a discounted rate, saying that if she was going to be doing a lot of cleaning, she deserved a volume discount. She also thought Mrs. Mac approved of what she was doing. As time passed, they became close. Charlotte considered her a good friend and loved to stop in for a chat, even when she didn't have a wedding gown in tow.

It only took a few minutes to enter the downtown area of Jennings. It was understandably busy on a Saturday afternoon. Luckily, someone pulled out from a spot not too far from the bakery, and it was a quick walk to the store. Walking in the doors of Pie in the Sky made her mouth start to water again. Everything smelled incredible and looked so appetizing. From personal experience, she knew it would all taste delicious. She could see the owner, Marilyn Spadoni, or Mrs. S as she liked being called, working in the back room, pulling yet another tray of pies from the oven. People came from the surrounding towns to have Pie in the Sky pies. During the holidays, the lines stretched out the door. Charlotte particularly loved her blueberry pie, but today just didn't feel like a pie day. As Lisa had said, something chocolate and decadent was in order.

Looking through the cases as she waited her turn to order, Charlotte heard her name called from the kitchen. Glancing up, she saw Mrs. S wave her back. Walking into the kitchen, she gave her a quick hug. "Hi Mrs. S. Those pies smell delectable! Then again, what in here doesn't?"

The older lady's face broke out in a wide smile. "Well, I try. It's nice to see you. You haven't been in for a while. Everything okay?"

Charlotte couldn't help but smile. Moving back to Jennings had been eye opening. Growing up, she'd never felt like she fit anywhere, so when the Jennings community embraced her completely, it was surprising. The belonging she missed as a child was here in spades. It just took the adult her to realize it. "Everything's been good Mrs. S, just busy. Lisa decided today was the day for something special, so here I am. How are you doing?"

"I'm delightful, dear." Mrs. S. patted Charlotte's arm. "I just finished a new batch of macarons that I know you'll love. I've been tweaking the pistachio recipe, so you'll have to tell me what you think." Of course, Mrs. S. knew Charlotte's weakness for macarons. She'd been feeding her sweet treats for years.

In the end, Charlotte compromised. A few macarons because she liked those almost as much as her pie; a small chocolate peanut butter cake covered in a rich ganache for tonight; and a last-minute addition, a fresh blueberry pie. It would have been downright criminal not to buy it. She could split it with Lisa. Well, at least one piece of it. A sizeable piece… maybe.

Giving Mrs. S. another hug, Charlotte gathered her packages, dodging around people as she navigated to her car. She hoped the dry cleaners wasn't as busy.

Making her way back to the east side of town, she pulled into the cleaner's parking lot and was happy to see there weren't a lot of cars. Swinging open the door, the bell rang over her head and Charlotte was engulfed in the smell of the dry cleaning. Years ago, the shop had switched to greener cleaning products, but even those had a distinct citrus smell. Given how often she was here, the smell was becoming a happy association.

One thing Charlotte appreciated about Mrs. Mac was how she approached each dress and discussed thoroughly what process would work best. What stains Charlotte couldn't remove herself, she turned over to Mrs. Mac and her team.

Other than the one customer in front of her, the shop was empty. To the side of the counter was a small table and chairs where she and Mrs. Mac would sit and visit. Normally, it held a plateful of cookies or other small pastries for customers. Mrs. Mac said it worked magic on kids bored with their parents' endless errands. They could look forward to something when they arrived at the cleaners.

As the customer in front of her completed their transaction, Charlotte went to approach the counter and instead took a step back. Mrs. Mac was nowhere in sight. In her place stood one of the most handsome men Charlotte had ever seen. He was tall, around six feet or so. He had dark wavy hair, almost black, and he had the most unbelievably vivid green eyes that seemed to go right through her. Especially now when they were staring at her.

Snap out of it, say something. "Um, hi." Great opening, Charlotte. Very sharp. Very witty.

"Hi. Can I help you with something?" Mr. Tall, Dark, and Handsome said.

She felt the rush of heat flame her cheeks. It was a curse that her fair complexion telegraphed any major emotion. Embarrassment, anger, frustration—they all marched across her face as a living billboard to her emotional state. Deep breaths. Just be cool. The blushing will subside.

"Yes... please." She took a breath, hoping it didn't sound like a gasp. "Sorry. I was actually expecting Mrs. Mac."

"Do you have an appointment?"

"No, I don't. I just thought she'd be here. I came to pick up something, and we usually have a bit of a visit if it's not busy. Is she okay?" She couldn't remember the last time she'd stopped into the store and not seen Mrs. Mac working behind the counter. Logically Charlotte knew the older woman couldn't possibly work every shift; it was just jarring not to see her there. Especially when instead of Mrs. Mac there was a guy whose hotness level was off the charts.

"Oh, she's fine. My dad had a few appointments she wanted to go to. I told them I would watch the store. I'm Adam, by the way."

Leaning over the counter, he stretched out his hand. "It's nice to meet you."

Reaching out, his strong fingers engulfed Charlotte's hand, and she felt it all the way down to her toes. It was like a small electrical spark that danced over her nerves, radiating out from where he touched her. The shock of it rocked her back on her heels slightly, and she took an involuntary breath. The feeling left her unsettled and bewildered.

Since her breakup with Todd a year ago, she hadn't found herself attracted to anyone, and she definitely had never had that type of reaction before. Although given Adam's looks and his piercing gaze, she wasn't surprised. She wasn't dead. A gorgeous man could make even the sanest person a little breathless.

Was she imagining it or was he prolonging this handshake? Could he be as affected as she was? The thought almost made her snort with laughter, which, thankfully, she didn't. That was just what this experience didn't need. She was distracted again as he drew his hand away. Small calluses on his palm brushed across her fingertips. She wanted to know how he earned those calluses, and more importantly how they would feel as they caressed her skin.

Adam paused, looking at her with interest. As the moment stretched on, he raised his eyebrows and gave her an expectant look.

"Oh," she said with a little smile. "Sorry. I'm Lottie."

"Lottie?"

"My friends and family call me Lottie. It's a nickname my Gram gave me when I was a little kid. It was her nickname, and I'm named for her, so she called me that, and now everyone does." Charlotte couldn't stop the nervous laugh from escaping, but she managed to snap her mouth shut after. You're babbling. Stop it. Stop it. Stop it. At his confused expression, she finally said, "I'm Charlotte."

He smiled. "Charlotte it is then."

Not many people called her by her full name. Just her mom,

in fact. The way her mother said it always made her tense. But when Adam said her name, it made her think of long afternoons cuddled in front of a fire.

It's official. She'd lost her ever-loving mind.

Trying to find even ground again, she latched on to the first topic she thought of. This guy was messing with her head. "So, you're Mrs. Mac's son?"

"Yes, I am."

"Oh, that's great." Charlotte vaguely remembered Mrs. Mac mentioning a son once or twice, but for the life of her she couldn't remember a thing about him. "I didn't realize you worked here."

She must be completely slaying him with her amazing repartee.

"Well, I haven't been working here long. I just returned to the area. I'm usually in the back."

Oh no. Here we go.

Here was the bad side of Mr. Wonderful. Did he live in his parents' basement and have abandonment syndrome? Was he working on finding himself? Adam was simply far too good looking not to be harboring some deep, dark issues. Wasn't that always the way it panned out? The more lovely the outside the more messed up the inside. Todd had taught her that much.

"So, what brings you here? Jennings, I mean, not the front counter."

"I worked at a consulting firm in Phoenix, but the company failed to land a few key projects. It's a new firm, so without those contracts, they had to let a few people go. It seemed like a best time to visit with my folks, so, here I am."

"I'm sorry to hear that," Charlotte said shifting uneasily. So potentially not a deadbeat. Actually, she felt bad for him. Getting let go from a job was never easy. "What kind of consulting do you do?"

"I'm a Senior Data Analyst. It means I look at all sorts of information and help companies or organizations make better decisions on what products to create, how to market to their customers, and things like that."

Now she was fascinated. He was drop dead lovely to look at and intelligent. "I had no idea you could get so much information just from data."

Adam laughed and a shiver run down Charlotte's back. The slightly husky tone paired with the richness made her want to hear that laugh every day, all day. A picture of him cooking in her kitchen chuckling at something she'd said flashed through her mind. Even better, Mr. Tall, Dark and Handsome laughing as they both reclined in her bed.

Her body flushed in response, and she licked her lips.

Adam smirked. "You sound like most of our clients. It's startling what you can learn. I enjoy helping companies work more efficiently. An acquaintance of mine started the consulting firm a few years ago. It's been a great place to work.

"Anyway," he said, bringing them back to the matter at hand. "As I said, my mother and father are out, but I'm sure I can help you with what you need. Do you have your claim ticket?"

Again, Charlotte found herself flustered. Mrs. Mac knew her. She never needed a claim ticket. "I don't have one."

"That's okay. I can look up the number. What's your last name?" He moved over to the computer terminal. When she didn't immediately respond, he glanced up.

How was it that this simple errand was proving to be this difficult for her? "My name won't work," she replied. Seeing his eyebrows raise, she tried to clarify. "My name isn't in the system. I mean it is. I'm a customer, so I'm sure it's there. There just isn't a ticket." Her explanation wasn't going very well. One last try. "It's not that I forgot the ticket. I mean that would be understandable. People do that all the time."

Focus! Focus, Charlotte. "It's that I... um... I don't have one. I mean your mom doesn't give me them. Because I don't need them. She knows it's me. Well, of course she knows it's me; I'm standing here." Surely there was a hole somewhere in the universe that could swallow her up right about now. If there was any justice in the world, that's what would happen. She paused hoping for that justice to appear, but when it didn't, she took a deep breath and tried again. "What I mean is, when I drop things off, there's no need for a ticket."

Adam couldn't have understood her explanation, but he seemed to roll with it. "Okay... that might make it a little hard for me to track down your item. But I'll give it my best shot. What are you picking up?"

"A wedding dress," she replied. It popped right out of her mouth and hung in the air between them.

Adam's smile faltered. "I guess congratulations are in order." His tone was lacking some of its previous warmth. "Were we cleaning it for the big day or preserving it for you?"

"Oh, there's no need for congratulations." Charlotte was so focused on trying not to blush or do anything dumb that she missed the bewildered look on his face.

"No?" Adam asked tentatively. His glance darted to Charlotte's hand and presumably bare ring finger. After a moment's pause, he said, "Oh, so you're picking up for a friend?"

"No, it's mine."

Adam's mouth was open as if he was going to say something, head tilted as if trying to decipher her words and translate them into something logical.

"I'm sorry, I'm not explaining myself very well." Another deep breath, again hoping it didn't sound like a gasp. "I rescue wedding gowns and fix them up. Your mom cleans them for me. She works with me on any stains to see if we can remove them." Charlotte stopped and looked at him expectantly, relieved that she'd finally managed to explain herself.

If anything, Adam looked more confused. "You rescue dresses? Are they being held for ransom?"

Charlotte's face broke into a bright smile, and she laughed. It was not a polite little twitter some people have but a full, delightfully rambunctious laugh that her mother was forever shushing her over. Luckily, Adam didn't seem put off, rather his face broke out into a wide grin, as well.

"No. No." Charlotte responded shaking her head. He was really funny. She'd have to tell Lisa that one. "I shop at a lot of thrift stores, vintage markets, and antique malls, and I seem to have this knack for finding old wedding gowns. They look so sad, I just have to buy them. With work, I'm sure they'll find a bride and get their second chance. That way their story continues."

Adam nodded but appeared unconvinced. "I think I understand the rescue part now, but I fear you've lost me again with the story part."

She hesitated. She was going to sound crazy, but as Gram liked to say, "in for a penny, in for a pound." This guy probably already thought she was a few donuts short of a dozen, might as well tell him the whole thing. Maybe not the whole thing—enough to explain but not enough that her crazy showed... any more than it already had.

"When I find a gown, I can't help thinking about the story surrounding it. Who wore it? What was the wedding like? What was the marriage like? How did it end up in that particular store? How many brides have gotten married in it? For me, each dress has its own story. It kills me to see them wasted in a store. People can't look beyond age or damage to see it could be beautiful again."

"And that's where you come in," Adam said, catching on to what she was saying. "You find these gowns—sorry." He grinned, charming Charlotte yet again. "You 'rescue' these gowns. Clean them up with the help of my mom. Then you reconstruct them into new dresses that people love."

"Yes. For the most part. I reconstruct and change the dresses to modernize them. So far, the 'people loving them' part is not a reality." The bell over the door rang, interrupting them. Glancing back, Charlotte saw a customer was approaching with an arm full of clothing, so she turned back and said quickly, "The dress I'm picking up wasn't preserved, just cleaned. It's a floor length, ivory lace sheath dress with spaghetti straps."

Adam glanced at the incoming customer, a flicker of annoyance crossing his face. Was he annoyed that their conversation was interrupted? Probably not, but it was wonderful to think so.

He turned and walked into the back of the store. He must have been able to spot the dress easily, as he was only gone for a moment. Bringing it back out front, he quickly rang up the sale and turned to Charlotte for payment.

Would the embarrassing parts of this errand never end? "Um, actually Adam, your mom has a special discount rate that she charges me. Because I bring in so many," she added hastily. Charlotte hated to say anything, but her gown budget was tight. She needed to watch every expenditure to make the numbers work.

"That makes sense." He paused and then continued. "I don't know what rate she charges you. I also don't know the pricing code she enters for that sale in our computer system. Why don't you take the gown and stop back in to settle the bill?"

"Are you sure? I feel bad walking out without paying."

"I'm absolutely sure," he responded with a big smile. "It's no problem. It will actually help me out, so I don't mess up the system by entering the wrong code."

His smile flustered her again, but, hearing the other customer right behind her, Charlotte didn't question him further.

"Thank you, Adam. That's kind of you. Please let your mom know I'll stop back in to settle up." She turned to leave then glanced back. "It was nice to meet you."

His eyes lingered on hers. "It was very nice to meet you, too, Charlotte."

◆ ◆ ◆

Adam attempted to focus on his current customer. It certainly had been an unexpected pleasure meeting Charlotte. His gaze kept wandering out to the parking lot where she was carefully laying the dress out across the back seat. She obviously cared a great deal about it. He stifled the urge to laugh again. She rescued wedding gowns? Was that even a thing? Granted, he wasn't all that knowledgeable about wedding stuff.

Wishing his customer a good night, he glanced out to catch Lottie pulling out of the lot. Nope. Not Lottie. Charlotte. He liked that better. She looked more like a Charlotte. And she rescued dresses of all things. He knew working in his parents' store again would be interesting, but meeting a wedding gown rescuer was beyond anything he could have predicted.

Shaking his head, he turned and went to the kitchenette they had in the back. A cup of coffee and a pastry would hit the spot. He had dinner plans with his folks tonight but needed a little something to tide him over. When Adams Marketing Consultants had laid him off, he couldn't have imagined he'd be back in Jennings. At first, he couldn't imagine anything at all; it had blindsided him. After a talk with his boss and company owner, Matt, he knew they were hoping to get him working again as soon as possible. Good to know he was on the recall list, but did he want to go back? Should he look for another job? Maybe in another city?

In the past, Adam would have done just that—pick up, move, and start again in some place new. When his career needed a boost, it was nothing for him to move to another state. Since graduating college eleven years ago, his resume read like a cross-country map of America. His mother called it his nomadic lifestyle.

Adam reached into the cabinet for a clean mug as the coffee maker finished brewing at last. Those first years after graduation, his parents had questioned his career path numerous times. He'd spent a great deal of time making it clear to his parents that his life choices had nothing to do with Abigail. They weren't convinced. Pushing down the ache he felt whenever thoughts of Abigail surfaced, he poured himself a cup, grabbing some cream and sugar.

What his mom saw as nomadic, he saw as an adventure. He liked to change things up every couple of years. Eventually his mother stopped trying to discuss it and seemed to accept his refusal to stay in one place too long.

His coffee fixed, he opened the Pie in the Sky bakery box,

hoping there was still something left inside. His lucky day obviously; there was a large cinnamon roll left. Coffee and pastry in hand, he went out front to sit at table his mom kept there. He could have his coffee break and still watch for customers. The first bite was packed full of sugary cinnamon goodness. He should have heated it in the microwave but didn't feel like getting up to do it now. Hot or not, the roll was exactly what he needed.

Sipping his coffee, he looked back out at the empty parking lot, shaking his head. Never in a million years would he have pictured himself back here. When the layoff dumped him on his ass, he had to eventually admit perhaps unemployment had come at just the right time. He'd been feeling unsettled both personally and professionally for a while but figured it meant it was time to find the next adventure. The only problem was, the thought of starting over in a new city left him cold, and that scared him more than he wanted to admit. Taking a sip, he shifted in the seat trying to ease the tension in his chest. He'd thrived for years on relocating to whatever spot the job took him. He didn't know how to process what he was feeling now.

Not surprisingly, he'd jumped at the chance to escape the white walls of his condo and return home when he heard his dad wasn't feeling well. Within a few days, he was back home working in his parents' store. Perhaps he just needed a change of pace to get over whatever was going on with him.

Stepping back from his real life was a welcome change. He could finally take a deep breath and think big picture with no distractions. Unbidden, Charlotte's face flashed into his mind. He'd unquestionably found their conversation distracting, but he enjoyed every moment.

When she'd walked into the store and spoken with him, she was clearly flustered. Was she always that nervous? Nervous or not, she was very attractive. Her wavy brown hair floated around her face, little tendrils caressing her cheeks. Her pale blue eyes were striking, the color tending toward ice blue. Those eyes had a sparkle that intrigued him. And that blush. It made him feel things he didn't want to feel.

When he thought about their conversation, he realized he had shared a lot. Adam wasn't averse to chatting with customers. He enjoyed it, actually. But making small talk was one thing; discussing everything going on in his life right now was a different story all together. Something about her drew him in and made him keep talking. And that made her trouble.

Gripping the coffee mug, he reminded himself again that he wasn't here to get distracted by anything or anyone. He needed to remember that and not be thinking of how amazing the sound of her laugh made him feel. It had traveled up his spine and swirled inside his brain like a firestorm.

Trying to pull himself away from thoughts of Charlotte, he grabbed a pen and paper from the table and wrote himself a note. If he didn't write it down, he'd forget to ask his mother about the discount. Next time Charlotte came he wanted to be prepared. An unknowing smile curved the corners of his mouth. He'd have to ask his mom if conversations with her were always so confusing. Confusing but engaging, his mind offered, making him frown.

Glancing down at his watch, he realized more time had passed than he thought. Grabbing the dishes, he put them in the kitchenette and started walking through the store's closing procedures. He found the familiar routine calming as he moved about locking doors and closing out the register.

Working at the store had been a surprisingly positive experience so far. There was something comforting about being back in Jennings and working here again. He hadn't expected that. He had fully expected to be bored beyond belief. Thankfully, that hadn't happened. Even if it had, it wouldn't change anything. He was more than happy to pitch in and help while his dad dealt with his health issues.

Adam frowned thinking about the recent testing his dad had undergone. Growing up, he'd believed nothing could stop his bear of a father. His dad was a hard worker who had built this business out of nothing. Long hours and hard work never phased him. Returning home to see his dad tired and stressed had shaken him. They didn't have the best relationship, and Adam found it hard to put his concern into words.

Hopefully his parents would have good news tonight regarding his dad's doctor's appointment. If not, Adam promised himself he'd do whatever was necessary to get his dad back to his old self, before Adam moved on to his next location.

CHAPTER THREE

Charlotte

Charlotte checked the clock again, wincing when she saw how late it was. She needed to hustle if she was going to leave the office on time. She'd made plans to meet Lisa and Rachel at happy hour and didn't want to be late. Since the evening on the deck, the three women had gotten together a few times for dinner or drinks, each time better than the last thanks to Rachel's sense of humor. Her stories always had them laughing and tonight, Charlotte was looking forward to a relaxing evening. It had been a tough work week.

As a project coordinator at Cullinan Marketing, Charlotte had a lot of things she needed to monitor. Her job depended on the details, which was something she found equal parts rewarding and challenging. But if she rushed, inevitably, something would fall through the cracks.

How her career had unfolded still surprised her. Her first job after graduation was in a marketing department working as an office manager. From there, she'd continued on a project management track, working her way up at a few different companies. While she rarely used her degree in graphic design—a detail her mother noted often during their infrequent phone calls—she was a valuable sounding board for design decisions. That's why she'd jumped at the chance to work at Cullinan. She could still use some of her design knowledge while also continuing her love affair with details, as Lisa called it.

Her roommate was convinced Charlotte's love of details was a by-product of her bridal fashion obsession. She was probably right. An ideal dress was all about the details: the structure and construction, the lace and embroidery, the fabric and the tulle. When Charlotte daydreamed of a bride walking down the aisle draped in one of her creations, it was always the details that stood out. The lace she would choose to overlay the skirt. The tiny cap sleeves highlighted with embroidery and pearls. Each element was unique and important in its own way.

Checking the computer monitor again, she read the list of highlighted projects. Looking across her desk, she grabbed the corresponding project folders and made her rounds. The company was small and did external marketing for local companies. Although, over the past few years, they'd been able to land a few larger regional brands. It made for steadier income but an almost unbearable crush of additional work.

The office was set up in a horseshoe shape around the front reception area. Her boss, Karen, who owned the firm, didn't believe in the crappy open-concept cube-farm design. That meant everyone had their own office space. It was an aspect of the job that she loved.

Her office was on the far right-hand side, so she made a practice of walking the horseshoe to check in with the project managers and various designers. She could have done it with a few emails, but she liked to interact personally with everyone instead. Making eye contact tended to get her better answers. Besides, it was hard not to get a response when she was standing in the doorway. An added benefit was that she could catch up with everyone and see how they were doing.

Dropping off various folders, picking up whatever they had for her, she talked to nearly everyone on the team. As she approached her desk, she heard her phone ding with a message.

You're coming, right? No fires?

Leave it to Lisa to know her well enough to check for new fires. She quickly texted back.

No fires. Checking off last items, then leaving.

Before she could even put her phone down, Lisa texted back, *Hurry!!*

With a few more things done, she wished everyone a

good night and hustled out. Walking out of the building, she took a deep breath. What a great time of year. Everything was blossoming, and, while that created a nightmare for her allergies, it was breathtaking to smell flowers again after the winter they'd had. It gave her a little extra pep in her step. She didn't mind winter; it was when it ran long that she got cranky. One of the cool things about living in New England was the four distinct seasons. She loved them all, though she wished this time of year lasted a little longer before the summer heat descended.

Her company, located in downtown Hartford, was in what people referred to as the Gold Building. Not too original, as it was covered in gold glass, but it made it an easy landmark. Walking past the last corner of the building, the gold-glass facade was throwing off some serious rays in the late afternoon sun. Two quick blocks later, and she was at the bar. As she was about to enter, her phone pinged in rapid succession with messages from her cousin, Alex.

Where are u

Have news

Wedding 911!

Charlotte gave a little laugh. If she had a dollar for every wedding emergency Alex had, she'd be wallpapering her bathroom with the bills. The closer the wedding got, the more dramatic Alex got. Charlotte couldn't blame her though; her cousin's wedding was going to be a big event and had a lot of moving parts. Growing up, she and Alex hadn't been that close, but as adults they had reconnected, especially over the past few years. Charlotte was happy to have such a deep connection with Alex, drama and all.

While she'd love to hear the latest wedding nightmare, that was guaranteed to be a long conversation. Best to call her when she got home. Charlotte shot off a text.

At City Steam happy hour. Talk tonight. Be home by 8.

Turning the phone on vibrate, she tucked it into her bag, and entered the building. Even in the dim lighting, it was easy to spot Lisa and Rachel in the back. They'd commandeered a booth and had ordered the first round. Tugging on her sweater hem, Charlotte tried to adjust her outfit inconspicuously. Lisa and Rachel always looked so put together, especially decked out in their office wear. She should have checked how she looked before dashing over. Too late now. Running a quick hand through her hair to tame the wonky waves, she threaded her way through the tables and greeted her friends. Sliding into the booth across from them, she quickly ordered a hard cider from the passing waitress.

"Hi, Rachel! How have you been?" Charlotte asked.

"Busy but hanging in there." Rachel glanced over at Lisa. "We're almost past the crazy season. While I love the energy of all this work, I'll be relieved to see it slow down." Both Lisa and Rachel worked in a big accounting firm. Handling both corporate and individual accounts, the firm had a predictable cycle of business. They both seemed to enjoy it, although at the end of the busy season, Lisa always looked a little worse for wear. Charlotte was concerned her friend was going to burn out one of these days. That said, she seemed to thrive on the office energy.

Charlotte's drink came, and the women settled in to catch up on everything. Midway through their second round, Charlotte caught a flurry of movement out of the corner of her eye. Before she could turn her head to see what was going on, she heard someone yelling her name. Turning, she spotted Alex, heading their way fast, arms waving.

Charlotte couldn't believe her eyes. What was Alex doing here? Had she actually hunted her down at happy hour? This was crazy. Charlotte started to slide out of the booth and stand, but Alex got there first, looming over her. Sitting back down, Charlotte inspected her cousin's face. Alex's eyes were red, tears and mascara ran down both cheeks. Whatever it was, it was bad.

"Charlotte," Alex sobbed. "Charlotte. I'm sorry. You didn't answer your phone. And I've been calling and texting. I need to talk to you."

"Alex, I'm sorry. I didn't realize." Charlotte paused. She was having trouble processing her cousin's abrupt arrival. "Are you okay?" she asked. She tried to stand again, but Alex was standing too close. "What's going on? Is this about the wedding?"

Charlotte hadn't realized Rachel and Lisa had stood up from the booth. She saw Lisa take off towards the ladies' room, while Rachel approached Alex and laid a hand on her arm.

"Alex, is it?" she asked, waiting until she turned to look. "Hi. I'm Rachel. Why don't you take a seat right over here?" Rachel snaked her arm around Alex, directing her to sit in the booth across from Charlotte.

Once she was seated, Rachel put her arm around her and slid in next to her. "It's going to be fine, sweetheart. I promise. You just need to take a deep breath and pause for a moment." Rachel's voice was magic—soft and soothing, the epitome of calm. Rachel continued talking weaving a tapestry of calming presence. "Whatever it is, we'll figure it out. We're here for you and there is no problem too big we can't solve it together." Alex's breathing slowed, as did her tears.

Lisa returned with a stack of tissues and napkins, sliding in next to Charlotte. "I grabbed some tissues and also placed an order with our waitress. I don't know what Alex drinks, so I asked for a glass of wine. I also ordered some appetizers. I'm thinking we're going to need food for this."

"Thanks, Lisa. That was smart," Charlotte murmured her attention focus on Rachel's soothing nature with Alex.

"I'm just going to ask the waitress for a glass of water for you," Rachel said. She passed Alex the tissues before rising from the table. "Stay here and just breath. Take a moment to collect yourself, Alex. I'll be right back."

Watching Rachel make her way through the restaurant, she had to ask Lisa, "Does Rachel always know the right thing to say?"

"As far as I've seen," Lisa offered. "She's the go-to person in the office if you need to talk through an issue."

While Alex was still visibly upset, she no longer looked like she was on the verge of a breakdown. "She should have been a counselor," Charlotte said watching her cousin swipe tears from her face.

"I think she thought about it, but after..." Lisa paused. "Her sister got in a dangerous situation. Rachel blames herself for not catching the problem earlier and helping. I think that's what kept her from pursuing any sort of counseling training."

Charlotte didn't want to pry. Obviously, that was Rachel's story to tell. "Well, she's certainly helping here." Alex had stopped crying and when Rachel returned, her cousin took a few sips of water, looking better for it.

Now that her cousin was calm, Charlotte leaned forward, "Alex, honey. What's going on?"

Her cousin sniffed and wiped her eyes again, smearing a little more mascara across her cheek. "I was calling to confirm the fitting appointment for my dress." Alex's voice tightened. "I couldn't get a hold of anyone."

Rachel rubbed her hand on Alex's shoulder. "Deep breath. Breathe in and all the way out. No matter what, we'll get through this."

Offering a small smile, Alex continued, "I couldn't get a hold of the store, so I decided to just stop by today on my way home and…" Tears flowed down her face, but Charlotte could see her taking a deep breath like Rachel had suggested. "And the store is closed," she finished in a rush.

"Closed?" Charlotte asked. "As in for the evening? Or closed, closed?"

Alex's lip trembled as she confirmed, "Closed, closed. There was a sign on the door that said the store was out of business."

Silence hung over the table, the shock palpable. Their waitress arrived with their drinks, and Alex grasped her wine glass, taking a large sip. "I looked in the windows, and they'd cleared the whole place out. The note said they apologized for any hardship this created. A hardship? Can you believe that? I have eight weeks till my wedding, no gown, and they call it a hardship. It's a catastrophe is what it is!"

"There has to be some sort of recourse against the bridal

salon," Lisa offered.

"There may be," Alex said dejectedly. "But by the time I track down someone who can help, I'm going to run out of time." Alex swiped the tears off her cheek. When Rachel pressed a fresh tissue into her hand, she nodded her thanks and took a moment to dry her eyes again.

"When I saw the business had closed, I went online to see if I could find any other information. Their website just restated that they were closed, but I could find a few online reviews." She paused seeming to struggle with the next words. "I found reviews from other brides detailing all the things they've tried to find their gowns." A small sob escaped her. "People have tried contacting the owners but have heard nothing back. One woman said they had sold all the gowns in the store at auction. In one case, someone even called the gown designer to get her gown, only to discover her order had never been placed. I read through all of them. No one has been successful in locating or retrieving their dress." Alex took a long sip of wine and looked at Charlotte.

"My mom is pushing me to order this other dress I tried on while I was searching. But I don't love it. I mean it's fine, but it isn't special. I don't like how the neckline is cut, and it's just blah. It's not what I dreamed of walking down the aisle in. But the company says with a rush order it can get here in time."

Charlotte placed her hand on Alex's. "I'm so sorry. I can't imagine what you're going through. Rachel's right, though. We're going to get through this. We'll go out first thing tomorrow and scour the stores until we find you another dress."

"It's going to be hard to find a dress in such a short time frame. Most gowns take five to eight months to order, so my options are going to be severely limited. I'd have to buy something off-the-rack or a sample gown, which might work if we had lots of time to scour stores near and far. But given the lower selection of dresses available, sizing issues, the needed time for alterations, and how long it took me to find my first gown, it's just not realistic to think I'll be able to find something I love in time."

The waitress arrived with several plates of appetizers. It

looked like Lisa had ordered enough to feed a small army. At Charlotte's look, Lisa shrugged. "I wasn't sure what everyone wanted, so I ordered a bit of everything."

As Lisa handed out small plates, Rachel turned back to Alex. "I'm sure there's a dress out there for you. Something you can get in time but is also exactly what you want. You just have to do a little searching."

"Actually," Alex glanced at Charlotte. "That's why I'm here."

Charlotte did not like the way Alex was looking at her. "No. Absolutely not."

"Please, Lottie? Please?"

Rachel was looking between the two women, clearly not following the conversation, while a slow smile spread across Lisa's face.

"I think it's a fantastic idea," Lisa chimed in, earning herself a kick from Charlotte.

"Oh!" Rachel's eyes lit up with understanding. "That is a good idea!"

"Not you, too," Charlotte groaned. She could feel a band around her chest tighten every second this conversation continued.

Dropping her head into her hands, she searched for the words to make them all understand what a bad idea this was. "I want to help, Alex." She looked up to meet her cousin's hopeful eyes. "I really do. But I don't sew professionally. My gowns are something I do on the side. They're just..." She paused for a moment. She hated saying the word. It brought back too many bad associations. "It's a hobby."

While the thought of finally seeing a bride in one of her creations was a powerful draw, even stronger was imagining all the ways it could go wrong. Her stomach clenched as she envisioned her worst nightmares. A seam could split, the lace or embellishments could fall off. What if the zipper split right in the middle of the vows? What if the hem wasn't straight and everyone in church noticed?

And her mother. Her mother was going to be at this wedding.

She'd see every flaw. Charlotte's stomach did a slow flip, making her nauseous. No way in hell was Charlotte signing up for that. "There has to be another way, Alex," she pleaded, her shoulders slumping knowing how disappointed Alex was going to be with her refusal.

"There is another way." Alex shrugged one shoulder, her cheeks still wet with tears. "I could order that gown my mother wants and just be unhappy with my wedding dress."

Ouch. Charlotte flinched. She felt that in her soul. How could she sit through a wedding knowing how Alex felt about the gown?

"I know you want to help, Lottie. I mean—come on—I'm family after all."

Charlotte knew she was being manipulated. She knew it and yet, it worked. Alex was family, and you didn't turn your back on family.

"What if Alex just comes and looks at your gowns?" Rachel offered. "It's possible she won't find one she likes."

Charlotte scowled over at Rachel. Could she kick her underneath the table, or would she just whack the table leg? A glare would have to do. On the surface Rachel's suggestion sounded reasonable, but it still made Charlotte feel far too vulnerable.

"That would work," Lisa piled on, all too happy to push Charlotte into taking the next step. "Why don't you pop over tomorrow, Alex, and take a look?"

"Whoa. Whoa. Whoa," Charlotte tried to interject, waving her hand at the three of them. She had to pump the brakes here. This was flying out of control quickly.

Undaunted, the conversation continued around her.

"That would be great, Lisa!" Alex's face lit up with a smile.

"We could make it a thing," Lisa continued. "I'll put together a delicious lunch, and we can sit out on the deck if it's nice weather."

"Oh, I like this more and more," Alex laughed.

Charlotte liked this less and less. She tried again, "Guys, wait.

This isn't a good idea."

"You're against lunch?" Lisa asked, her eyes wide with innocence. "It's just four lovely women getting together to share a meal and then look at some wedding gowns."

"Four? Wait. Am I included in this?" Rachel asked.

"Oh, hell yeah, you are!" Charlotte's proclamation made everyone look at her. "This was your crazy idea," she continued, spearing Rachel with her gaze. "You aren't getting out of this now."

Her friends looked at one another and then turned to her with radiant smiles. Realizing what she'd said, Charlotte threw up her hands. "Fine. Lunch tomorrow, and we'll look at the gowns," she grumbled.

"Thank you, Lottie!" Alex beamed at her. "You're the best cousin ever!" Not waiting for a response, Alex turned to Rachel and the two women started discussing the wedding in earnest.

"It's going to be fine, Lottie," Lisa whispered.

Glancing over at her friend, Charlotte couldn't keep the worry from her voice. "What if she finds something she likes?"

"Then you sell your cousin a dress she'll be proud to wear on her wedding day. It's time, Lottie. I know you don't feel you have enough experience or that your designs are skillful enough, but they are. You've put the time into honing your craft. It's time to push yourself to take the next step."

"Does the next step have to be in front of my family? If she wears one of my gowns, my whole family will see it and judge it." Her voice waved. Swallowing hard, she tried to shake off the flood of emotion.

"I think you mean your mom will judge it." Without letting Charlotte respond, she pressed on. "Listen, you're getting ahead of yourself. It's a lunch and looking at some gowns. Focus on that. Besides," Lisa cast a glance over to where Alex and Rachel were chatting like long-lost friends. "Look at how happy you've made her. At the very least, we'll have a fun day she can remember about planning her wedding."

Charlotte's eyes lingered on Alex's face, seeing the happiness reflected there. Lisa was right about a few things, perhaps. At the very least, the four of them would have a yummy lunch and give Alex fun wedding memories.

"You're right." Charlotte sighed in resignation. "We'll do it, and I won't worry about what'll happen down the road." She forced a smile. "I'll focus on having a terrific day with friends."

She reached for her cider and took a large sip before muttering, "I won't worry about public humiliation and epic failure at all."

CHAPTER FOUR

Charlotte

"Lisa, Lottie, I can't thank you ladies enough for having me over. This lunch was just what I needed." Alex raised her wine glass saluting each of them. "For your gracious hospitality. Cheers."

They all joined in the toast, clinking glasses before taking a sip. When Rachel and Alex had arrived, it became apparent that last night wasn't a fluke. The two women got along famously. In fact, the four of them had a fun time. Charlotte was relieved they would be spared any awkward or stilted getting-to-know-you phase. Sitting through a meal like that would be torturous.

Even though there hadn't been a lot of time to prepare, Lisa had pulled together a mouthwatering chicken Caesar salad and with the weather so delightful, eating outside had been a simple decision. As they started filling their plates, Charlotte had to ask, "Alex, you said at happy hour that gown shopping wasn't a great experience. You never said anything before. I thought it went well the times I went with you. Why didn't you like shopping?" While she knew Alex had gone to many stores, she'd never indicated that the search had been difficult. If there was going to be a problem, Charlotte wanted to get ahead of it.

"Oh, Lottie." Alex shook her head in disgust. "What a mess. Eleven different stores. You know, I tried on everything from a ball gown to a mermaid. It was fun when you came with us, but after a while I was really worried I wouldn't find anything that I loved. But thankfully, that last store had a beautiful dress. It was a trumpet silhouette with a lace overlay. It would have looked pretty going down the aisle. Although I'm not sure if I was totally in love with it, or if it was just the first dress my mother and I agreed on."

Charlotte cringed. Aunt Jennifer could be stubborn and was very concerned with appearances. Charlotte's mom, Katherine, and her sister Jennifer were undoubtedly cut from the same cloth. Although, while Katherine could be critical at times, Aunt Jennifer seemed to have the sharper tongue. She didn't envy Alex that shopping experience. While she hadn't heard her aunt say anything outright when she'd been with them, that didn't mean she hadn't. Charlotte should have known finding the gown would be difficult.

"Alex..." Charlotte considered how to phrase what she wanted to say. "I don't want to be rude, but have you considered that part of the issue is Aunt Jennifer? I love her, but she has no filter. Whatever she thinks, she says. She's always been critical of your wardrobe, especially because your tastes are so different."

Alex put her wine glass back on the table and played with the stem of the glass. "You're right. I know that. I pretty much knew that the first dress in." She sighed. At the others' questioning looks, she laughed a bit and seemed to struggle with whether to share. She must have known she was in safe company because she continued, "Mom and I were in the first store, and we had picked a few dresses for me to try on. I was pleased we were finding ones that had potential. The first dress was a beautiful all-over lace gown with these darling little sleeves. I thought it looked elegant. Three steps out of the dressing room and my mother told me it looked like I had a two-by-four strapped to my chest."

The ladies shared a chorus of shocked and sympathetic responses. Charlotte's heart dropped. She'd had no idea. When she'd accompanied them there had been a little tension, but nothing like what Alex was describing.

Alex continued, "The next dress, according to my mom, made my boobs look like fried eggs. Every store and almost every dress I tried on there was something wrong with it. One made me look like a burlesque dancer shaking her hips. She didn't like the lace pattern on another. The next one made me look like I was stealing towels from a hotel. I'd nearly reached my limit when she said she didn't like where the shoulder ended on a particular dress. The problem with that was where the shoulder ended was where I ended."

Charlotte wasn't sure who laughed first, but someone did. That started them all laughing, Alex the hardest. Lisa even snorted. As the laughter subsided, Alex wiped her eyes. "I sorely needed that," she said.

"At some point, you have to throw your hands up and see the humor in it," Lisa said.

"Well, now that we know what not to say when we look at dresses. Why don't you tell us about your wedding and what you picture yourself wearing," Rachel asked.

Alex's face lit up. "It's going to be so incredible! I've got the entire color scheme planned out. Soft grays with touches of blush and light pink. The cake is going to be five tiered with chocolate and red velvet layers. Jason has a large family, so it's a good-sized wedding, about 250 people."

Charlotte's mouth went dry hearing the number. So many potential people to fail in front of. Half of them her own family. As her throat started to feel tight, she remembered a favorite mantra. Deep breath in. Slow breath out.

Alex chatted on, unaware of Charlotte's panic. "We tried to cut down the guest list but obviously had little success. Honestly, I don't care how many people we have there. It could be fourteen or four hundred. I'm just so excited to be marrying him."

Looking at the joy in her cousin's eye, Charlotte felt a momentary jolt of jealousy. She loved Alex and wished her every happiness, but she couldn't help thinking that if things had been different, this might be her wedding they were discussing.

"What's Jason like?" Rachel asked.

Alex's eyes took on a dreamy soft quality. "He's amazing. He makes me laugh. When we first met, I thought he was super serious and stiff. I didn't like him that much," she laughed. "We had dinner and afterwards were walking around the town. The more we talked, I saw he was so much more.

"He has a wicked sense of humor and the biggest heart. Seeing him with his family, all that love, and loyalty made me fall for him." Alex paused, caught up in her memories. "His family is Scottish and very proud of their heritage. We've incorporated some of those traditions into the wedding. I'll have a sprig of white heather in my bouquet, and I'll even have a sixpence in my shoe!"

"That's charming that you're including those," Lisa offered with a smile. "Although that sixpence thing just sounds uncomfortable."

Alex laughed. "Right? Let's hope it's not too bad. Jason's grandparents are coming from Scotland to attend, so it was important to me that our celebration honored their culture."

"That's lovely," Rachel said. "And I'm sure he's tall, dark, and handsome too!"

Charlotte didn't hear Alex joyfully describing Jason's curly brown hair and hazel eyes. The moment she heard Rachel's description thoughts of Adam flooded her brain. Her own Mr. Tall, Dark and Handsome. Except he wasn't hers, and she shouldn't be pondering that. Just thinking about him made the blood rush to her face. So caught up, she didn't realize she was gazing into the garden with a big smile on her face.

"Earth to Charlotte," Lisa called.

"Hmmm," she responded, reluctant to let go of the tantalizing image of Adam.

"Charlotte? Where did you go? It must have been someplace superb because you're blushing," Lisa continued to press her.

"What," Charlotte stammered. Damn her fair complexion. Looking around she knew she wasn't getting out of this without an explanation. "Sorry. Rachel's description made me remember something."

"My description?" Confusion colored Rachel's tone. "Oh, you mean tall, dark and handsome?"

"Yes," she replied. "Whoever thought of that description? Probably something straight out of a fairy tale, don't you think?"

She fervently hoped she could direct the conversation away from her and her run-in with her own Tall, Dark, and Handsome.

"Yeah," Rachel replied thoughtfully. "It sounds like something from a fairy tale. But it's an apt description. When you run into it, you know it!" Earning her a laugh from everyone.

"You said you were remembering something," Alex inquired.

"Remembering something that made her blush," Lisa interjected, her eyes narrowing as she scrutinized Charlotte's face.

Damn. They weren't going to let this go. She could see Lisa's assessing look. "It's nothing. I saw someone the other day that fit that description."

"Oh, do tell," Lisa said gleefully. "And don't for a minute think you can get away with not telling us everything. You're blushing, and I want to know why!"

Charlotte took a sip of wine, letting the sweet flavor linger on her tongue, as much to enjoy its taste as to give herself a moment. "I was at the dry cleaners the other day and there was a guy there. When I saw him… I called him Mr. Tall, Dark and Handsome in my mind. When Rachel said the same thing, it just made me think back to meeting him."

"You thought of him and blushed?" Lisa was relentless.

Charlotte threw up her hands. "Yes. I guess I did." She shook her head at Lisa's tenacity. Leave it to her best friend to grill her on something so insignificant. Although, it was hard to think of anything about Adam as insignificant. It may have been a brief interaction, but from his hot looks to his sense of humor, the meeting had left an impression. She felt the corners of her mouth twitch upwards. "But damn," she relented. "He really is tall, dark and handsome."

Alex clapped her hands. "This is so cool! Did you talk to him? Does he have a name? When are you seeing him again?"

This conversation would never end. Again, why couldn't the earth swallow her up? Because that would be very convenient right about now.

"It's not like that," she tried to explain, but three sets of unbelieving eyes stared back. They weren't going to make this easy. "Fine! His name is Adam. He's Mrs. Mac's son." Glancing at Rachel, Charlotte explained. "Mrs. Mac owns the dry cleaners. She's a great lady and a friend."

"Are you going to see him again?" Lisa asked.

"No. Yes. I don't know. Maybe?" Why was such a simple question so hard to answer?

Lisa searched Charlotte's face before asking, "But you want to see him again?"

If Charlotte were being honest, she'd known the answer to that from the moment she first saw Adam. She couldn't deny she was hoping for another opportunity to see him. "I'd really like to," she admitted.

Both Lisa and Alex couldn't hide their surprise. "Really?" Lisa asked gently. "I haven't heard you express interest in a guy since Todd." Glancing at Rachel, she explained, "Charlotte's ex-boyfriend."

Rachel looked at Charlotte, sympathy softening her face. "I'm sorry. Breakups can do a number on you. How long ago since you broke up?"

Charlotte cringed, her hands tightening into fists. It infuriated her that the mere mention of her ex made her relive all those feelings of embarrassment, anger, and hurt. "It's been a little over a year now." Not wanting to rehash the breakup yet again, she hurried to add, "Let's just say it ended badly."

"Now Mr. Tall, Dark, and Handsome has entered the picture," Lisa teased.

Charlotte felt her face flame again. Her friends laughed at her obvious discomfort. Joining in, she shook her head, "I'm not sure he's in the picture, but I can't deny there is something about him."

Before she could say more, Alex's phone rang. Making a face when she glanced at the screen, she said, "I'm sorry I have to get this. If I don't, she'll just keep calling." Alex moved off the deck onto the lawn.

Charlotte stood and cleared the plates, but stopped when

Alex's voice raised a few octaves. Snatches of the conversation were easily heard. "I understand, mother… No, I know. I've told you, I don't like that dress. Do not put the order in. I want to see what Charlotte has… They are not used gowns. Charlotte redesigns them. You don't know that!"

Charlotte's chest tightened. She didn't want to imagine the other side of the conversation. Just hearing one side was making her regret having lunch.

"Well I trust her!" Alex said, then ended her call abruptly. Turning she saw everyone watching. "Sorry, I didn't realize that was going to get loud." Walking up the steps to the deck, she approached Charlotte. "Lottie, I'm sorry. But you know what my mom's like; she doesn't trust anyone. She's just all stressed out about the wedding. Obviously, we both think you're very talented. She just has an attitude when it comes to buying vintage."

Charlotte appreciated Alex's attempt to smooth things over. Honestly, she needn't have worried. She was used to the criticism, although that didn't dull the pain she felt at her aunt's obvious judgement. If her own mother got wind of what was going on, Charlotte was positive their conversation would have been even worse.

"It's fine, Alex," she replied, keeping her voice steady to hide the hurt. Later she'd let herself feel the sharp pain her aunt's comments left behind. It annoyed her she could be so wounded by a stray comment. She should be used to this by now, having had years of her own mother's disapproval to toughen her up. "My own mother isn't my biggest fan either, why would her sister be any different?" Charlotte offered. "Although I had hoped Aunt Jennifer would be a bit more open."

Alex looked even more distressed and unshed tears pooled in her eyes. "I'm so sorry I pulled you into this and put you in such a bad position. I wish I was a better person who would say never mind, let's not do this, so you wouldn't have to be in the middle between my mother and me. But I'm not that person." A tear escaped Alex's eye, breaking Charlotte's heart into a million pieces.

"I'm desperate and selfish," Alex continued. "The gown my mother wants has to be ordered by Monday or the store can't guarantee it will be here on time. I know I can't have my original dress, but I just wanted something I could love." Alex dissolved into tears.

Rachel jumped up and placed her arm around Alex, guiding her back to her seat. "It's going to be fine. Really, it will. This is all going to work out." She glanced over at Charlotte. "First things first. Let's focus on seeing if Lottie has a dress for you. Until we know that, it's not worth getting upset over."

Charlotte and Lisa gathered up the dirty dishes and took them into the house. They could hear Rachel talking to Alex and by the time they came back out, Alex had stopped crying and looked calmer.

Lisa topped off everyone's drinks while Charlotte placed some cookies on the table. Charlotte wondered which was worse, the tightness in her chest or the lead balloon sitting in her stomach. But Rachel was right. Worrying about everything was useless.

Sitting back down at the table, Charlotte grabbed Alex's hand and squeezed. "Let's talk about fun things. What are you looking for in a gown?"

Alex gave Charlotte a weak smile. It wasn't the greatest, but it was an improvement over the tears. "As I said, it's a large wedding, so the event venue is pretty big. That's part of what makes picking a dress so challenging. I want a dress that will stand up to such a grand location. You know, something that makes a statement in a large room, but not too large that the dress overpowers."

Seeing Charlotte's nod, Alex continued, "As far as details, it doesn't have to have a ton of embellishment, but I would like some. I'm mostly drawn to ball gown designs. There's just something about them. Oh, and I know it's super impractical, but I love long trains."

Charlotte felt her heart leap and grinned. A girl after her own heart. To her, the train was the best part of the dress. "I have to agree with you. It's hard to resist a dress with a long train." She paused to take a sip of her wine. Courage. Have courage and dive in. "I know you know what I do, but I just want to make sure you understand. I work with the dresses I find. I don't have an enormous selection..."

"You sure about that?" Lisa interrupted, giving them all a much-needed laugh. It broke the tension, allowing them to relax.

Charlotte shot her a glare but continued. "I have a handful of dresses,"—she looked pointedly at Lisa— "that I've reworked. You know I'm not a professional seamstress." Charlotte looked Alex in the eye. "But my work is good. You won't have to worry about your dress falling to pieces when you're out there busting a move and dancing. I may not do this for a living, but I've sewed for years. You don't have to worry about the quality of my stitch work."

Charlotte felt strange, like her skin was too tight. It made her uncomfortable to say it, but she was proud she'd taken ownership of her skills. It also felt good to get the disclaimer out in the open. She wasn't a trained designer but looking objectively at her projects, she would concede that her work was solid. Not professional, but strong for someone who didn't have any formal training. That was the rub, wasn't it? She hadn't gone to school for this, and she certainly hadn't had any training. So much of it felt like flying by the seat of her pants.

Alex smiled at Charlotte's assurances about her dance moves. "I understand, Charlotte. I really do. Thank you again for letting me look. At the very least, this has been a terrific afternoon, and I think I have a better perspective on my dress search."

"Fantastic! Now that that's settled, let's go upstairs and start looking," Charlotte said as she stood. "Lisa, grab the bottle of wine, would you?" If the dress search didn't go well, the wine would be a necessity.

◆ ◆ ◆

As they entered the workroom, Charlotte heard Alex gasp behind her. Looking around, she could see where it might be a lot to take in. She couldn't remember the last time her cousin had been in the workroom, and her collection had grown a great deal this past year. Alex stood in the doorway for a moment before walking over to the mannequin in the center of the room, Charlotte's current project.

Running her fingers reverently over the gown, Alex said, "This is beautiful, Lottie."

"Thanks, Alex. I'm pretty happy with how it's coming out. If the dress were a little larger in the bust, I would say try it on. But I fear that's a narrow bodice."

"Isn't that something you can fix?" Rachel asked. She and Lisa had set themselves up on Charlotte's sewing table, complete with wine and the platter of cookies.

"Potentially," Charlotte responded slowly as she eyed the dress. "I'd have to dramatically restructure the bodice and all the lace appliqué work, and even then, I'm not sure I could make it work. Given the timeline we're working with, it's best to stick with gowns that have already been reworked."

Walking to the dress rack on the far-right wall, Charlotte started unzipping the white storage bags. "This side has all the complete dresses. Take a look. If anything strikes your fancy, let me know. You can try it on."

Alex started looking and almost immediately pulled out a gown. "This is gorgeous, Charlotte. Did you do all these embellishments on the top, or did you find it like that?"

Alex had pulled a square neck princess line dress with illusion long bell sleeves. The bodice was adorned with simple but elegant embroidery. "I wish," Charlotte answered. "The gown had that already in place when I found it. I can work with most everything on a dress, but I don't do embroidery. Why don't you go try it on?" Charlotte indicated a screen in the corner of the room. "Call me if you need help with the zipper."

When she returned, Charlotte couldn't contain her sigh. Alex looked exquisite. She went to stand in front of the full-length mirror propped against the wall. The fabric of the dress flowed delicately over her body as she moved and while the bodice was a bit loose, it wasn't anything they couldn't fix easily.

Walking up behind to make sure the zipper was closed, Charlotte laid a hand on her cousin's arm, "Alex, you look stunning."

"Thanks, Lottie. This dress is lovely. I love the way the fabric moves." Turning to Rachel and Lisa, she asked, "So? What do you think?"

"I love the design," Lisa said. "I agree, you look stunning. Although," Lisa paused for a moment, considering the gown. "I think it may be a bit bohemian-looking for you."

"Oh, I was thinking it had a renaissance flair," Rachel interrupted.

Alex laughed. "Either way, it's beautiful but not what I'm going for. Besides, the train is almost nonexistent."

"Well, we can't have that," Charlotte joked. "Let's keep going."

As Alex looked through the remaining gowns and tried on two more, Charlotte was pleasantly surprised. She'd been worried about how she would feel when her gowns were passed over, but she was fine when Alex wasn't drawn to any of them. A dress search really was exceptionally personal.

As they came to the last of the finished dresses, Charlotte was relieved, but also disappointed. It would have been a navigational landmine to traverse through all the pitfalls of Alex wearing one of her gowns. But she'd survived her first bridal appointment, and that was a win in her eyes.

"I'm sorry you found nothing, Alex," Charlotte said with a sigh. "Maybe you can go shopping at a few stores on Monday to see if you can find anything. I'd love to come with you and help."

"What about all these other dresses?" Rachel gestured to the other dress racks in the room.

"Those are gowns I haven't redesigned yet. There just wouldn't be time to reconstruct one and have it ready for the wedding."

Alex glanced around the room. "Could I try some on just for

fun?"

"Yes," Rachel exclaimed clapping her hands.

At the same time Lisa said, "Great idea!"

Charlotte wondered how much wine those two had consumed while she and Alex had been busy with the gowns. Although, she had to agree, just trying some of these on would be fun. Looking at Alex's hopefully expression sealed it. "Of course."

Alex jumped over to the racks opening bag and after bag. The first dress she tried on was a 1950s short dress with a full skirt. When Alex twirled out from behind the screen, they all laughed. As cute as it was, she looked like she was on her way to a very fancy sock-hop.

Next was a sophisticated slip dress that hugged Alex's curves a little too tightly. When she turned to show them the deep plunging back, they couldn't help but notice the rather obvious stain on the left cheek of the gown. The bride had obviously sat in something. Alex's sashay back behind the screen set them laughing again.

As Alex tried on a few more dresses, Charlotte thought through her inventory and when the answer came to her, she gasped. She hoped no one heard because the idea she had was a terrible one. If she'd known she'd compound this bad idea with another one later, she would have called a halt to their day right then.

"Aha!" Lisa exclaimed. "I know that look. You have one in mind, don't you?" Turning to Rachel, Lisa explained. "Besides rescuing dresses, I'm convinced she has a sixth sense about pairing up women and wedding gowns. We had a college friend get married a few years ago. A bunch of us were gown shopping with her. She must have had fifteen dresses on by then and rejected them all. Lottie walked into the store, pulled one gown and told the bride that was the one."

"It wasn't exactly like that," Charlotte interjected. She'd listened to all the things her friend wanted in a gown and paired that with her knowledge of dress fitting. Looking through the racks she hadn't been positive the dress would work, but she knew it would look nice and check off most of the bride's criteria. She'd gotten lucky. Okay, she'd gotten lucky a few times. Could she help it if she had a knack of knowing what would look good?

"It was just like that," Lisa continued. "The gown she picked didn't look fabulous on the hanger, so we were all surprised Lottie pulled it. When our friend tried it on, we knew the moment she stepped out of the dressing room. I don't know how Lottie knew it was the one, but she was right. I've watched her do it a few of times now; it's fascinating."

Looking back at Charlotte, she added, "Too bad you can't use that power for good, say for picking lottery numbers or something."

"Hilarious," Charlotte shot back. Looking at Alex, she said, "I do have a dress in mind. It might give you an idea of some elements to look for when you go shopping. Or perhaps you can have something added to the gown your mom wants. There's always a chance you can make a few minor changes to the dress your mom wants you to buy, and it could become the dress of your dreams.

"You're going to have to use your imagination with this one. I haven't had time to take a crack at removing the stains. Plus, the design is super dated. Try not to get hung up on all that."

Alex nodded. "I promise. I'll keep an open mind."

Charlotte turned and went into the walk-in closet. With so many gowns, this closet had been pressed into service months ago. Although Lisa might think the workshop was pure chaos, there was some order. For example, the gowns in the closet were ones she hadn't had time to clean or catalog the condition, but knew they needed a large amount of help. The closet dresses were the enormous projects.

"You have more in there?" she heard Lisa cry. "I guess I'm lucky you haven't taken over my closet!"

"Don't tempt me," she yelled back. Finding the gown she wanted, she pulled it out into the room. Unzipping the protective white bag, she lifted the dress out.

"Dear lord, that's hideous," Rachel blurted. "Sorry Lottie." She looked a little embarrassed by the outburst but kept the pained look on her face. Not a good sign.

Lisa looked the gown over for a bit and then chimed in, "I have to agree here, Lottie. Heinous-ahoy."

It was an eyeful, that's for sure. The dress was a full ball gown made from satin and embellished with lace. The sleeves had high-pouffed tops that seemed to strain to reach the sky. Charlotte thought they were called mutton sleeves, or more accurately, leg of mutton sleeves. Whatever Sunday dinner they were named after didn't matter; they visually dominated the top of the dress.

The gown had a square neckline, and the entire bodice had lace embellishments and crystals. Additional lace accents showed up on the full skirt, but it was hard to focus on those. What caught your eye immediately was the five dark brown stains that scarred the beautiful white fabric.

Turning it around, Charlotte made a point of shaking out the train. It was one of the reasons she bought the dress—stains and all. The train was long, cathedral length, and had delicate cut out lace appliqué accents. She grabbed the edge and fluffed the train out to its full length. She heard Alex sigh. Catching her cousin's eye, she asked, "What do you think?"

"It's exquisite, Lottie. That train is breathtaking."

Lisa leaned over to Rachel and whispered, "Did she say exquisite?"

"Pretty sure she did," Rachel whispered back.

Alex glanced at the two women. "It is! Look at all that lace work and the sparkle on the embellishments. It's astounding. I can see why you bought it, Lottie." Hearing the other two women snicker, she allowed, "Yes, the dress is dated, and I would have to agree that between the outdated design—lord help me, those sleeves—and the stains, it is... What did you call it, Lisa?"

"Heinous-ahoy."

"Okay, yes. There are major parts of it that are heinous-ahoy, but overall, there's more good about it than bad."

"Are you sure about that?" Lisa whispered, but Charlotte ignored her. Finally, someone who had vision enough to see past stains and imperfections to the true beauty of the dress. If she hadn't been so caught up in the moment, Charlotte would have realized she was about to have her second bad idea of the day.

"Go try it on, Alex," she suggested. "You can get a feel for a dress with a long train." Alex took the dress and disappeared around the screen. There was a lot of fabric rustling and perhaps a few choice words, but it didn't take her long to emerge.

As Alex appeared, Charlotte focused on the fit of the gown. Dresses always looked different on an actual person than on the hanger. It was fascinating to see how this looked and moved. Taking the train, she fluffed it, sending a puff of air under the skirt, settling it perfectly. She backed up and laid the train out across the floor for the full effect as Alex went to face the mirror.

The ballgown skirt was very full, but it still had enough movement to make it appear Alex was gliding across the floor. The bodice seemed to fit well enough, and surprisingly, the hem only dragged on the floor slightly. Someone of Alex's height might even wear a small heel. So caught up in her assessment, she almost missed Alex's question.

"How would you redesign this?"

Still examining the various elements of the gown, Charlotte answered automatically. "Get rid of the sleeves first thing. While that design is making a comeback, those are terrible examples of the style. Instead, I'd have it sleeveless with a wide strap or maybe a cap sleeve. Nothing strapless—between the interior construction that would have to happen and the fact that it's a lot of dress to hold up, strapless isn't the best idea."

Caught up in the dream of possibilities, Charlotte continued, "I would soften the neckline by moving a bit of lace to break up the visual line. There aren't a lot of changes needed on the train. For the skirt, if the stains won't come out, I'd have to think up a way to design around them. Maybe hide them with lace or remove some fabric from the skirt," Charlotte mused.

Leaning down, she grabbed the lace edge of the train. "This

is what I was talking about when I said small embellishments make a big difference. I think this lace pattern used in the train may be a Scottish thistle." Charlotte continued, Alex's small gasp unheard, "I'm not that familiar with lace design, but I remember seeing something years ago with a Scottish thistle on it. This is quite similar. You could have something like this added to your gown. It may make all the difference in how you feel about the dress."

"It has Scottish thistle," Alex said reverently. "Did you know the thistle is the Scottish national emblem? Jason told me while we were researching traditions to add into the ceremony. And one of the highest honors the country can bestow is called the Order of Thistle."

"I didn't know that," Charlotte responded, her focus still on the train of the dress. "That's nice."

"That's not nice, that's mind-blowing! The national emblem of Scotland on my dress? That's perfect. It's magical!" she exclaimed, her face suffused with joy.

Charlotte dropped the fabric and stepped away. "That's what I'm thinking of off the top of my head. There are lots of possibilities. That's why I love working on these; it's very rewarding. With a little effort, or a lot in this case, you give a gown a second chance at being fabulous." Charlotte looked over at Alex and froze.

How many times had she seen that look? Alex was staring into the mirror, her eyes shimmering as her fingers delicately ran over the beadwork of the dress. Damn. Damn. Damn. That was a stupid mistake. She never should have let Alex put this on. If she'd been thinking, she would have realized the risk. If Alex hadn't put it on, she would have never fallen in love with a dress she couldn't have.

Alex turned from side to side taking in all the aspects of the dress, "It's perfect, Lottie. Just perfect. And it has Scottish lace on it. It's a sign. This is my dress. It's so beautiful and so different from any other dress I've seen!"

Charlotte wasn't sure, but she thought she heard Lisa mutter something about just how different it was already. Ignoring her friend, she struggled to find the words. This couldn't be her dress. "Alex, honey," she began. "Alex," she said again, waiting until Alex looked her in the eye. "This isn't your dress. This is just an example of what you can do to that other dress to make it your own."

"Oh no," Alex said, running her hands over the full skirt as she turned back to the mirror. "This is it, Lottie. This is my dress. It's everything I wanted. And it has Scottish lace on it! It was meant to be."

Charlotte tried again, "It's very possible I'm wrong about the lace. Don't take that as a sign or something. Besides, this dress hasn't been redesigned. There's only eight weeks till your wedding. There's not enough time to redesign it and have it ready. I'm so sorry. I'll go with you to see the other dress. I can work with the seamstress there, and we can incorporate some of these elements into that dress."

"It won't be the same," Alex argued. "This dress has it all: a ballgown skirt and this beautiful train. Can you imagine what it will look like as I walk down the aisle? That other dress doesn't have a train like this one! And this one has Scottish lace! I know it does; I can just feel it. It's like the universe is sending me a message. This is my dress!"

Charlotte kicked herself again for letting things get so out of hand. If the universe was sending a message, it was that she'd messed up, and now she was going to break her cousin's heart.

Realizing what was going on, Lisa and Rachel came to stand with them. "Can you really not get it done in time?" Rachel asked.

Charlotte sighed. "It may not sound like it, but there's a lot of work that would have to be done. Even on minor projects, I take about three to four months to complete a gown."

"Well, that's with you working full time," Lisa offered. When Charlotte shot her a glare as if to say, not you, too, Lisa shrugged. "I'm just pointing it out," she added. "You never use your vacation time. And you once said your ideal vacation would be to work on your dresses... so here you go. Win-win."

Note to self. Suffocate Lisa in her sleep.

"I can't take six weeks off from work," she said, her mind churning with possibilities against her will. "Although I do have a decent amount of vacation time. I guess I could take a few days off here and there and maybe take a full week off."

Why was she even thinking about this? It was impossible, vacation time or not. This conversation had taken a sharp left turn. She had to bring it back to reality. Before she could once again list all the reasonable arguments, Alex turned and grabbed her hands.

"Lottie, I know it's a big ask, even for a family member. I don't have any right, but I'm asking anyway. Please."

The simple entreaty paired with the reminder about family made Charlotte pause. Could she pull this off? Conflicting emotions threatened to overwhelm her. She wanted to do this for Alex, but she was so afraid of failure it was almost paralyzing. What if the dress wasn't done in time? What if the design changes she made looked horrible? All she could picture was a church full of relatives judging her as Alex walked down the aisle.

Her internal debate must have shown on her face because Lisa interrupted her thoughts. "You got this, Lottie. You can do it."

"I haven't known you long, Lottie," Rachel offered. "But I know you can do this. I've seen your skill and passion. You'll make it happen."

The silence stretched between them when Alex added softly, "Should I remind you that you love me, and I'm your favorite cousin of all time?"

Rolling her eyes, Charlotte felt the last of her resistance fade. You don't abandon family. Sighing, she said, "Well, I have a lot of vacation time saved up."

Alex yelled and threw her arms around Charlotte, giving her a big squeeze. "I'm so excited! Thank you! Thank you! Thank you!"

"No celebrating yet. We have a lot to do. Lisa, can you take some notes?" When Lisa nodded and disappeared in search of pen and paper, Charlotte turned to Rachel, "Can you help me look to see if the train already has a bustle?"

"I don't know what that is, but whatever you need."

Looking back at the dress, Charlotte started making plans in her head. She'd have to tackle the stains first to see if they would come clean. If not, she could shift some lace from the sleeves to cover. Bending down to look closer at the train, she spotted a loop hidden amongst the lace.

"See this loop, Rachel? Look for similar ones on your side." After they'd located a few of them, Charlotte reached down, grabbed the center loop and attached it to a tiny white button hidden on the dress's waistline. Rachel followed suit and in short order, they had the train bustled. Alex clapped her hands and turned in the mirror so she could see how the dress looked.

"Well thankfully the bustle's done. A victorian bustle at that."

"Is that what we want?" Alex asked.

"It's right choice for showing off all the intricate detailing on your train," she replied. Seeing that Lisa had returned, Charlotte turned to Alex. "So, here's the deal. If we're going to have any hope of getting this done, you'll need to compromise." At Alex's nod, she continued, "First thing is your shoes. They'll have to be a certain height to make this hem and bustle work. Looking at it, I would say at least an inch to an inch and half. We'll have to experiment."

"Understood."

"Also, I'm not positive the lace on the train is a Scottish thistle pattern."

"I know," Alex interrupted. "It's just so romantic to think it is. Besides, I can feel it is. I can't wait to tell everyone!"

"Well," Charlotte softened. "I can do some research to confirm. For now, let's list out the needed changes. Ready Lisa?"

"Fire away."

"Well, obviously, sleeves removed. Then new straps created either with fabric from the sleeves or some other material. I'll have to see. Change the neckline to soften the appearance, maybe a slight sweetheart neckline. I'll have to do some internal structural changes to the bodice. After that, we'll have to have the bodice fitted a little better. We'll do a fitting at that point. I'm guessing we'll need to take in the seams a little around the waist. I'll want to tighten the bustle attachments as well. And of course," Charlotte finished. "The big unknown. I don't know if we can clean the stains or have to redesign the dress in order to remove them."

There was more, but they were small enough that they could be left off. The list was already giving Charlotte hives. If everything was on there, she might just hyperventilate. "Why don't you go change out of the dress. We can finish up downstairs. I think I need something stronger than wine."

Wrapping up the details, Charlotte tried not to get overwhelmed with everything that had to be done. She'd write out a detailed project plan tonight. That would make her feel better. She and Alex discussed the timeline and budget. Since this was Charlotte's first real commission piece, she wasn't sure what to charge. Thinking of the other gowns she'd worked on, she gave Alex a wide range of potential final budget numbers, but that seemed okay. In the end, they agreed on a deposit to start and to reevaluate pricing as the genuine work started.

It was all done so quickly, it made Charlotte's head spin. Before she could comprehend the magnitude of what she'd agreed to, Alex and Rachel were leaving. Charlotte and Lisa walked both women out.

Before Alex walked to her car, she threw her arms around Charlotte and pulled her into a big hug. "I meant what I said to my mother," she said into her ear. "I trust you. More than that, I believe in you. My dress is going to be breathtaking." She pulled back and held on to Charlotte's arms, squeezing them reassuringly, "Don't worry about my mom. I'll get her onboard. She'll love it as much as I do."

Alex's validation made Charlotte tear up and filled her with affection. It was so satisfying to hear a family member stand up for her. It was a gift she would not forget. She'd make sure Alex's dress was perfect.

As Rachel and Alex both pulled out of the driveway, Lisa looked at Charlotte and smiled. "Well, you sure have your work cut out for you."

Charlotte's stomach dropped, making her regret again her food choices for the day. Glancing at the deposit check clutched in her hand, she hoped she was up for this challenge.

"And to think this was all my idea," Lisa said. "I'm positively giddy with myself!"

"All your idea? How do you figure that?"

"I've been telling you for years you were skilled enough to sell your gowns. And here you are now," Lisa nodded toward the check. "A professional wedding gown designer. You can thank me at any time," she said smugly.

Charlotte paused and then just had to laugh. Leave it to Lisa to take credit for the whole thing. "I'll try to remember it was all your idea when I'm wrestling with those damn dress sleeves!"

Turning back into the house, Lisa shot back over her shoulder, "Speaking of which, I was thinking they'd look amazing on me!"

CHAPTER FIVE

Charlotte

Even though it was a Saturday, Charlotte's eye popped open before 6 a.m. She would have enjoyed staying in bed a little later, but there was a lot to accomplish. She'd probably be saying that for the next seven weeks. The countdown to Alex's wedding had almost become a constant clock ticking in her mind. Hard to believe she'd already lost a week. At least it had been a productive one.

Even thought it was early, it looked to be a beautiful day. A brief glance out the window and Charlotte felt compelled to be outside. Dressing quickly, she left the house quietly so as not to wake Lisa.

She loved her early runs: the quiet, the stillness of the neighborhood, the riot colors that lit up the sky. It was an invigorating experience, and one she cherished.

As she ran, her thoughts turned to the dress. The first thing she'd done once Alex and Rachel had left was to pull together a project plan. There were a lot of steps and moving parts, but on paper it was possible. She'd taken all day Sunday to work and rework the plan until she felt it was as efficient as possible. That also allowed her to plan her vacation days. Thankfully, the office was going into slow season, so they approved her vacation day requests.

During the evenings, she worked on the dress. She'd spent the majority working on the stains. Actually, she tackled the stains after she removed those sleeves. Those sleeves! Charlotte smiled, thinking of how Alex looked in them. They were beautifully crafted, but the image of the lace topped sleeve reaching almost to the top of Alex's ear made her laugh.

If only the stains were that easy. She'd tried several formulas, but even with all her work, two stains remained. They'd faded but were still visible. The dress would need to be spot cleaned. Hopefully, the last of the marks would come out, so it wouldn't need a drastic redesign.

If there was more time, she'd have the dress fully cleaned, but the timetable was just too tight. The project plan called for a full cleaning two weeks before the wedding. By that point, she should be pretty close to being done. *My lips to God's ears!*

That meant, according to the plan, her first errand today was to drop the dress off at the cleaners. Charlotte tried to ignore the small flutter in her stomach when she thought about returning to the cleaners. She was positive Adam wouldn't be there, or at least that's what she told herself. She also gave herself a stern talking-to about wanting to see him. This was no time to get distracted by a gorgeous, funny, intelligent guy. This was the time to focus on making her dreams reality.

Rounding the corner of her street, she slowed to a walk, taking in the subtle spring changes in the neighbors' yards. Even though Charlotte had no gardening skills, surely not like Lisa possessed, she could still appreciate the effort people put into their landscaping.

One last breath of the fresh morning air, and she walked into the house. As she entered, the smell of flowers was replaced by coffee, which was unusual. Normally on a weekend Lisa didn't emerge from her room until at least 10:30. She must have an appointment Charlotte didn't know about.

Walking into the kitchen, she found Lisa at the table hugging a mug of fresh, still steaming coffee. "What are you doing up? Are you going somewhere?"

"No," Lisa grumbled. "I just woke up and for the life of me I couldn't get back to sleep. And on a Saturday! That's simply unfair."

"Sorry, Lisa. I know you cherish your late mornings." Many times in college, Charlotte had to push, pull, and roll her roommate out of bed to make it to class. These days, Lisa had created a strict routine during the weekdays and was never late to work. But on the weekends, she caught up on sleep.

"No one is more disappointed about this than I am," Lisa sighed, taking another sip of coffee. "We should do something fun today. You've been locked in that workroom all week. I've barely seen you. Besides, I need something to turn this day around," she finished dramatically.

"Okay, okay. I have to drop the dress off at the cleaners this morning, but why don't we have some fun when I get back? Do a little shopping and then go out for lunch? Maybe at the winery? It looks like it's going to be a beautiful day."

"Oh! Now, that does sound perfect. That's the reason my eyes popped open this morning." Looking slyly over the mug, she continued, "I gather you're up and running this morning for an entirely different reason. Seeing Adam?"

Charlotte felt her face flush. "I have no plans to meet with him. I mean, he might be there. I don't know. But I'm not going to see him, see him," she floundered to a stop. Ignoring Lisa's laugh, she tried again, "I mean, he may be there. But I'm only going to drop off the dress. I have a schedule to keep."

Refusing to rise to her friend's ribbing, she grabbed a mug of coffee and sat down. Taking the cream and sugar, she spotted Lisa's eye roll, although she didn't comment. Lisa was forever teasing her about her coffee preferences. It just so happened that Charlotte happened to like a lot of cream and sugar. She would make no apologies about it. "I'm also going to visit Ethel this afternoon. Do you want to come along? I'm taking the dress sleeves over. Hopefully she can tell me if the lace pattern is a thistle design. I'm sure Alex has informed the entire world that it's Scottish, and I need to verify it. Although Alex is right. It would be fantastic if it turned out to be Scottish. It would elevate that dress to the stratosphere."

If anyone could shed light on the lace pattern, it was Ethel. Her years of experience and knowledge of fabrics were invaluable. She was the reason Charlotte started sewing in the first place. For most of her adult life, Ethel owned a seamstress shop right in downtown Jennings. When Charlotte was younger, Ethel had come to her school for career day. Hearing the details and description of how she fixed and sewed pieces of clothing, Charlotte found her imagination soaring with possibilities.

To take such simple items as fabric and thread and create something was a wonder. Small decisions could change a piece from fancy and intricate to something designed to be comfortable and cozy. To Charlotte, that was power. That was magic. From that moment on, she was almost always working on some project.

Later, when her skills became more refined, she became a frequent visitor to Ethel's shop. Over the years, Ethel had become a mentor, showing her more advanced sewing techniques and stitches. When Ethel retired, Charlotte visited her every month. They would have a cup of tea and catch up. Her hands afflicted by arthritis, Ethel didn't sew, but appreciated seeing the projects Charlotte brought by. In turn, Charlotte appreciated Ethel's vast experience and opinions. Decades may span between them, but Charlotte considered her a close friend.

Happily, Lisa and Ethel got along famously as well, like long-lost friends. With the same quirky sense of humor, they could swap stories for hours. "Thanks for the invite," Lisa replied, "but I'll have to pass. You and Ethel will be all gown talk. While I love you both, I would go crazy if I had to sit through more conversation about a dress.

"Besides," she said with a smile. "When I woke up this morning, I promised myself a nap this afternoon."

Charlotte shook her head and laughed. "I love that with your eyes barely open you're already promising yourself a nap."

"It's important to get your priorities in order first thing, Lottie. That way, you know the day will unfold as it should."

Leaving Lisa to linger over her coffee, Charlotte ran upstairs to get ready. After her shower, she refused to consider that she was taking longer with her hair than normal. And if picking an outfit seemed more difficult today, she chalked it up to whimsy.

It positively had nothing to do with possibly seeing anyone special today. Nothing at all.

Bundling the dress into the bag, she hurried downstairs to grab her purse and keys. The dress was quickly loaded up, and she drove over to the cleaners. Since it was still early, the parking lot was virtually empty, which suited her just fine. No need to worry about other customers needing assistance. It would be pleasant if she and Mrs. Mac could have a visit and perhaps look at the dress together. There was also that outstanding bill she wanted to take care of. If she didn't handle that now, she would forget.

Opening the door, she heard the familiar ring of the bell and was happy to see Mrs. Mac already seated at the little table off to the side. Trying to not look obvious, she glanced around to see if Adam was there. She was safe. But that fact didn't make her as happy as she thought it should. She tried not to feel disappointed. Giving herself a mental shake for silliness, Charlotte smiled and walked over to the table. A three-tiered plate sat in the middle, and while she couldn't make out what was there, she knew it would be delicious. As was her habit, Mrs. Mac was enjoying a cup of tea. Hopefully, she wouldn't mind Charlotte intruding.

"Hello, Lottie!" Mrs. Mac called. "How wonderful of you to stop by. I was just having another cup of tea before it got busy. Will you join me?"

"I'd love to," Charlotte smiled back, savoring the warmth of her greeting. Sometimes it still surprised her how welcomed and, frankly, loved she felt by the community here. It was such a stark contrast from her childhood.

"Your regular tea?" Mrs. Mac asked.

"That would be wonderful, but please don't go to any trouble on my account." Mrs. Mac waved her concerns away and walked behind the counter to get another teacup.

Charlotte loved Mrs. Mac's earl grey tea. No matter what she tried, Charlotte could never reproduce the marvelously aromatic cup. Funny how even with the same ingredients and recipe, each cup was different. She couldn't get an earl grey tea that was even close to matching the ones she enjoyed here. Mrs. Mac said hers tasted better because it was sipped with a friend. How could she not agree with that?

It took a few minutes for Mrs. Mac to return, and the two women settled down at the table. While she waited, Charlotte had hung the dress on a nearby rack. They could discuss it in a minute. For now, it was time for tea and cookies. Looking over at the tiered plate, she had to ask, "Are these from Pie in the Sky?"

"Of course! Marilyn would hit me if I went elsewhere, besides you have to support your friends. They're fig roll cookies. Marvelous! Please help yourself. We won't have a lot of customers today, and we have way too much. Now that you're here, I'm hoping you'll take a few back with you. I'm sure Lisa would love some. My husband bought them this morning, so they're very fresh. He can't buy a little of something, he has to buy a bunch! He assumes with Adam here we need double the amount of food."

Before she could blink an eye, Charlotte felt her face flush at the mention of Adam. With this blasted complexion of hers, she might as well just put a neon sign on her forehead. All she could do was hope Mrs. Mac didn't notice. "That was very nice of him. And it's kind of you offer. I'm sure Lisa would love a few cookies. I'll take some with me." She paused, not sure if she wanted to open this box, but she couldn't help herself. It was just a question. "I actually met your son the other day. I had to come in and pick up a dress—which reminds me, I still need to pay you for that. Adam wasn't sure of the pricing, so he said to stop back in to settle up. I haven't seen him here before. He works here in the store for you?"

"He does," Mrs. Mac said, taking a small sip of tea. "He also spends a fair amount of time over at the commercial location. It's so enjoyable to have him home, but I worry about him. He's at the store so much, I don't think he's had time to reconnect with old friends. Surely that's not the first time you met him. You're both around the same age. Didn't you know each other in high school?"

I wish, was her first thought. What would Adam have been like in high school? Probably too cool for her, but it was a nice thought anyway. "I lived over on the east side of town, so I went to Chapman High. I'm guessing he went to Jefferson?" she said tentatively. She wasn't sure where Mrs. Mac lived, but she would have remembered Adam if they'd met before. He must have gone to the other high school in town.

"Oh yes, that explains it. He did go to Jefferson. The way he talked about you, it seemed like you two knew each other. Well, that's too bad. I'm sure the two of you would have gotten along well in high school."

Butterflies danced in Charlotte's stomach. Adam had talked about her? Was that what Mrs. Mac had just said? Did he say nice things about her, or was he venting about the wedding gown rescuer weirdo that stopped in? She wanted to know, but at the same time didn't.

Charlotte wasn't sure where to go from here. She didn't want to ask any more questions about Adam because, really, she didn't care. That's right. She didn't care if he was single or seeing anyone. No need to get that information. Taking a sip of tea, she decided her best bet was to change the subject. "I'm sure we would have, and I'm sure he'll find the time to connect with all his old friends. Speaking of time, I have a dress that needs a quick spot clean. Some stains aren't responding completely."

"Certainly, dear. We're closed tomorrow, but I can have Cynthia look at them on Monday. Is this a new rescue? Any big plans for this gown?"

Charlotte couldn't keep the exciting news to herself. "Actually, there are some big plans. I have a client! Well, it's my cousin Alex, but still a paying client."

Mrs. Mac's face lit up. "That's marvelous news, Lottie! I'm so proud of you." The older woman leaned across the table and laid her hand over Charlotte's arm, squeezing it gently. "You're very talented. It's delightful to see you sharing it with the world. Tell me everything!"

As she unpacked the dress, Charlotte filled Mrs. Mac in on how the project had come about. As they looked over the gown, examining the stains, Charlotte detailed the planned changes. "You wouldn't happen to know anything about lace patterns, would you, Mrs. Mac?" she asked hopefully.

"Oh, no I don't. I'm so sorry. Why do you ask?"

Grabbing a piece of the hem, Charlotte showed Mrs. Mac the lace. "I thought that this may be a Scottish thistle pattern. It would mean so much to my cousin if it were, as her finance's family is from there. It's one of the things that drew her to the dress."

"That would be lovely. Sorry to say, I don't know that much about lace."

"I just thought I'd ask while I was here. I'm going to visit Ethel this afternoon. Hopefully, she'll be able to shed some light on it." Charlotte was reaching for a cookie when she felt him. Was it possible that she could feel his eyes on her? Could she sense him before he was even in the room? Apparently, it was. Her chest tightened as she turned to look toward the back doorway. Adam was there. And he was staring at her.

She couldn't help but notice he looked even better today. The deep purple polo he was wearing just intensified the green of his eyes. Beautiful green eyes that were staring right at her. Her heart threw in a few extra beats and her stomach, for some reason, decided to vacation down in her toes. It was a horrible and exciting feeling all at the same time.

Meeting his gaze, she felt herself blush. How long had he been standing there? Had she sounded like an idiot going on and on about the dress? As she was trying to remember every word, she'd said in the past five minutes, she realized that Mrs. Mac had been speaking. She hadn't heard a word.

Turning back, she said, "I'm sorry. I didn't hear what you were saying."

Mrs. Mac smiled, her eyes looking past Charlotte to Adam, who was walking toward them. "Not to worry, dear. I was just saying that I know little about lace pattern origins, but you're right, Ethel would be the best person to ask. She's far more familiar with the subject and may even give you a quick answer. Give her my best when you see her, would you?"

Although she could hear Adam's footsteps, Charlotte kept her eyes and focus on Mrs. Mac. "I'll let her know."

By now, he'd reached their table and was towering over her. Turning to acknowledge his presence, she couldn't meet his eyes directly, so she smiled slightly in his direction, praying her cheeks didn't look as red as they felt.

"I thought I heard voices down here. Nice to see you again, Charlotte."

Just the way he said her name sent a small shiver down her spine. His voice seemed to draw out the pronunciation as if it was a luxurious piece of chocolate. "Hi, Adam. Nice to see you as well. I was just visiting with your mom and discussing my latest project." She needed to get his attention off her and on to something else. Any more time in his direct focus and she'd either burst into flames or melt into a puddle. Neither option sounded very appealing.

Snagging a nearby chair, Adam sat next to Charlotte, his arm brushing hers as he settled in. Looking over the gown, he asked, "Are you leaving it with us to clean?"

She watched him pull the dress fully out of the bag. Charlotte was mesmerized by his hands, watching them trace and feel the blemishes on the delicate material. It was as if she could feel his hands on her body, his fingers gliding up the sides of her thighs. When he stopped to caress the formerly stained fabric area near the hip, she nearly fell off her chair.

"The fabric is beautiful," he continued. "Do you mind if I look at the rest?"

"Not... not at all," she stuttered. "Please. It's a very ornate gown, especially the train." Clearing her throat, she took a big sip of tea and immediately regretted it. The hot tea only exacerbated the heat her thoughts of Adam were generating.

As Adam stood up, Mrs. Mac turned to her son to explain. "Lottie usually treats and removes as many of the stains as she can. It helps her keep the cleaning bill down to a minimum. Even with the volume discount she gets, it can be expensive."

Adam was examining the lace work on the train but looked over and smiled as his mom spoke about the volume discount. "I believe I've heard something about that volume discount." He glanced at Charlotte and winked. His attention returning to the dress. "This is beautiful work. I assume this is one of your 'rescue' gowns?"

"Yes. I picked it up a few years ago. With the dated design and the stains, it was doomed to sit and die in that thrift shop. I couldn't let something that beautiful waste away. With all the lace and cutouts, it would have been criminal."

"Criminal for sure," he said, catching and holding Charlotte's gaze. "What made you decide to work on this now? Do you have a lottery system to pick the next dress? Or is it whatever has been with you the longest?"

Although she recognized he was probably teasing, she wasn't sure how she felt about it. Was he simply joking with her in a good-natured manner, or was he making fun of her? The grin he gave her and the mischief in his eye led her to believe he was just having some fun. "Actually," she said with a hint of attitude, "I have a client who wants this dress." Let him make fun of that.

"That's fantastic news," he said, sitting down again, invading her space with his warm body. "I didn't think you were selling gowns." His gaze stayed locked on her face, his expression sincere. She felt her shoulders relax in response; he wasn't mocking her and her work.

"Well, I haven't been selling them. This is really a first. My cousin's wedding gown was never ordered. The bridal salon went out of business. I wasn't expecting to be involved, but things just sort of happened." Charlotte shrugged. "Here I am with eight weeks—no, seven weeks now—to redesign a gown for her."

"Why didn't you say no?" Adam asked, leaning across to snag a cookie bringing him closer to her still. She could smell his cologne, the woodsy sent causing her temperature to spike yet again. It should be illegal for a man this good looking to smell like a deep pine forest after a rainstorm. Would he taste as good as he smelled?

Distracted by Adam's nearness and her reaction, it took a moment for her to find the words. "I couldn't say no. I mean, I could have, but that wouldn't have solved anything." She considered what she wanted to say. Why did she say yes when it was such a Herculean task?

"At the end of the day, Alex is family. I want her to be happy, and if this is what she wants, then I'll do it. For me, family means being there and supporting one another. Whether it's by blood or by choice, it doesn't matter. You don't turn your back on family."

Mrs. Mac grabbed Charlotte's hand and gave it a squeeze. "I couldn't agree more, darling. It's well past time you shared your work. Your designs are beautiful, and this dress is going to make a stunning gown. Now, tell me what we can do to help."

Charlotte's eyes teared up, moved by Mrs. Mac's support and faith. Family by choice, Charlotte was blessed to be surrounded by remarkable people. Clearing her throat, she reached into her bag and pulled out her planning notebook. "I put together a plan to get this all done. I'd like to confirm from a cleaning standpoint that I've allotted enough time.

"If you spot clean the gown, I have a half day on Thursday and can come pick it up. I'll have it in time for the weekend when I'm doing the bulk of my work. I've made plans to have the dress in for a thorough cleaning two weeks before the wedding. Does that sound doable?"

"That sounds like a solid plan," Adam chimed in, his eyes lingering on Charlotte. "The spot cleaning will let you know what you're working with and get some of these deeper wrinkles out. That should make the alterations easier and more precise."

"Two weeks before the wedding is suitable for the full cleaning," Mrs. Mac added just as her cell phone rang. Looking down, she smiled and stood up from the table. "Sorry, I need to get this. Lovely seeing you, Charlotte. Adam, will you watch the front?" Without awaiting a response, she answered the phone and went into the back.

Charlotte stood and began clearing the cups and plates from the table.

"That's okay," Adam's deep voice rumbled in her ear. He leaned past her to take the dishes from her hands. His touch left a trail of heat over her skin, and she could feel her body reacting to his proximity. She felt breathless, her heart thumping as heat and awareness of him curled down her spine. She needed to leave. Being around Adam made her feel things. Great, but uncomfortable things.

"I'll just take these in the back," he said.

As he walked away, Charlotte took advantage and started packing up the dress.

"I thought you were leaving that with us?" Adam asked as he returned.

"Oh," Charlotte stood back from the dress. "Yes, you're right. Not sure what I was thinking." You were thinking about a certain hot guy who smells like a forest, makes you feel all tingly, and you want to climb him like a tree. That's what you were thinking. Now stop being ridiculous and get a handle on yourself.

Pep talk complete, Charlotte moved to take the dress back out, but Adam beat her to it. He reached in to scoop the dress out, and her eyes again became fixated on his hands. There was something about his fingers trailing over all the lace and satin that was sending electric sparks through her. What was wrong with her? This was by far the weirdest thing she'd experienced, but she couldn't stop. Nor could she seem to look away, not that she really wanted to. Seeing such a muscular guy hold and caress the lace with such reverence was making her insides get all hot and bothered. As Adam turned back, she prayed none of what she felt showed in her face. She wouldn't be able to live with that level of humiliation.

"I can feel that you've done some treatments on the spots already. I can only imagine how bad they were when you started."

Taking a slow breath, Charlotte tried to get herself on level footing. Focus on the work and only the work. "Some of them put up a fight. Do you think you'll be able to get out that last bit? I mean, not you, but whomever you have working on the gown?"

He stood up and let the fabric fall from his hands. "Definitely not me. I don't have the right touch for something this delicate. Cynthia works on gowns. I'm sure she has several tricks up her sleeve to tackle it. Then I would think a cold-water wash with conditioners should put it in good shape."

"Your mom has mentioned Cynthia. She's worked on most of my other gowns, I believe."

"You can't go wrong having her work on your pieces. She has advanced training and has also received many honors. In fact, the DCL presented with the Master Spotter Award."

"Master Spotter Award? You're kidding, right? That's not really a thing," she sassed him.

Adam laughed. "I kid you not. It is a thing. Awarded by the Dry Cleaning & Laundry Institute or DCL as we refer to it." Dropping his smile, he frowned. "We take cleaning seriously here, Charlotte."

She thought he was joking again, but perhaps she had insulted him and his work. "I know you take this all very seriously, Adam. Everything I've ever brought here was done brilliantly. And when something couldn't come clean, your mom went over it with me."

Adam caught her eye, his look warming her. "I was kidding. Even I can see the humor of a Master Spotter Award. Not to take away from Cynthia's accomplishments. She worked damn hard to get them."

Assured he was joking, Charlotte beamed at him, unaware Adam's breath had hitched when she looked at him. "Well, I won't take up more of your time. Thank you and your mom for your help."

Not waiting for a reply, she turned and walked toward the door. Right before she made it, she whirled around and just about landed in Adam's arms. She hadn't realized he had been following her.

"Oh... um. Sorry," she stammered, looking up into those startling green eyes. She felt her skin tingle beneath his hands as he reached out to steady her. "I wanted to pay my bill... for the dress cleaning. The one I picked up the other day."

He gazed down at her and seemed to hesitate for a heartbeat. "That's okay. I'll just add it to the bill when you pick up this gown. I know I'll be seeing you again."

Trying not to read too much into his words, she nodded and left. Inhaling, she tried to center herself. Something about him put her off balance. Walking to her car, she risked a quick glance back. Adam remained where he was, watching her walk away. The sight sent her pulse racing again. What was it about him? Why did he affect her so much?

CHAPTER SIX

Adam

As Charlotte pulled out of the parking lot, Adam shook himself. He must look like a complete idiot or like a deranged stalker standing by the door watching her leave. This was the second time he'd found himself observing her. Hopefully, she hadn't noticed.

When he'd heard her voice in the shop, his first thought was to go see her. Before he had even taken two steps, he made himself turn around and go back to what he was doing. He shouldn't be this interested in her.

His resolve had lasted for all of five minutes before he made his way to the front of the store. He felt an inescapable attraction to her. She was enchanting. Even though he swore he would just say hello and leave, he found himself settling down right next to her.

Turning from the door, he finished logging the gown. Rescue gown, he corrected himself. Just thinking about their conversation made him smile. He wasn't sure which he loved more, that she blushed so easily or the steel in her spine when she felt he wasn't being respectful. Both were delightful to watch. Just as he was finishing, his mom returned.

"Sorry, honey, that was your dad."

Adam was immediately on alert. "Is he okay? I thought he was taking today off?" Thankfully, his dad's test results were better than expected. There wasn't a problem with his heart or anything… yet. The doctor had been clear. The stress in his dad's life needed to change, along with his diet and lack of exercise. If he didn't make some different choices, there would be trouble down the road. The thought of anything happening to him left Adam shaken.

"He's fine, honey," his mom responded. "He's at home; trying to cook some new recipe." His mother scowled. "I swear, if he destroys my kitchen again trying to cook, I'm going to kill him."

Adam laughed with relief. This sort of problem he could handle. "Mom, it's going to be slow today, and we close early anyway. Why don't you go home? I can handle things here."

"That's kind of you, Adam, but I don't want you to have to cover the whole day," she said dismissively. "But I appreciate you offering."

If he was going to win this argument, he was going to have to negotiate and maybe pull out the big guns. "I tell you what, Mom, I'll make you a deal." As the idea formed in his head, he liked it more and more. It would make everyone happy.

Seeing her skeptical look, he continued, "I didn't have time to grab anything before I left my condo this morning. Why don't I take a walk to Pie and get something now? When I get back, you can take off. That way I'm not here all day, I have a pleasant walk, and you leave early. Everyone wins."

When she didn't immediately argue with him, he pulled out his ultimate weapon. "You can go home and supervise Dad's cooking, so he doesn't trash your kitchen." He fell silent, letting her think that through. Surely, she had to be considering it, especially when her beloved kitchen hung in the balance.

His dad wasn't a big cook, but he seemed to be taking the doctor's orders seriously. Looking for healthier options, his dad's few cooking attempts, according to his mom, had ended in somewhat edible food. The cost being an Armageddon-like outcome for her kitchen.

He could see the moment he'd won when his mother smiled. "I see what you did there, but I'm more afraid of what will happen with my kitchen than arguing with you. So, off you go! Say hi to Marilyn for me. Tell her I'll call her later so we can catch up."

A quick kiss on his mother's cheek, and Adam was out the

door. Thankfully, their shop wasn't far from downtown where Pie was located. On such a beautiful day, it would be an enjoyable walk. Setting off towards town, he tried to push away his anxiety about his dad's health.

He'd have to call his sister Julie and tell her about dad's attempt at cooking again. She'd get a kick out of that. She lived in Pennsylvania with her husband and two kids. When she'd heard about their dad's health issues, she was all set to come back to Jennings, but Adam assured her he'd be there and keep her in the loop.

Now the challenge was to get his dad to slow down. With both a retail and commercial side to the business, his parents had their hands full. There had to be a way for Adam to help. In the past, he'd made suggestions about improvements and ways to streamline the business, but his dad stubbornly refused to change. No matter what he suggested, his father never listened. Adam shouldn't have been surprised. Communication had never been their strong suit.

When Adam was a kid, talking to his dad had been somewhat easier. As the years passed, it got harder and harder to find common ground. Mom did an admirable job of bridging the gap, but there was always that space between them.

Taking a deep breath, he blew it out and even shook out his shoulders, trying to release some of the tension. It just felt like he there was no clear path on how to help his parents. Ultimately, what it came down to was even if his dad fought it, the business had to change. And the data didn't lie. Perhaps he'd take another deep dive into all the business information and see what it said. It was his specialty, after all. Maybe with solid data behind him, he'd get his dad to listen.

Entering downtown, Adam walked through the town common. All the familiar sights lifted his spirits. There was something about coming home that made even bad days better. These were the same streets he marched as a kid during the Memorial Day parade. There was the hardware store he and his dad would go to. The town green and rotary brought back memories of arduous driving lessons learning to navigate through the spoke and wheel town center. Looking at it all now, he appreciated its elegant design and the feeling of home it inspired.

Spying an open bench in the shade, he sat for a moment to enjoy the day. Checking his phone, he saw nothing from his employer. He had hoped they'd have those contracts signed by now. It would be nice to know when or if they were expecting to recall employees back to work.

The lack of news was a bit unsettling. What would happen if they didn't land those jobs? He hadn't even let himself consider that possibility, but as time went on, that outcome seemed possible. Did he return to Phoenix and get a new job there? Should he look for a new job in a new city now? Honestly, the idea of starting over in a new city or a new job didn't thrill him. And he didn't know why. That thought alone made his anxiety ratchet up.

Adam sprang up from the bench, needing to be in motion. Just the act of walking again made him feel better. He was far too agitated by his thoughts to be sitting still.

The other exciting thing about being home was visiting all his favorite places. As he entered the door of Pie in the Sky, he heard the bell on the door jingle his arrival. Thankfully, since he was here between breakfast and lunch, there wasn't a line.

As he scanned the cases, trying to decide, Mrs. S. came out of the kitchen door. "Adam!" she said, enveloping him in a big hug. "It's nice to see you. How are you doing? I haven't had a chance to visit with your mom recently, so I haven't gotten the latest gossip on your life."

Leave it to his mom's friend to get to the heart of the matter. "Hey, Mrs. S. It's great to see you. The bakery looks marvelous, as usual. It smells divine. Mom sends her love and wanted me to let you know she'd be calling you. I'll tell her you're running low on gossip."

Laughing, Mrs. S. went behind the glass case and asked, "What can I get you today?"

"I'd love one of your raspberry cream cheese turnovers, and how about a piece of the lemon lavender pound cake?" Not the healthiest options, but there was no way he could leave the bakery without those.

"Sure thing. You up for trying one of our experimental recipes?"

Adam felt his mouth water in response. Some of his fondest memories were of coming to the bakery with his mom. As the two women chatted, he would be tasked with eating whatever new recipe was being tried. He would then give a full opinion report to Mrs. S. She called him her number one taste tester. "I'd love to. What are you trying today?"

"Meat and bean chili turnovers. We've perfected the recipe with beef, but I want to offer one with turkey, as well."

"Sold! And can you also put together a box for my mom?" Adam paused. Maybe he should get something his dad wouldn't be tempted to eat. Mrs. S. had healthy options available, but he wasn't as familiar with those. His best bet would be to get some of those macarons the bakery made. His mom loved them, and best of all, his dad didn't. "Maybe some of those macarons she loves? She's leaving early today to supervise dad's experiments in her kitchen; she'll need sugar to get through it."

Mrs. S. quickly gathered his order together while Adam looked through all the display cases, impressed by how much more they offered these days. When he came to the healthier options, he studied them closely, noting the names. He'd do research and see what was best for his dad. He also knew that if he let Mrs. S. know what was going on, she would start testing recipes that wouldn't sabotage his dad's diet restrictions.

"The chili turnover is a bit hot, but it'll be just the right temperature by the time you get to work," she said, ringing up all his purchases. "Give my best to your mother. Tell her we need to have a girls' night sometime soon."

"I'll do that. Thanks again. Have a good day, Mrs. S." He leaned over the counter, kissing her cheek. "I can't wait to try the new turnover. I'll be sure to give you a full report."

Leaving the store with a smile, Adam headed back. Mrs. S. had been his guiding light growing up in Jennings. His mom's best friend, she was not afraid to call him out on his occasional teenage punk behavior, but she'd also been a sympathetic ear when he needed one.

Heading back to the store, he let his mind wander, just enjoying the day. For all his anxiety about his dad and his own job situation, he caught himself singing bits and pieces of different songs. It startled him to realize he was actually feeling better today than he had in the past few weeks. Charlotte's face drifted into his thoughts. He shook his head, his lip curling. To think seeing her had anything to do with his improved mood was ridiculous.

Granted, seeing her this morning had left him feeling a little off. He was magnetically pulled to her and wanted to discover why. It wasn't just his physical reaction to her, although that was unsettling as well. She had some luscious curves that drew his eye. And her blue eyes seemed to look through him. Add to her good looks the fact that he enjoyed their interactions. He'd dated his fair share of woman over the years, but something about Charlotte felt different, and that made his chest tight. She was dangerous.

He'd purposely sat close to her at the table this morning, crowding her. All he could think about was getting a whiff of her perfume. Today it was a deep floral note but had undercurrents of coconut. He wondered if that was her shampoo or perhaps body lotion. Brushing her soft skin as he reached across for a cookie had sent a spark directly to his groin. He'd had to stop himself from touching her again just to see if he'd have the same reaction.

Running his hand through his hair, he shook his head. He had to stop thinking about her. He lengthened his stride; the quicker he could get back to work, the quicker he could distance himself from thoughts of Charlotte. He shouldn't be thinking about her anyway. He couldn't afford any distractions. He was here to get his head straight and decide his next move.

Since college, he'd loved moving around and trying unknown places. He had a solid career and a great life. Meeting new people, living in different places, that's how he liked to live his life. He wasn't a settling down type of guy. If that was no longer true, what did it mean?

Deep down, he wondered if his parents had been right; did his nomadic lifestyle have anything to do with Abigail after all? Could that one event have dictated his life choices for the past decade? He pushed the thought away as he arrived back at the store. Abigail was in the past, and he was over it.

"I'm back, Mom," he called as he entered. "I bought you a little something."

Looking at the various boxes he carried, she said, "I can see that. How's Marilyn today?"

"She seems to be doing well. She wants to plan a girls' night. Let me just grab my work files upstairs, and I'll take over the front desk."

"No rush, honey. Your dad called. He's going to pick me up in an hour or so. He needs some stuff, so we're going to go to the grocery store together. Maybe I can steer him toward options that don't require every pot in the kitchen to be dirtied." She shook her head in futility. "We also need to swing by the warehouse on the way." She held up her hand before he could even say a word. "It's nothing big. We just need to sign a contract and send it out. Nothing stressful. So, take your time and eat. I'll give a yell when your dad gets here."

"Okay. But call me if it gets busy."

"Sure thing."

Adam disappeared into the back, stopping to grab a cup of coffee in the kitchen. Walking past the large washing machines and dryers, he climbed the building stairs. Most of the everyday retail cleaning and pressing was done here on site. For their larger commercial business, they had a warehouse just outside of town. That location housed the larger capacity cleaning equipment and was much easier for their trucks to do pickups and drop-offs. The business had a solid base of commercial accounts from local hotels, hospitals, and restaurants. The steady business of linens, uniforms, and towels was much of their income.

A few years ago, Adam had tried to convince his dad to expand the use of commercial trucks and offer it to residential clients. If they maximized how pickups and deliveries were made, he was sure they could free up at least two days a week to offer to clients. While not every residential customer needed delivery, Adam felt there were enough to make it profitable. But like his other suggestions, the idea had not excited his dad. Rather than butt heads again, he'd dropped it.

It was hard to rein in his passion for problem solving. It was part of what he loved about his career. Often, he was translating customer data so a company could respond better or improve in some way. Many times, he was finding solutions for problems that had plagued a company for years.

Walking down the hallway, he entered his office. It wasn't large by any means, but more than adequate for his work. His desk faced a pair of windows, which provided wonderful light, but meant his back was to the office doorway. He hated that, but there wasn't room to move the desk. Besides, he was only here temporarily.

Once settled, coffee in hand, he took a bite of the chili turnover. Mrs. S. was onto something with these. They were outstanding. Maybe a touch more garlic, but they seemed pretty damn amazing as is.

As he ate his way through the turnover, he listed out what he wanted to accomplish today. The inventory lists were straightforward, so that shouldn't take long, then he could look at the customer data and come up with some more ideas to streamline the business. Maybe if he kept himself busy, he wouldn't worry so much about his own job, his dad's health or any super attractive dress rescuers that he couldn't seem to shake from his mind.

CHAPTER SEVEN

Charlotte

Charlotte sat back in her seat, pleasantly full. The superbly relaxing lunch at the vineyard was the break she didn't know she needed. Amazing food, a beautiful day, and marvelous views had worked their magic. "Thanks for coming out with me today, Lisa. I really needed this."

"What? You needed my expertise to help pick out which tin of Danish cookies to bring Ethel? For the love of everything good and decent, please don't tell anyone I had anything to do with that."

"Don't be a cookie snob! Those tin cookies happen to be her favorites." Secretly, Charlotte agreed, but damn if she'd disparage Ethel's favorite cookie. Besides, every time she saw the iconic blue tin it made her think of Ethel and smile. For some reason, her friend loved those cookies. She said they were unpretentious and went beautifully with her afternoon cup of tea. No arguing with that. Charlotte didn't want to show up empty-handed, so she'd bought a tin on the way to lunch.

Taking a sip of wine, she took another look around the vineyard. From this vantage point, they had a breathtaking view of the surrounding rolling hills. It was a sight that filled her with a wonderful sense of calm. "This is turning out to be a remarkable weekend."

"Well, any time with me is always well spent. But since I know that's not the only reason, what else is making this an over-the-top weekend?"

"Well, this, of course," she smiled and toasted Lisa with her wineglass. "And I have a visit with Ethel today and as you said, it'll be all gown-talk. I'm hoping she'll give me good news on the Scottish lace, which would make my weekend complete."

"And it has nothing to do with a certain someone you may or may not have run into this morning?" Lisa asked slyly. "Don't think I didn't notice your failure to discuss the dress drop-off." Seeing Charlotte's blush, Lisa crowed, "I knew it! I knew it! Spill!"

"There's nothing to spill," Charlotte tried to deflect. "I had a brief visit with Mrs. Mac, and she loves the dress. I asked her, but she knew nothing about the lace. She thinks Ethel may know." She was blathering, and she knew it. Worse, Lisa knew it. There was no way Lisa was going to let this go.

"Fine. I saw Adam. He came in while I was visiting with Mrs. Mac," she conceded, feeling her body flush with warmth. The man was so damn attractive.

"Annnndd?"

Charlotte hesitated briefly, torn between not wanting to acknowledge what she was feeling and needing to talk to someone about it. Lisa may joke with her a lot, but she knew her friend would always be there for her. Glancing out over the vineyard to collect herself before turning back to Lisa, she said quietly, "I'm so confused."

Lisa's eyebrows shot up. "Confused? I didn't see that one coming. What's going on?"

"I've just met Adam, but my reaction to him is so crazy strong. He makes me feel nervous and disorientated but fantastic at the same time. And yeah, he's attractive," she paused, thinking of how enchanting he'd looked this morning. "Okay. So very attractive. But it's more than that. I enjoy talking to him. He's funny and appealing. And it's crazy!"

"And that's what's confusing?"

"Yes. No. I mean all of it. All of it is confusing." She wasn't making much sense. "I barely know him. This instant over-the-top chemistry isn't me."

"Well, it has been over a year since thing ended with Todd. You haven't been dating at all. Perhaps your reaction is simply an overreaction to finding someone you're attracted to."

"Maybe you're right," Charlotte replied, toying with the stem of her wineglass. "But…" She bit her lip, wondering if she should just get it all out. "I've never felt quite like this before. Even with Todd." Shifting forward in her seat suddenly, she shook her head. "It doesn't matter anyway." Seeing that Lisa was about to argue, she continued, "I have a very large, very important project that requires 110% of my focus."

"Agreed. But at some point, you're going to need to get past Todd," Lisa added quietly. "I know he did a number on you, but you need to let go of the fear and let yourself get close to someone."

Charlotte pretended not to hear Lisa's comment. Her friend may be right but that didn't make it any easier to hear. Thinking about Todd and how things had ended made the lovely meal she'd just consumed sour in her stomach. She didn't want to think about any of this. Instead, she changed the subject, and like the loyal friend that she was, Lisa let her. By the time they finished, Charlotte was able to resurrect her positive attitude.

Dropping Lisa at the house, Charlotte grabbed the dress sleeves and drove to Ethel's. She had always loved Ethel's home. It was a small Victorian, the outside painted a cheerful yellow with a white picket fence that circled the yard.

Opening the gate, Charlotte admired the flowering plants lining the front steps. With Ethel's arthritis, there was no way she had planted them. It must have been her son who lived the next town over. He and his twin boys ensured the house was well kept and provided Ethel with everything she needed.

Tucking the sleeves and cookie tin under her arm, Charlotte walked up the front steps and knocked on the door before entering. "Ethel? It's me, Lottie," she called.

A voice called from deeper in the house, "Come in, darling. Come in. You're just in time. I made a fresh pot of tea."

Passing through the tidy living room, Charlotte made her way to one of her favorite places. The kitchen wallpaper was old and faded terribly, the linoleum floor was cracked and worn, but to Charlotte it was the most beautiful place in the world. Here she was accepted just as she was. Unlike her mother, Ethel was easy to talk to and always had a sympathetic ear.

As usual, the magic of her friend's kitchen relaxed her even further. Ethel was at the stove, pouring hot water into two flowered teacups.

"Hi, Ethel," Charlotte said, leaning over to plant a kiss on her cheek. "Let me take those cups to the table."

"Yes, please. I can manage one but I'm not so steady on my feet to make handling two a possibility."

As they settled down at the round kitchen table, Charlotte set the tin of cookies on the table, prying off the cover. "You must have known I was coming, cookies-in-hand."

"I might have had a feeling you were coming with something delicious," Ethel mused. "Thank you for bringing me my cookies. They go so well with a tea." Taking a cookie, she took a bite, and closed her eyes to fully enjoy the flavor. "Delightful. Is there anything better than an afternoon tea and cookie?" Not waiting for Charlotte to answer, she continued, "So, how have you been? Anyone tall, dark, and handsome in your life yet?"

Adam's face jumped to mind, but as unnerving as her involuntary thoughts of him were, it was worse to realize this was the third mention of that exact phrase. She refused to consider that the universe was sending her a message. Although Adam fit that bill incredibly well. But she'd had enough of talking about him today, so she pushed him out of her mind. "Not tall, dark, and handsome," she replied playfully. "I'm in a serious relationship with long, white, and sparkly."

Ethel laughed, "This I have to hear."

"I sold a wedding gown!" It felt so fantastic to say that out loud.

"Oh, Lottie dear! That's wonderful, wonderful news. I'm so happy for you. I knew it was just a matter of time. Your designs are glorious."

"Thank you, Ethel," she said, touched by her mentor's praise. "That means a lot to me. It's for my cousin Alex. As it turns out, her wedding gown was never ordered, so I didn't really have a choice but to step in and help."

"You certainly had a choice," Ethel said with some heat. "And because of the magnificent person you are, you said yes." Ethel smiled at her. "Your cousin is lucky to have you. Now, tell me all about the dress!"

Charlotte described the gown down to its very last detail. It was energizing to talk to someone who knew and understood all the intricacies of a wedding gown. As she finished, she brought out the two dress sleeves. "I looked through a bunch of my bridal books and did some online searching to see if this is a Scottish thistle pattern, but I have had little luck." She ran her hands over the lace of the sleeves. "I saw some thistle designs on tablecloths and linens, which sort of look like this, but nothing conclusive. I was hoping you'd take a look."

"Of course, dear," Ethel said, reaching for the fabric. "My, these are heavily embellished. Point out to me the pattern you think is a thistle design."

Once Charlotte pointed to a specific area, Ethel brought the sleeve up close, running her stiff and bent fingers delicately over the lace. "This is beautiful." She inspected it for several more seconds before saying, "Can you run to the bookcase in the front room? There's a comprehensive book called Couture Bridal."

"Sure thing," Charlotte said, jumping up to retrieve the book. Once in the living room it was surprisingly easy to locate. She quickly thumbed through the book. It looked like a valid source for all things bridal sewing. Handing it over, she took a sip of tea and crossed her fingers. Alex wouldn't be the only one crushed if it the lace turned out to not be Scottish. The idea of the gown having Scottish lace was so right and so romantic. It had to be true.

Ethel checked a few different pages before closing the book. "Hmm. Nothing in there. It certainly talks about lace, but just the different types, like Chantilly, Alençon and Duchesse. Nothing in there about Scottish patterns used in lace-making." Picking up the material again, Ethel said, "I can't say for certain whether this is or isn't a thistle pattern."

Seeing Charlotte's disappointment, Ethel gave her a sympathetic look. "Listen, my eyesight isn't what it used to be. Before you give up hope, you should talk to someone more knowledgeable about lace patterns.

"I have a friend, Mary, who's worked in the fabric industry in New York for years as a buyer. She's very well-informed about high end fabrics, lace, and embroidery. She'd be able to give you a definitive answer. I'll give you her contact information. Take a detailed photo and email her. I'll call her and tell her to keep an eye out for it."

Charlotte slumped back in the chair. "Thanks, Ethel. It's kind of you to offer." Dropping her chin on her hand, she sighed, "I've got my heart set on having that element in the dress. Sure, it would mean a great deal to Alex and Jason, but beyond that, the symbolism of having it incorporated into the dress takes the design to another level."

"Let's not give up hope just yet," Ethel replied, reaching for another cookie. "What's meant to happen will happen. You just have to have a little faith."

A little faith, a lot of luck, and fast sewing skills, Charlotte thought. Toasting Ethel with her teacup, she said, "As always, you're right. Now, tell me what you've been up to."

◆ ◆ ◆

It took all of Charlotte's patience to wait a few days before emailing Ethel's friend, Mary. It also gave her far too much time to fixate on the Scottish lace. She'd agonized over photographing it, laying the dress out carefully with different lighting scenarios, trying to capture the lace pattern perfectly.

With the latest round of photos on her phone, she jogged downstairs in search of Lisa. Not finding her in the house, she went out back. If Lisa wasn't in the kitchen, then chances are she was in the yard, working on her gardens. Spying her friend kneeling beside one of the planting beds, she made her way over.

"The gardens are looking fantastic this year," Charlotte said.

Lisa sat back and gazed up, pulling off her gloves. Looking out over the yard, she nodded. "They're shaping up quite nicely, I think."

Standing, she arched her back, rubbing it with her hands. "I spent too long hunched over the herb garden, but I'm determined to get rosemary to grow this year."

Charlotte tried to hide her smile. Lisa's ongoing feud with rosemary had lasted years. It was one of her favorite herbs, but each attempt at growing it had ended in epic failure. Lisa took it as a personal affront. She must have not been too successful in hiding her amusement, because Lisa stopped, her gaze narrowing.

"You had better not be laughing," she said vehemently. "I will win."

"I know you will be victorious," Charlotte replied, lacing her voice with sarcasm. "For no one strikes fear in a rosemary plant quite like you."

Charlotte ducked as Lisa's gardening gloves went sailing past her head. Lisa's aim was getting better. She must be practicing.

Smiling back at her friend, Charlotte said, "Come, weary warrior. 'Tis time for lemonade."

"You're a freak," Lisa replied, her lips twitching upwards. "But I am thirsty, so I'll take that lemonade."

Walking into the house, Charlotte went to the refrigerator while Lisa grabbed glasses. Settling down at the kitchen table, she waited until Lisa had taken a long sip of her drink.

"So, can you take a look at these photos of the dress," she started.

"Of the lace?" Lisa asked, her eyebrows raising. At Charlotte's nod she shook her head. "What is this, like round fifteen of photo shoots?"

"I'm just trying to get it right so Mary can see it clearly."

Lisa reached out for the phone and started scrolling through images. Looking up, she said, "These look fine to me. Why are you so worried about this?"

"It's important to Alex. She's so convinced it's Scottish I'm afraid she'll be terribly disappointed if it isn't. I have to admit, I've kind of got my heart set on it too," she ended with a sigh.

Passing back the phone, Lisa took another sip. "The photos look good. You've given Ethel enough time to get in touch. Go email that lady and find out already. Waiting is only going to make it worse."

"You're right. I'm going to go take care of it now."

Running back upstairs, Charlotte grabbed her laptop, sat down on her bed and crafted an email to Mary. Attaching the photos, she read through the text one last time.

"Here's goes nothing," she muttered as her finger hit send.

CHAPTER EIGHT

Charlotte

Charlotte checked the time again as she entered the final numbers into the spreadsheet. Saving the file, she closed it and started wrapping up at the office for the day. Waiting for Thursday to pick up the dress had been torture. Four whole days lost not working on it. She planned to make up for that time this afternoon. The pickup should be quick, and then she could spend the rest of the day working.

Within a few moments, Charlotte was out the door and heading home. As she drove, she replayed the various scenarios in her mind. If all the stains came out, she was golden; changes could proceed as planned. If the stains remained, she had a few options. Each option had its own pros and cons. She'd just have to wait and see it before deciding.

Pulling into the cleaners, she had a moment of panic. What were the chances Adam would be in today? Checking her hair before she got out of the car, she tried to tame a few errant hairs. She surely wasn't primping for him. She just wanted to look professional. At least that's what she told herself. Even if she didn't buy it.

Mrs. Mac greeted her with a big smile and immediately led her through the back. Charlotte had never even been behind the counter before. She tried not to gawk as Mrs. Mac crossed to a smaller room on the left. Once they entered, Charlotte was sure she was in heaven. A few wedding gowns hung in various places around the room, but there were also scores of other formal gowns and outfits. It looked like everything from baptism gowns to evening wear. She longed to go examine everything closely.

Right in the middle of the room was a table with her gown displayed on it. A petite woman with shoulder-length blonde hair was bending over the table inspecting a portion. Charlotte's body stiffened. Was something wrong with the gown?

"Cynthia," Mrs. Mac called. "Allow me to introduce you to Charlotte. Charlotte, this is Cynthia. Why don't you two get acquainted while I get Melissa to watch the front counter. I'll be right back."

As Mrs. Mac moved off, Cynthia stuck her hand out. "Charlotte, it's nice to meet you finally."

"Same here," Charlotte replied, shaking Cynthia's hand as her gaze darted around the room at all the different gowns. "This is the best room I've ever seen," she laughed.

Cynthia smiled. "It's easy to get sidetracked in here."

Before Charlotte could ask questions on the various gowns, Mrs. Mac returned. "Sorry about that. Melissa's got the counter, so shall we dive in?"

Moving toward the table, Cynthia indicated Charlotte should follow. Alex's wedding gown was face-down on the table. She'd know those lace cutouts anywhere.

"I wish I had better news," Cynthia started. "I wasn't able to get all the stains out of the front. They're a little lighter now, but there's still discoloration."

Charlotte restrained her sigh. She should have known this project would take the harder road. The new design would need to work around the discolored fabric.

"I was afraid of that," Charlotte offered. "It was a long shot. I appreciate you trying."

"My pleasure. I wish I'd been able to remove them." Cynthia frowned as if the dress had disappointed her, personally. "I also wanted to show you a few areas I'm concerned about. Before starting a project, especially something with vintage material like yours, we give it a complete examination to make sure there are no other stains or problem areas. In looking at some of the lacework on the dress, I've found areas of weakness. My concern is that during a regular cleaning, which I assume you'd want before the wedding,"—Cynthia paused until Charlotte nodded—"there's a possibility that some sections could sustain damages."

Charlotte felt the breath freeze in her body. Had she heard that correctly? What did that even mean? Blinking rapidly, she tried to reconcile what Cynthia was saying.

"Here, let me show you what I'm talking about." Cynthia took a section of gown's train in her hands, flipped it, and pulled it closer. Leaning toward Charlotte so they could both look at the underside, she ran her hand down until she came to one of the lace cutouts. Bringing that section closer to her face, she ran her fingers over the edge of the stitching. "I can feel it more than see it, but the thread on these embellishments is frayed and thin. And the edge fabric is far sheerer than I'd like."

Charlotte couldn't see any visual difference, so she ran her fingertip over the area. "I think I can feel what you mean about the edge fabric. Is this the only section that has the issue?" She forced her limbs to relax and inhaled. Now was not the time to panic... even though part of her mind screamed it was the perfect time to panic.

"Unfortunately, no. There are a few different areas." Placing the dress back down on the table, Cynthia pointed out the other cutout sections on the train and a few areas on the bodice.

"Any idea why it's like this?" Charlotte was proud that her voice was even and calm, even if she didn't feel that way. On the inside she was screaming, arms flailing, and in a full-on run.

"Well, it's any number of reasons. Age, any solvents or cleaners previously used, or even something used in the manufacturing of the original elements. It could just be poor quality thread that's degraded over time. There are just too many variables and it's passed through too many hands to be sure."

Charlotte continued to stare down at the dress letting Cynthia's words flow over her. While disappointing, it wasn't shocking that areas of the gown were a bit threadbare. Working with vintage gowns presented its own set of challenges. And it wasn't as if the dress was ruined... at least not yet. Straightening her shoulders, Charlotte looked over at Cynthia. "So, what's the worst-case scenario?"

"Well," Cynthia said, glancing over the fabric. "Worst case is the fabric in those areas fails and the embellishments become detached from the dress. That said, I don't think there's a high probability of that happening, but it is a possibility I wanted you to be aware of. Unfortunately, I can't predict how the fabric will respond."

Well, that didn't sound as bad as Charlotte feared. Just something to be aware of, but it would be better if she could remove even the possibility of an issue down the road. Even as she thought of solutions, she dismissed them just as fast. Looking at the various areas of the gown she'd have the work on, she shook her head.

This Saturday was a mere six weeks before the wedding. There simply wasn't time to complete all the work to change the dress and reinforce those areas. She'd just have to press on. If there was time, she'd go in and reinforce what she could, but other than that, she'd just have to pray.

"Couldn't you sew them again?"

Charlotte started at the sound of Adam's voice from behind her. She'd been so focused on the gown she hadn't noticed him come in. Glancing over, her eyes took in the way his light blue button-down shirt hugged his chest, accentuating his broad shoulders. He undoubtedly had a swimmer's build she thought to herself, her eyes followed the line of his body as it tapered to his waist. Hell, even his ordinary gray pants looked delicious hugging his thighs. He probably would still look smoking hot if he wore burlap.

Determined not to drool, she glanced up to find him smirking at her. Eyebrow cocked, his eyes twinkling with humor, he was obviously having a lot of fun with the fact that he caught her checking him out.

Turning back to the dress, she started fiddling with the fabric. "Um," she stammered, mentally kicking herself for letting him get to her. "Ah, if only sewing it were that easy," she finally answered, pausing as she realized what she'd said. Duh. "Well, technically it is that easy," she started again, keeping her eyes glued to the dress. "Sewing and reinforcing are pretty straightforward."

She steeled herself, then met his gaze and was drawn in by the depth of his green eyes. Her mouth went dry. How was it he had such long eyelashes? Had she ever looked at a guy's eyelashes before? She didn't think so, but it was hard to unsee how delightfully long and dark his were.

"The issue is time." She licked her lips, hoping no one was aware of how flustered she was. Who knew she'd have to take a pause in the game for eyelash appreciation. The thought made her want to laugh out loud. Yup, she was officially losing it.

"My project plan is very tight, especially now with the stains not coming out completely. I'll need to design around them."

"Ah, yes. The project plan," he smiled.

Charlotte could see the merriment reflected in those damn eyes. Was he mocking or joking? "Yes. A complete breakdown of all tasks, timing, and deadlines."

Thankfully, Mrs. Mac chimed in before Adam could respond. "Do you have any ideas on how you're going to work around the stains?"

"There are a few options," Charlotte replied, her brow furrowing as she considered the dress. "I could try to hide the stains with lace from the sleeves. Although, I might consider removing the damaged fabric and adding new panels on either side of the skirt. The bride likes the fullness, so I wouldn't want to just remove panels without replacing them. The issue there is finding something to match the current fabric."

"Oh, well," Mrs. Mac smiled. "If you need fabric, you need to go see our friend Barry. He owns Cord Textile Company. They have a large fabric warehouse here in Connecticut. If you're looking for something special, that's the place to go." Her smile fell, "Although their warehouse is rather tricky to find."

"I'm sure that won't be a problem," Charlotte interrupted. "Thank you for the tip. I'll have to check them out."

"Adam," Mrs. Mac continued as if Charlotte hadn't spoken. "You can drive Charlotte to the warehouse and introduce her to Barry. You remember where it's located, right?" Without waiting for a reply, she barreled forward. "Now tell me how the Scottish lace mystery is coming along. Here, we can pack up the gown while you give me an update."

Charlotte blinked a couple of times, trying to process everything Mrs. Mac had said. It was considerate of her to order Adam to drive her, but there was no way that was going to happen. Given her reaction to Adam, an outing together sounded both stimulating and panic-inducing. And to have him ordered to take her was the most embarrassing thing she could think of. She'd let Adam know he was off the hook, but first she needed to bring Mrs. Mac up-to-date on the Scottish lace.

In short order, the gown was packed, and Charlotte had told the story of the lace. "So, I emailed Mary photos, and I'm just waiting to hear from her. Fingers crossed she can identify the pattern as Scottish."

"It sounds like you're in the right hands," Mrs. Mac replied. "When you see Barry, you may think of asking him as well."

Best to clear the air about the Barry trip. "Thank you so much for suggesting Cord Textiles. I'm sure I'll be able to find it if you just give me the address. Or I could look it up."

"Nonsense." Mrs. Mac waved her hand. "Adam will get you there. It's tucked away in an industrial park down by the shore. Now, I have to get back to the counter. Take care, dear. Adam," she called as she sailed out of the room, "coordinate with Charlotte on getting her down to see Barry."

Before she could say anything, Cynthia turned to her. "Charlotte, it was a pleasure to finally meet you. I'm looking forward to working with you more. Take care."

"Cynthia, I can't thank you enough for your care and effort on all of my dresses. I really appreciate it."

"I'm a big fan of your work and can't wait to see what you do with this one," Cynthia replied before leaving the room.

Now Charlotte was all alone with Adam. No way around it,

she needed to put the kibosh on the warehouse trip. Drawn to him or not, there was no need for him to drive her. The fact that she had such a physical response to him just made it imperative that she not go out of her way to spend time with him.

She knew it was fear holding her back. Was it so wrong that she didn't want to be hurt again? It had taken her so long to get over what had happened with Todd, she wasn't sure she could survive another heart break.

Best to dive right in. "Adam, you really don't need to take me down to the warehouse." She made eye contact and was again mesmerized by his gaze. Did he always look like he was up to mischief? Ignoring the jump in her heart rate, she continued, "You can just send me the address. I'm sure I can locate it.

Ignoring her question, Adam stepped closer. "I'm really sorry we weren't able to get all the stains out," he said softly.

The change in topic didn't unnerve her as much as his nearness. She tried slowing her pulse by taking a deep breath. That only made things worse as she inhaled his intoxicating scent of a deep pine forest, but there was something light and floral about it as well. Lavender? Citrus?

Feeling the heat creep up her neck, she turned to stare down at the gown, trying to avoid him seeing her blush. Fingering the dress bag, she tried to remember what they were discussing. "Um. The dress looks great."

"Cynthia is very proficient at what she does. If anyone could have gotten those stains out, it would have been her."

Stains! That's what he'd said.

"Cynthia is a miracle worker. I'm sure if there was any way to remove them, she would have." She felt a little more in control when she didn't look at him, but she needed to make sure he understood about the warehouse. She risked a glance and was struck by just how close he was standing. Clearing her throat, she regrouped. "So about the warehouse..."

"Why don't you give me your number?"

"What?" Did he just really ask for my number? This conversation is becoming like an out-of-body experience.

"Your number. I'll text you so we can coordinate the road trip to see Barry."

"Adam, you don't need to take me. As I said, I'm more than capable."

"You heard my mom, right?" he offered.

"Yes," she replied slowly.

"Mom said."

"Mom said?" A giggle escaped her lips even as she wondered if she'd heard him correctly. As arguments went, 'because Mom said' was pretty weak.

Hearing her laugh, his face lit up with a smile as he leaned over to grab the dress bag. His arm barely brushed hers, but it sent a spark of desire through her. Bag in hand, he straightened, maddeningly close. He paused, staring down into her eyes with an intensity that both scared and thrilled her. The heat of him reached out to her, wrapping around her body. She wanted what she should not want. His touch. With only inches separating them, she could see the rise and fall of his chest. Was it possible she was not the only one affected by their closeness?

Her tongue flicked out to wet her suddenly dry lips. She watched as his eyes darkened and dropped to her mouth. The heat of his gaze set her on fire, the warmth pooling in her belly. Her breasts felt heavy even as she could feel her breath quickening.

A loud bang from outside the room broke the moment, causing Charlotte to take a step back. With a last dark look at her, Adam folded the dress bag over his arm and walked toward the door. "Mom said, Charlotte," he called over his shoulder. Turning at the door to look at her, he arched an eyebrow. "While you may be more than willing to blow that off, there's no way in hell I'm going to."

It took a moment for Charlotte to shake herself loose from the spell his proximity cast over her. When she ran through what he'd said, it was all she could do not to laugh. Which was good because she might snort. As it was, a giggle still escaped as she shot back, "You're really going to drive me because your mom ordered you to?"

Adam's face was the picture of innocence. "What's so funny about that?" The corner of his mouth twitched up.

He was kidding with her, and she liked it. A lot. Was there anything more attractive on a man than a sense of humor? "It's just interesting to meet a man so afraid of his mommy," she laughed.

"Darn right," he said, turning back to leave the room. "And if you mess with my mom's plans, don't think I wouldn't throw you under the bus in a heartbeat," he deadpanned as she came up beside him.

"Oh, would you now?" she poked, enjoying the banter between them. Making their way to the front, they brushed against each other, sending tingles up and down Charlotte's arms. "And how would you do that?"

"Oh, I'd tell her it was all your fault."

Following him toward the storefront, Charlotte didn't dare reply with Mrs. Mac standing right there working with a customer. Adam rounded the counter and started walking toward the exit. "You wouldn't dare!" she hissed, catching up with him.

Opening the front door, he moved to look her in the eye and whispered back, "Count on it, sweetheart." A huge grin broke out across his face, and his gaze danced with merriment.

So keyed up by the conversation, Charlotte didn't even miss a beat when he called her sweetheart, although she stored it away for later analysis. Following him down the outside steps, she knew he had her. She would hate for Mrs. Mac to think she turned down her generous offer. It made her so frustrated she wanted to stamp her foot and yell. Thankfully she refrained, her shoulders dropping as she sighed. "Fine. We'll go together," she muttered, unlocking her car.

Adam laid the dress across the backseat, stood up and took out his phone. "Digits, darling," he drawled.

She realized he was provoking her, but that didn't prevent her from giving him a scowl. It only made his smile bigger. Reading off her number, she quickly climbed into the car and started it as Adam walked back toward the store.

Before she could start driving, her phone rang. She answered it automatically.

"Would it really be that bad, Charlotte?" The seriousness of his voice surprised her.

Turning, she saw him standing across the lot by the door.

"If you don't want to go, I'll understand."

She could hear the something soft and vulnerable in his voice. She swallowed and said, "No. It'll be better if we go together. Thank your mother for offering you."

His smile was back. "Just text me when you want to go. My schedule seems to be a lot more flexible than yours," he chuckled. Disconnecting, he put the phone in his pocket and went back inside.

Charlotte took a breath. It felt like forever since she'd inhaled deeply. Both hands on the steering wheel, she took a few more. Guess I have a date. Is it a date? Technically his mother set it up, so perhaps that disqualifies it. She hadn't dated in quite some time, so she wasn't as knowledgeable on the date/no date protocols.

Maybe Lisa would know.

CHAPTER NINE

Charlotte

Adam picked Charlotte up at eight-thirty sharp on Friday morning. Too early for a date, though Lisa insisted otherwise. Still, if this place was as amazing as Mrs. Mac said, it would be an invaluable resource. Charlotte and Adam had texted back and forth for a bit before finalizing plans. She found herself enjoying that as much as their in-person banter.

She also realized that date or not, she was looking forward to taking the trip with him. The idea of spending all that time with him in close quarters made her palms sweat and butterflies erupt in her stomach, but she somehow knew they would have a fun time.

Grabbing a hoodie in case it was cooler by the shoreline, she locked up the house and walked over to the driveway. Adam was leaning against his car, arms folded, just watching her. She thought he'd looked hot in his blue button-down shirt. Well, it didn't hold a candle to Adam in a black t-shirt and jeans. His dark hair was windblown but still looked soft enough that she wanted to run her fingers through it. As she got closer to him, she had to remind herself to keep both hands pinned to her sides.

She loved Adam's car on sight. "A Volkswagen GTI. I love it."

He grinned. "A lady of good taste."

"I'm partial to VWs myself," she said, admiring the 4-door white Volkswagen. He held the door open as she self-consciously slid into the passenger seat, leaning in so he could close her door. After he settled into the driver's seat, he turned and asked her the all-important question.

"Music preferences?"

"Well, I always follow standard road trip protocols. I'm not sure if you do," she said, lifting an eyebrow in challenge.

"Oh, so it's going to be like that," he joked, his smile growing larger as she laughed. "Fine. Driver's preference then. I'll do a shuffle of my music."

As Adam drove, they settled into a comfortable companionship. They talked about everything and nothing. Charlotte's worst fear was an awkward and stilted car ride, but she was relieved to find herself comfortable talking with him. As the miles rolled by, Charlotte felt herself relax.

When they arrived at the warehouse, she admitted it was a right choice to have Adam take her. Tucked away in a rabbit warren industrial park, she'd quickly lost her bearings as they took various turns. Adam was far too pleased with the admission.

Having never been to a fabric warehouse, she wasn't sure what she was expecting, but whatever it was, Cord Textiles wasn't it. The large, low, brick building was whitewashed and looked out of place with the rest of the industrial park. The building was older, although the peeling paint may have aged it prematurely. Perhaps the park had sprung up around the building. That would explain the dramatic difference.

While the entrance was as nondescript as the rest of the building, once through the doors, it was as if she'd crossed from black and white to color. The rows and rows of fabric bolts were a feast for the eyes. She let out a small gasp as she took in the kaleidoscope of colors stretching all the way to the metal roof. Her eyes bounced around, taking in the regal looking plaid patterns, the soft velvet cloth that begged to be touched, the sturdy heavy weave of wools, and the silken drape of silks. She'd seen nothing like it. It was like a fabric addict's Shangri-La.

Only a few steps inside the door, she stopped abruptly, overwhelmed by the sheer vastness of it all. Adam skirted around her and approached the counter and small office just off to the left. He started speaking to the employee there when a large man barreled out of the office and came around the counter. Tall and broad shouldered with an enormous belly, his speed and intensity were disconcerting.

"Adam!" The man grabbed him by the shoulders and pulled him into a big hug. Shifting back, he looked him up and down. "I can't believe how grown up you are! It's been far too long!"

A smile lighting up his face, Adam reached up to grasp the man's arms. "It's nice to see you, too, Barry. How have you been?"

"I'm good, I'm good." Barry's smile was as large as his personality, and humor danced in his eyes. This was a gentleman who enjoyed life. "Sophia sends her love. She's not here today, unfortunately. She's going to be upset she missed you. I couldn't believe it when your mom called to say you were going to pay me a visit."

Adam shook his head. "I should've known she'd call ahead." Gesturing back, Adam said, "Barry, let me introduce you to Charlotte. She's a very talented bridal gown designer in search of something special. As I'm sure Mom told you," he added.

"Mom and I both told Charlotte there's no one better than you."

"Jackie mentioned something to me yesterday about you bringing your girl around."

Adam shot a look over to Charlotte, eyebrows raised, clearly as shocked as Charlotte was. Then she saw the twitch of his lips and knew he saw the humor of his matchmaking momma in action.

Before she could correct Barry's assumptions, his giant stride ate the distance between them. Charlotte had a moment of panic when he was looming over her. He was an imposing figure, but then he smiled and held out his hand. "It's nice to meet you, Charlotte. Jackie tells me I'm to make sure you get only the best —as if I would have it any other way!"

Barry's hand engulfed hers, but his grip was gentle and warm. Dropping her hand and turning abruptly, Barry started walking toward through the rows of fabric. "Come on," he called over his shoulder. "I'll show you to the bridal section. It's in the back near the entrance to the other warehouse."

"There's another warehouse?" Charlotte hissed to Adam as they turned to follow. Adam didn't respond other than to widen his grin.

Metal shelving towered over them, filled with roll after roll of fabric. The sheer quantity of inventory was simply overwhelming. Her inclination was to just stand and stare, but Barry was striding off into the rows. For every step the man took, Charlotte swore she took three.

"I told you this place was the best," Adam said as he and Charlotte tried to keep up with the big man. "If he doesn't have a fabric, then it's probably not worth having." Adam increased his pace, looking over at Charlotte who struggling to keep up. "Let's see some speed. Barry's a force of nature that doesn't like to wait for us mere mortals."

"You think?" she huffed, trying to make her feet move faster while also stealing glances at all the fabric they were passing. "Barry seems to have personality to spare. I'm guessing he may be a force of nature, but a gentle giant."

The further they ventured into the warehouse, the harder it was to concentrate as they passed one gorgeous fabric after another. Her fingers itched to touch them, but no way could she do that and keep up. She promised herself a return trip so she could fully explore. Glancing around, she amended that. She'd need multiple trips.

Noticing his charges were falling behind, Barry slowed his pace, thankfully. Charlotte could take a breath and when he asked, she filled him in on her business and current fabric quest. She wanted to make sure he knew that today was a scouting mission. She hadn't committed to a specific redesign path yet. Before she could do that, she needed to understand all her options.

Exiting one of the last rows, Charlotte tripped over her feet, stunned by the sight before her. Adam reached out a hand to steady her, but her eyes were captured by the rows of silk and satins, the yards of lace and sequins—from plain to exotic all collected all in one space. The sheer beauty of it took her breath away. She never imagined this many options existed.

"Sort of overwhelming, isn't it?" Adam whispered in her ear.

"You have no idea," she managed to say. She hadn't realized he was so close. His breath caressed her ear, sending tendrils of heat curling into her stomach.

Barry turned and gestured. "From what you've said, you should start here on the left. Those should be the closest to what you're looking for. As you can see, there's a lot to consider.

"If you have questions, or if you're ready to have something cut, just pick up the yellow phone on the wall there. Someone will come help you. I have some things to attend to, so if I don't see you before you leave," he held out a hand to Adam, "it was nice seeing you. Stop by more often. Although Jackie and I have discussed a date for a get-together, so I could be up your way soon. It's been far too long since we've seen your parents."

"Charlotte," Barry extended a hand to her as well. "It was a pleasure. I've never heard of a business like yours, and I confess, I'm intrigued. I hope we'll see you here again. When we get together with Adam's folks, perhaps you can bring one of your dresses by so me and the Mrs. can see it. I can already tell she's going to be fascinated by what you do."

Before she could respond or do more than thank him, Barry swept up the row and disappeared. "You weren't kidding about the force of nature thing," she said, watching Barry disappear into the aisles.

Looking fondly at Barry's retreating back, Adam smiled. "No. He is that, for sure. But a nicer man you'll never meet. And his wife Sophie is a delight. She and my mother get along famously. The running joke is that when they retire someday, they're going to terrorize the senior citizen cruising community."

"Oh, I'm sure they will. You better start saving cash now," she joked. "I hear international bail money is pricey." Looking around at the fabric, she speared him with a glance. "Now, no more talking. I must dive in to all this loveliness."

Charlotte started where Barry had indicated, skipping fabrics she knew would never work. Adam started further down the row and would occasionally pull a fabric for her to look at. Working their way toward each other, it was an exercise in concentration, as all the different materials seemed to call out to her. She let herself indulge, running her fingers over a bolt of Chantilly lace, her fingertips following the delicate curves and swirls. It seemed so fragile, but she knew from experience it was tougher than it looked. This pattern would look amazing on another dress project she had in the workroom.

Her mind started running with ideas of how and where she'd incorporate the stunning lace. She wished she'd brought her design book so she could sketch out a few ideas. The final result was so clear to her, right down to a dream bride walking down a sun dappled aisle, the lace falling softly over the train.

Lost inside her world of fabrics and lace, it startled her to hear Adam laughing. Confused, she glanced up to see what was so amusing. He was standing just a few feet away, looking at her. Did she have something on her? A quick visual inspection eased that fear. One solid glare in his direction, and he explained.

"Are you aware that you hum and mutter while shopping?"

"I do not," she said hesitantly. Lisa had accused her of the same thing when working on dresses. But she would have realized if it was a habit, especially if she did it in public.

"Oh, you do, Charlotte. You really do." His tone was teasing as he moved closer. "I've been trying to make out what you're saying, but it seems to just be bits and fragments about the dress, I think."

Charlotte felt herself flush. He must have thought she was daft. The nervous butterflies in her stomach returned, and her palms were sweating like crazy. Before she could reply, he jumped in.

"I think it's magnificent, Charlotte. I'm convinced it's the sign of a creative mind," he offered. "Now, I've been writing down the fabric I found that you said were possibilities. Why don't you give me the information on the ones you found? That should make it easier if you decide to come back and get some."

Focusing on the task at hand and not the nearness of Adam,

Charlotte read out the information from a few different bolts of fabric. If she went this route, she had options. "I think that about does it," she said. "Your mom was right. This place is a gold mine. Thanks for bringing me."

Adam looked into her eyes. "It was my pleasure." He glanced at her lips before meeting her gaze again, his eyes darkening. It was as if the world slipped away and all she could see was him. The intensity of his look made a shiver of heat travel down her back. How was it the interaction between them could fluctuate so quickly? One moment it was comfortable and casual; the next, it was heat and passion.

His hand brushed lightly over her jaw, making her skin tingle and erupt in goosebumps. Her lips parted as she tried to steady her breath, even as his nearness stole it from her. He captured a loose strand of hair, winding it around his finger before releasing it and tucking it behind her ear. His fingers trailed down her neck, and she could feel every fluttering thud of her heartbeat as it echoed in her ears. She prayed he wouldn't be able to feel her racing pulse as his hand lingered on her neck.

She ached to return the caress, to feel the slight stubble of growth along his jawline. She imagined running her hands across his wide shoulders and down his chest, which would, of course, prompt him to wrap his arms around her and pull her to him.

He was already so close; she could smell the unique scent that was Adam. She could feel the heat of him reaching out to her, curling its way into her body. All she'd have to do was stretch up on her toes and she could taste his lips. What would he taste like? Would he kiss her back?

She would bet her last yard of lace that he was a great kisser, almost groaning out loud with the thought of his mouth on hers. What her life needed was more toe-curling, breath-stealing, shiver-inducing kissing. It had been far too long since she'd kissed a man—not since Todd had left her.

The echo of Todd's betrayal sent a shaft of pain through her heart, causing her to step back. "So," she said, her voice coming out weird and high. She wanted to kick herself. Kissing Adam was not a smart choice. Even daydreaming about kissing Adam was a dumb move. But more than that, what she hated was the reminder of Todd. The pain and humiliation burned in her stomach. She needed to steer clear and get things back on track. Clearing her throat, she tried again. "So, we best be going."

Adam paused, his shoulders dropping, before glancing around. "Wouldn't you like to look around some more before we go?"

Kind of a stupid question, because of course that's what she wanted to do. As much as she wanted to say yes, she knew she couldn't. This moment was awkward enough, prolonging it would be torturous. "I wouldn't subject you to that," she joked, hoping to get them back to the comfortable friendship zone they had enjoyed.

"Well, at least look around here so you know more fully what they have," he offered, his voice flat. "You never know what you may need down the road," he added with a small smile.

If he was going to be all logical with her, who was she to fight it? "That would be wonderful, as long as you don't mind," she asked even as she started walking toward the lace and tulle section. Hearing his laugh, she took that as a yes. "Put the timer on 20," she threw over her shoulder. "If I go longer than that, pull me out!"

His laughter ringing in her ears, she spent a delirious ten minutes touching and looking at all the different options. Elbow deep in fabric, her mind whirling with possibilities for projects, it took a moment to realize her phone was vibrating. Digging into in her bag, she saw Alex was calling and swiped to take the call.

"Alex, I'm at the most incredible place. You should see..." she started to say, but quickly fell silent as Alex talked over her. She listened for a few minutes as her cousin wailed about having to get Aunt Jennifer's approval. "No. No, I understand. But Alex..." She fell silent again as Alex cut her off.

Adam was now standing in front of her, eyebrows raised. He

mouthed, "Everything okay?"

She wasn't sure it was, but she nodded anyway. Alex was upset, her voice shrill and talking fast, so she let Alex continue hoping she'd vent the worst of her feelings. Maybe then Charlotte could circle back and ask questions.

Why was Alex talking about getting Aunt Jennifer's approval? What did that mean? Wasn't Aunt Jennifer on board already? At their initial lunch, Alex said she'd take care of that.

"I know it's a lot to ask, Lottie. I really thought we were past this," Alex said, her voice breaking. "I've tried talking to Mom, but she's not listening. I thought she was fine with everything, but I guess she wasn't. She's been going to bridal salons looking for dresses. Without me!

"Out of the blue, she announced at dinner that she'd found my dress. She has a bridal salon holding it for me. She even put down a deposit!"

"I didn't think there was time to get something ordered?" Charlotte asked when Alex took a breath.

"It's a sample dress, so it doesn't have to be ordered. I'd buy it off the rack, provided it fit. But that's the point, I don't want to buy it. I want the gown you're making."

"Alex, it's going to be fine," she soothed, trying to calm both Alex and herself. If the pit in her stomach hurt any worse, she thought she might be ill. This was not the moment to fall apart. She needed Alex to take a breath so she could explain the entire situation. So far, it felt like she'd only told Charlotte part of it. "Please, just explain what you meant by your mom's approval."

"I'm sorry," she sniffed. "I'm not making much sense. As you can imagine, Mom and I got into a bit of an argument. Well, it got so bad that dad stepped in, and he negotiated a compromise."

Charlotte sighed in relief. Uncle Bill was the levelheaded one in that family. And he had an intense dislike for drama. God bless Uncle Bill. Hopefully he hadn't made a terrible deal.

"Mom and I agreed that she'd come, with an open mind, to see the dress you're making. I know once she sees it on me, she'll have to agree it's the best option," Alex finished breathlessly.

"I hear what you're saying, but Alex, the dress is all torn apart. I'm in the middle of alterations." Charlotte tried to keep the panic from her voice. "Do you know what specifically she objects to? Is it the style? We can't change a lot, but perhaps we can make a few minor adjustments."

Alex sighed. "I think one of the major issues is it's a used gown. I keep calling it vintage. She keeps calling it second hand. She just has a hangup about it." Alex stopped, but it sounded like there was more.

Charlotte had to ask, "What are her other issues?"

Alex said nothing.

Charlotte felt the punch in her gut. Turns out, Aunt Jennifer and her own mom actually were cut from the same cloth. "Let me guess," she said bitterly. "Her issue is me." It was so hard to say those words out loud, and damn if they didn't make her feel worse once they were verbalized. She wanted to believe she was wrong, but she knew in her heart she wasn't.

"Oh Lottie, no," Alex exclaimed. "Not you. She loves you."

Right now, this didn't feel much like love. She should have known this was going to happen. Aunt Jennifer didn't think she could do it. She was kidding herself if she thought her family would look at her as anything other than some amateur with a cute little hobby.

Maybe they were right. Maybe this was a bad idea. Here was her chance to scrap the whole thing. Did she really need this level of crap in her life? And it wouldn't stop here. Even if she could somehow convince Aunt Jennifer she was up to the task, that argument would never go away. Eventually, her mother would hear she was involved, and she'd be facing this all over again. She'd never be good enough, and they'd never see her as a capable designer. How many times did she have to fight this fight?

Alex continued, unaware of Charlotte's inner despair. "It's just that it's a tight timeline, is all. That's all."

Charlotte bit back her heated response. This wasn't Alex's fault. "You don't have to sugarcoat it for me. You and I both know what's going on." She was almost successful in keeping the hurt out of her voice. "So, Uncle Bill has negotiated a summit. When?"

"Can you do it next Saturday?" Alex asked timidly.

"Next Saturday!" she exclaimed. That was crazy. What had Uncle Bill gotten her into? "And to imagine, I thought he was on my side," she whispered.

"Charlotte," Alex pleaded. "I know it's last minute. I know the dress isn't done. And I know this isn't fair. I apologize for dragging you into this. I'd love to just pull the plug and say I'll get the dress my mom wants. But I can't do that. And honestly... I don't think you want that either. I know how you feel about what you do. For you, the magic is in the story of each gown. All that love and well-wishing is stored up in the fabric. With this gown, I feel like that too.

"The dress you're making is the right choice, and you know it. It was meant to be. I knew it the moment I saw it. And what about the Scottish lace? It doesn't get better than that! You just need to believe in that and believe in yourself, and we can change my mom's mind. I'm sure of it."

Hearing her cousin plead her case was a straight shot to her heart. Hearing her verbalize how they both felt about this dress put her over the edge. "Fine. Fine, Alex. You win. We'll have an Aunt Jennifer Summit on Saturday."

Charlotte couldn't help but smile hearing her cousin's joyous squeal. Assuring Alex she'd call so they could make plans, she hung up and looked over to find Adam staring at her.

"That sounded like an interesting call."

Shaking her head, Charlotte walked over to where he was standing, "Sorry about that. But yeah, it was an interesting call to say the least."

"Trouble in wedding gown land?"

"You could say that." She reached out to caress the silk duchess satin fabric bolt closest to her. Feeling the smooth material slip through her fingers relaxed her. She could do this. "My aunt isn't on board with the idea of me making Alex's dress from some 'used' gown someone tossed away. My words, but basically her sentiment."

They turned and started walking down the aisle. "So, you're having a summit with said aunt?" he asked.

Charlotte blew out her cheeks. It sounded even worse when he said it out loud. "Even though the dress isn't done, we need to get her approval before we can continue. She went behind Alex's back and has a dress on hold at some bridal salon." Charlotte felt her jaw tighten. Aunt Jennifer was out of line, both with shopping behind Alex's back and also for discounting Charlotte's skills.

Taking a deep breath, she shook out her clenched hands and focused on breathing out all negative thoughts in her exhale. Alex wasn't wrong. This dress was the right one, and Charlotte was the right person to create it. Now she just had to hold on to that thought and stay positive.

Adam grabbed her hand. "Charlotte." He pulled her to face him, staring down at her with those intense green eyes. She could get lost in them forever. Were those little flecks of gold she saw or just reflections from the overhead lights? Gold flecks, she decided. Definitely gold.

"Charlotte, I believe in you." Adam reached out and tucked that same errant strand of hair back behind her ear, causing her breath to hitch. If it meant that Adam would always touch her like that, she would train that hair to fly out of place regularly.

His fingertips left a sizzling trail of quivers which blossomed into a stream of heat that traveled through her. Her awareness of him bubbled to the surface again, but his words echoed in her mind, leaving their own trail of warmth across her psyche. He believed in her. Did he really just say that? Could this man get any more attractive?

"You hardly know me," she couldn't help saying.

"I know enough," he whispered, his eyes traveling over her face. "I know you care very much for your cousin. I know my mom thinks you're super talented, and she's never wrong. You're smart and conscientious. And, most importantly, I know you're passionate about what you do. In the end, that's what matters most."

Charlotte felt rooted to the floor, allowing his words to flow over her. She'd never had a man see her so completely and deeply before. Her chest was tight; the emotions his words invoked were almost unbearable, to the point of being painful. What did people do with all these big emotions? She felt like crying and jumping for joy at the same time. It was all she could do to not throw her arms around his neck and kiss those tantalizing lips.

"Thank you, Adam," she whispered huskily, praying that none of her internal agitation showed. "That means a lot to me."

He looked a little flustered and gave her hand a squeeze before letting go. "Well," he said turning away from her to walk again. "I meant every word." Clearing his throat, he continued, "Are you ready to leave?"

"Let me just take a few things to the front counter and get a small sample so I can see how it plays with the dress."

As they made their way out of the store, she felt like she was on a teeter-totter. One moment she was replaying the conversation with Alex, her stomach in knots and plagued with doubts. The next, she remembered Adam's words, which filled her with happiness. Maybe she should just let the two different factions duke it out and leave her out of it.

Adam held the door and as she passed him, she heard his phone chirp a few times. Seemed like someone wanted to reach him. Adam grabbed it and gave the screen a quick glance. Whatever it was, he didn't seem pleased.

"If you have to get that, Adam, please do," she offered. He'd given up his day to bring her here; the least she could do was not hold him back from his regular life.

"No," he said, checking the screen one last time. "No need." He looked at her, all trace of displeasure gone from his face. Perhaps she had imagined it.

"I can deal with it later. Now," he rubbed his hands together. "I'm thinking about lunch!"

"Lunch? Already? It's not even 11:00 yet."

"I know, but it'll take us about forty minutes to get there. I'm thinking about the most astoundingly delectable, utterly unique cheeseburger. So juicy and tender, you'll cry it's so amazing."

Charlotte's traitorous stomach chose at that moment to rumble. Loudly. Laughing and holding a hand over her stomach, she said, "Tell me you didn't hear that!"

"Was that yours or mine?" he asked. "Doesn't matter. Have you ever had a steamed cheeseburger?"

"I beg your pardon?" She obviously hadn't heard him correctly.

"A steamed cheeseburger."

"That's not a thing." Now he was just making stuff up.

"No, really, it is. Instead of being grilled or pan fried, the burgers are steamed in small trays. I guess you could call it a regional food item. There's an awesome place on the way home. We'll stop, and you'll try one."

"A steamed cheeseburger?" She wasn't sure what to think about that. Why would that taste good?

"You're going to love it," he added with a bright smile, the twinkle of mischief back in his eye.

◆ ◆ ◆

Fifty minutes later, her mouth smeared with ketchup and cheese, she had to admit Adam was right. Looking at him as he munched on a french fry, she could see it in his eyes. He knew he was right too.

Swallowing the final delicious bite, she reached for her napkin. Before she could, Adam leaned over and wiped a bit of cheese from the corner of her mouth. His fingers slowed, and she could see his eyes linger on her mouth before he met her gaze. For a moment, they both sat staring at each other, not saying a word.

Their waitress returned with soda refills, breaking the moment. Sitting back against the plush booth seat, she took a sip of her drink to give herself a moment. It was scary how quickly the energy between them could change—as if it simmered below the surface all along and just needed a moment to leap forward.

She grabbed a fresh napkin and finished wiping her face and fingers. "That," she said roughly. Clearing her throat, she tried again. "That was astonishing. You were right. Thanks for bringing me here."

"My pleasure. I love introducing people to new foods. When I move into a new city, I love trying original foods or regional dishes. It's like a scavenger hunt for all the amazing places to eat."

"Have you moved around a lot?" she asked.

"I wouldn't say a lot, but my mother sure seems to think so," he laughed. He took on a more serious tone. "My career has taken me to some amazing places. I've lived in Boston, Tampa, Denver."

"Wow," she replied flatly, her heart falling. It sounded like Adam had moved every couple of years. "I hadn't realized you'd lived so many places. Doesn't all that moving around get tiring?"

"Well, some of the physical part of moving is a pain, but a new city means new adventures. Also, I've been able to advance my career by not limiting myself to one geographic area. I go where my career needs me to go, and that's important to me."

Charlotte didn't allow her disappointment to show. He was obviously committed to his career and didn't mind not putting down roots in any one place. There was nothing wrong with that, but for her, it would be a very lonely existence. In coming back to Jennings Township, she'd found her place and her people. They made her feel accepted and treated her like family.

Shifting her gaze to look around the restaurant, she wondered where his next career leap would take him. And even though it shouldn't matter to her, it did. Picking a piece of lint off her arm, she couldn't help but wonder how long until his next adventure.

She tried to shake off her mood as they finished up their sodas, but negative thoughts kept popping into her head. About Adam. About Alex and the dress. This whole situation with Aunt Jennifer. She could only imagine what her mother would say when she found out. As they walked back to the car, she tried to push all the doubts away and focus on all the things going right.

"I think this calls for a celebration," Adam said, interrupting her negative thought cycle. He was standing next to the car, arms over his head, stretching.

"A celebration? Not sure I follow you."

His smiled widened as he explained, "Well, you found fabric heaven. You got to try steamed cheeseburgers. And they were incredible." He wiggled his eyebrows at her, making her laugh.

"Yes," she smiled back. "They were delicious."

"We had a splendid meal, a fun ride, and a productive errand. All in all, it's been an awesome day." Adam opened her car door, leaning in with a roguish look. "That calls for a treat."

"Oh, you think so, do you?" She arched an eyebrow at him, more than happy to play along. She loved his sense of humor and how he saw the world.

"Yes, it does," he continued. "How else can I convince you to stop for ice cream on the way home? I'm really in the mood for a sundae."

Laughing, she slid into the car. Looking up at him, she shook her head. "How could you eat anything else after all we just had?"

"Watch me!" he laughed. "And to think we have your hobby to thank for this tremendous day."

Charlotte heard his words, and they carved a path of grief through her heart, taking her breath away.

Her hobby.

Her little hobby.

So that's what he thought about her work. Unbidden, the memory of her mother flinging those same words at her surfaced. As much as she tried to push the memory away, she felt the same crippling pain as it replayed in her mind.

There are thousands of talented kids slaving away, waiting for their big break. Do you really think you're better than them? That somehow you have what it takes when they don't? These outfits you make for yourself are fine. But it's just a nice little hobby. That's all it is.

Charlotte's hands clenched into fists. Her mother didn't

believe in her. Her aunt had made that very clear as well. To hear it from Adam was almost too much to bear. As the door opened and he slipped into his seat, she turned and looked out her window, blinking back tears.

"Thank you for the invitation for ice cream, Adam," she said, glad her voice sounded somewhat even with her throat so tight. "But I have so much to do. Can you just take me home, please?"

"Oh. Yeah, okay. If that's what you want."

Charlotte nodded but didn't turn back. She kept her eyes focused out her window, hoping he didn't notice as a stray tear escaped.

CHAPTER TEN

Adam

Adam wasn't sure what was going on. How could the mood of this outing change in such a short amount of time? He walked through the events again. They'd had a grand time bantering back and forth. He loved the way she joked around with him, comfortable enough to sass him right back. It was captivating, and she seemed to enjoy it as well.

He opened the door for her and used all of his charm and persuasive skills to convince her to get ice cream. He closed the door and walked to the other side of the car. It was that simple. What could have happened between the time he closed the door and when he got into the car? When he slid in next to her, it felt like a wall of ice was between them. She asked to be taken home. She gave one-word responses, and she refused to look at him.

Tightening his hands on the steering wheel, Adam tried to control his rising frustration. He'd asked if everything was okay, but her short answer of 'fine' didn't inspire confidence. Now she was staring out the window. He wasn't sure what had changed or what he'd done or not done, but something was definitely up.

The longer he thought about it, the more unsettling he found it. Why did he care so much, too much really, that he might have pushed her away? He was back in Jennings for very specific reasons, none of which was Charlotte.

Turning off the highway, his movements stilted as he navigated the streets of Jennings, he repeated the reasons to himself. He was here to help his parents out while they got his dad's health issues under control. That also meant he was here to help streamline and improve the store, so his dad had less stress.

He was here to take stock of his life. While stepping back from his normal existence hadn't been his idea, he knew now it had come at the right time. He needed to figure out what he wanted to do next. This time in Jennings was about looking at the big picture with no distractions.

As he pulled into Charlotte's driveway, he couldn't help but try one last time. "Home safe and sound," he said, putting the car in park. He turned to her, trying to catch her eye. "Are you sure you're okay? It seems like you're upset about something."

Avoiding eye contact, she woodenly responded, "I'm fine. It was just a long day." Opening her door before he could reply, she got out. "Thank you again for taking me. And please thank you mother as well. Goodbye, Adam."

She'd closed the door and gone into the house before he'd had a chance to stop her. Not that he would have. He couldn't figure out what had gone wrong. Drumming his fingers against the steering wheel, he shook his head. There was no rational explanation for what just happened, and he should stop trying the make sense of it.

Anyway, he couldn't get distracted by getting involved with someone, especially since he wouldn't be in town for that long. He needed to figure out his next career move. Hopefully, the email he'd received from the company today would help clarify things. Matt had also sent him a few texts when he was at the warehouse. He wanted to make sure Adam knew he was on the recall list and gave him the lowdown on the new contracts they were hoping to sign. He should go home and find out what the latest on the job front was.

Pulling out of the driveway, he took the long way home. He felt restless and unsettled. Driving his GTI through town was one of his favorite things to do, perhaps it would settle him. Lowering the window, he inhaled the fresh spring scents and felt a little better.

He contemplated stopping at the bakery for that afternoon treat, but the episode with Charlotte left him soured on the idea. Turning toward his condo, it frustrated him that he couldn't stop thinking of her. This was becoming a problem. He couldn't deny he was attracted to her. He desperately wanted to kiss her today in the warehouse. When she'd looked up at him with those wide, startlingly blue eyes, he wanted to devour her. A few more inches and he could have taken her mouth. Nibbled on her lips and teased her with his tongue. What little sounds would she have made as he ravaged her mouth and rained kisses down her neck? Just thinking about the possibilities caused his groin to tighten.

Shaking his head to rein in his thoughts, he pushed back the images of them together. But like a painful tooth you couldn't help pressing again and again, the ruthless side of him kept questioning. Why did he find her so hard to resist? Yes, she was smart and attractive, but he knew lots of women who fit that bill. He liked her humor and her spunk, but was that enough to draw him so inexplicably?

He pulled into the garage under his townhouse. He'd been lucky to find a short-term rental place with a garage. It wasn't the best complex, but it was tidy, and the neighbors were quiet. Under no circumstances would he move back in with his parents. He loved them, but every day under their roof was a recipe for disaster.

Jogging up the condo steps, he had a thought that almost made him miss a tread. Did he find Charlotte so enchanting because he was using her to avoid making the tough decisions he needed to make in his own life? That thought slowed his footsteps as he entered the condo.

He threw his keys on the counter and grabbed a soda from the fridge. Could it be possible that he was using her, not intentionally, but using her nonetheless, to avoid dealing with things? Was his fascination with Charlotte an escape from his memories of Abigail? A way to avoid considering his future? Was that why he found himself so drawn to her?

Shaking his head, he flopped down on the couch. Phone in hand, he looked at the text messages Matt had sent.

Email went out. Wanted to make sure you saw it

Looking good for closing the deals
Should have news soon

Adam laid his head back on the couch and closed his eyes, his brows knitted. Why was his life getting so complicated? He didn't understand why he was feeling this way. The old him would have already reached out to his network, seen what jobs were available and weighed all his options by now.

He couldn't even decide if he wanted to return to Phoenix or not. The thought made his stomach knot. He didn't want to move to a new city, nor was he champing at the bit to get back to Phoenix. Where did that leave him?

Lifting his head, he opened the company email on his phone. Nothing new in there, just legal clarification on the company's policy surrounding the recall list, assurances they were working to bring back the employees, and who to contact with questions. There was also an email from Zara, the company CEO. Scanning it, he deleted it. It was just her sending reassurances she was working hard to get him back.

Unable to be still a moment longer, he jumped up from the couch. He needed to be doing something. Sitting here wasn't getting him any closer to the answers he needed. Going up to his bedroom, he changed into running clothes and was out the door not five minutes later.

A few miles running would help clear his head, or at the very least, help him run off that steamed cheeseburger and the bitter ending of his day with Charlotte.

Purposely choosing a challenging route, he walked a bit to warm up and then began to run. It took a few moments, but his pace settled in, his breath found a cadence. Listening to the repetitive pounding of his feet on the pavement, he felt the tension slip from his shoulders and neck.

Thoughts swirled in his head, rising and falling as he let his mind wander, his family and career, Abigail and Charlotte. All the while he prayed that the familiar rhythm of the run would work its magic. At the very least, he may not have answers, but at least he'd be less stressed.

CHAPTER ELEVEN

Charlotte

The bell at Pie gave a sharp clang as Charlotte pushed through the door with a little too much gusto. She needed to get a hold of herself. But it had been a stressful week preparing for the Aunt Jennifer Summit, and she had the tension headache to prove it.

To make matters worse, thoughts of Adam and what he'd said plagued her. When he'd dropped her off, she'd ended up rehashing the day with Lisa. As usual, her roommate provided a solid sounding board and offered a different perspective.

"What if it was just a word, Lottie," Lisa had challenged. "It's not your profession or career, so what if he called it a hobby for lack of another word to call it? And rather than that word being a judgement on all you do and how talented you are, maybe... maybe it was just a word. Everything else about the day seems to be about him encouraging you."

The more she'd thought about what Lisa had said, the more she was convinced her friend was right. Adam hadn't been dismissing her passion and talent for designing wedding gowns. If anything, the whole day had been a celebration of his support. Looking back, she cringed with guilt over her behavior. Her overreaction had nothing to do with Adam and everything to do with an old memory. She swore, when lunch was over today and this damn summit was in her rearview mirror, she'd apologize to Adam. But first, she needed to survive today and Aunt Jennifer.

Looking over the cases of pastries, it was hard to decide. What would work best to sweeten her aunt's temperament enough to approve the dress? She bent to examine a beautiful red velvet cake. Did her aunt like red velvet? Would it make her see red figuratively and literally? She was overthinking this by a mile, but that seemed to be the theme of the day.

She'd been cleaning the kitchen early this morning, giving herself a pep talk that had turned ugly quickly.

Just show her the dress. It won't be any trouble at all. It'll be fun. She gave the counter another vigorous scrub. *Alex will try it on, show her mom, end of story. But it's not the end of the story. It's like the beginning of a horror movie. Where you watch the young stupid kid say yes to walking outside alone. Don't say yes. Don't be that idiot in the movie. We all know it's a bad move. Why can't you see that? Nope, you go ahead. You say yes, and WHAM you're in hand-to-hand combat with a knife-wielding psychopath.*

Luckily, Lisa had intervened to set her straight. "Lottie. You're muttering again."

"Sorry. I'm a little nervous."

"I'd tell you again it's going to be fine, but 'knife wielding psychopath' is a little daunting of a characterization," Lisa said with a smile. Walking over, she took the cloth from Charlotte's hand. "Your aunt is not a knife-wielding psychopath."

"Shows what you know," Charlotte muttered, clinging to her sense of doom.

"Listen," Lisa replied. "Go get dressed and run out to the bakery for dessert. When you come back, we'll do the final touches. And then we'll get a glass of wine and sit out on the back deck to wait. Think about it. A delightfully cold glass of Duplin sipped in the sunshine?"

"You fight dirty," Charlotte sighed. "But I love it."

It was enough to put her fears to rest while she dressed and headed out. Now standing in the bakery, all the fears and doubts were creeping back in. Grabbing her phone, she checked for the millionth time to see if Mary had responded about the Scottish lace. Even though it was too soon to expect an answer, she couldn't help but freak out she hadn't received a response. Thankfully, she heard her name called and was glad for the distraction.

Looking up, she saw Mrs. S. coming out from the back room. Her blond hair was held back with a bright green and pink scarf knotted at the top. As always, even dressed in an apron and dusted with flour, Mrs. S. looked lovely.

"Charlotte, honey," she said, coming around the counter to give her a quick hug. "You're in bright and early. What has you running around this time of morning, on a Saturday, no less?"

"Morning, Mrs. S. I need a miracle dessert. Something that will sweeten the crankiest disposition. Nothing messy or too crumbly. Something that says intelligence and skill while not being fussy."

"Sweetheart." Mrs. S. placed her hand on Charlotte's arm. "Are you sure you're looking for a dessert? 'Cause my treats are skillful, but that's a tall order for a pastry."

Charlotte closed her eyes. She sounded like a nut. This was going to be a long day if she didn't get a hold of herself. Looking back at Mrs. S., she smiled. "Sorry. I'm having lunch today with my aunt and the stakes are high."

"Oh, it's dress approval day."

Of course, Mrs. S. knew. Small town plus a close-knit circle of friends equaled everyone knowing everything. "You got it," Charlotte responded with a laugh. "So, what do you have that will tip the scale in my favor?"

"Again, an awful lot to ask from a pastry. And you don't need any help. Your work can stand alone. That said, I'm going to say madeleines." Walking to the far case, Mrs. S. indicated the top trays of cookies. "I have a variety of flavors and they look lovely on a platter. They're technically a cake, but easy to eat with your fingers."

Charlotte couldn't help but stare at the delicate shell-like patterned cakes. They all looked so tantalizing, "Wow. Those are amazing."

Reaching into the case, Mrs. S. started pulling cakes. "These are lavender earl grey covered with white chocolate and gold leaf. Visually, I'd pair them with these vanilla ones, which are glazed and then dipped in sugar and ground flower petals." Mrs.

S. took a few of the elegant pink-tipped cakes and put them in the box. "Finally, these. They have a delicious lemon curd glaze." Adding the last of the cakes, Mrs. S. taped up the box and handed it off to Charlotte. "As close to guaranteed as I can get to ensuring a successful afternoon."

As Charlotte reached to take the box, Mrs. S. looked her in the eye and said, "You're going to be impressive today. Don't forget that!"

"Thanks Mrs. S. Great reminder." Charlotte was blessed to have so many people supporting her and cheering her on. She needed to remember that. While she never wanted to take them for granted, it was easy to fall back into old patterns and not realize how lucky she was to have this family she'd constructed for herself.

After she paid, she gave Mrs. S. a last wave and left. Walking to back to her car, she gave herself a stern talking-to. Mrs. S. was right. Today was going to be a good day. She just needed to face Aunt Jennifer head-on and be calm. She had nothing to lose and everything to gain. Even with the short timeline and all, she wanted to make Alex's dress. She deserved to make it, and Aunt Jennifer was going to have to listen to her.

Fully engaged in the pep talk, Charlotte rounded the corner and walked straight into someone. Startled, she almost fell, but powerful arms wrapped around her, holding her upright. Glancing up, she was mortified to see Adam's handsome face.

"Adam," she said a little too breathlessly to save her dignity.

"Charlotte." His eyes danced with humor even as his mouth curved into a smile. "Better be careful. You falling would have put an end to whatever deliciousness you have in the bakery box there."

Charlotte was having a hard time putting together a sentence. Adam's arms were still wrapped around her, pulling her close. Skin tingling from where he touched her, she tried to respond, but his intoxicating scent was messing with her. What she wanted to do was wrap her arms around him and lay her head against his chest. And that scared her more than she wanted to admit.

Clearing her throat, she stepped back, and Adam released her. "I wasn't looking where I was going." Fabulous, another reason she owed him an apology. She just couldn't win with this guy. She should cut her losses and get out of there, but her sense of propriety kept her rooted to the sidewalk. He deserved an apology.

Shifting from one foot to the other, she screwed down her nervousness. She just wanted to get it over with. "I'm glad I ran into you, no pun intended," she laughed stiffly. "About the other day..."

Before she could continue, he interrupted, "Yeah, I'm sorry about that."

"You're sorry?" Why was he apologizing to her? She needed to apologize to him.

"Well, I think I may have said or done something to upset you, and I wanted to let you know I was sorry if that's what happened."

She glanced down, humbled by his forthrightness. "No, Adam. I'm the one who should apologize," she sighed. "The whole thing with my aunt and Alex's dress got to me. On my best day, I can be a little sensitive about my wedding gowns, but all of that piled together... I just reacted badly, and I'm sorry. I shouldn't have."

"I get that the situation with your aunt and everything could get to you. How could it not? But what do you mean that you're a little sensitive about your gowns?"

With Adam's hand on her elbow, they turned in unison, meandering down the sidewalk toward her car. She took a few steps before responding. "I've wanted to work in fabrics and sewing since I was a kid. Ethel took me under her wing and taught me all about sewing and designing."

"Is that what you went to school for?"

"No. I got my degree in graphic design." Adam said nothing but continued to look at her. Taking a deep breath, she added, "I wanted to, but that didn't really work out. I applied to RISD

—Rhode Island School of Design. I wanted to major in Apparel Design."

"What happened?" he asked gently. "Were you not accepted?"

She glanced away, tears filling her eyes. She needed to get past this. "No, I got in." She cleared her throat. "My mom didn't think it was a responsible degree. She thought I'd be throwing all that money down the drain on what she considered to be,"—she inhaled and exhaled sharply—"a nice little hobby." Her voice came out hard around those awful words. She saw the realization bloom on Adam's face.

"I'm so sorry, Charlotte. I meant nothing by that. What you do is amazing," he said earnestly.

His words were a balm to her soul as she tried not to hear her mom's voice yelling again, "It's just a nice little hobby. That's all it is."

"That's very kind of you to say, Adam. I'm sorry I overreacted the other day. It was out of line." There, she felt better now that she'd apologized. She hadn't realized how much their disagreement affected her.

"What did you do about school?" Adam asked, pulling her from her thoughts.

"I guess I could have ignored my mom. Maybe gone to a trade school for sewing. But she'd saved for my college tuition for years, so she deserved a say in how the money was spent." Charlotte rolled her shoulders, trying to release some of the tension. "In the end, I went along with what she wanted. I went to a state school here in Connecticut and majored in graphic design."

Adam reached over and grabbed her hand. "You did what you felt you had to, and now you have a business as a wedding gown designer."

Charlotte laughed at his emphasis. She looked at their joined hands. It felt wonderful, his hand enfolding hers. "It doesn't matter now. Or at least it shouldn't. It was a long time ago. But you're right," she smiled up at him. "I have a paying client. One step closer to a business."

By now they'd arrived at her car, so Adam released her hand. Missing his warmth immediately, she reached into her pocket for her keys. Opening the door, she placed the pastry box on the seat. Turning back, she said, "Well, I have to get back. Today's the Aunt Jennifer Summit. Lord help me."

Stepping closer, he leaned in and whispered, "Hey, Charlotte. You've got this."

Charlotte thought her heart was going to stutter to a stop. He was so close and so hot and so real. His piercing green eyes captured her, and the world dropped away.

"I believe in you."

Reading the sincerity of his words in his eyes, she felt something deep within her settle. Before she could let herself think about it, she rose up on her toes and kissed him. Her lips barely brushing against his but enough to send a spark racing through her.

Adam looked so flustered she was afraid she'd made a critical error, but before she could say anything, he blurted, "Have dinner with me." It was more of a demand than a question.

"Excuse me?"

"Have dinner with me," he repeated. He paused and seemed to realize what he'd said. "I mean dinner with me... and my parents."

Now she was confused. "You want me to have dinner with your parents?"

"Sure." He also sounded confused. "My mom would love an update on the dress."

As she considered his request/demand, she tried to think of a polite way to say no. Lisa kept saying it had been a year since her breakup with Todd, and she should start dating. But to her, it didn't feel like a year. It felt like yesterday. Although having dinner with his parents meant it was not a date, so maybe that was okay.

"Please, Charlotte," he said. "Really. Come to Sunday dinner. Not this Sunday," he clarified. "Mom would whack me if I sprang an important guest like you on her last minute. But next

Sunday."

He seemed sincere, and she couldn't find a courteous way to say no. If she were being honest, she wanted to go. It was with his parents, so that was safe enough. "I'd love to."

"Great." A slow smile spreading across his face. "Can't wait. Now, go blow Aunt Jennifer out of the water."

Laughing, she went to get into her car. Turning back to him, she said, "I'm glad I ran into you, Adam." He rewarded her with a laugh and a roll of his eyes.

Today might just be a good day after all.

CHAPTER TWELVE

Adam

"Have dinner with my parents," he muttered, shaking his head as he walked back to his car. What an idiot. Granted, he hadn't planned on asking her out, but after he'd blurted it, why hadn't he shut his mouth? Better yet, why did he ask her out in the first place?

It was that kiss. So innocent and quick, it barely counted as a kiss, but it just about brought him to his knees. Her lips were so soft, and he wanted so much more. Just that fleeting touch and his desire had roared to life.

He wanted to pretend it didn't matter, but he could only lie to himself so much. He wanted her. Every inch of him craved her, which scared him. That's why he'd choked and made it dinner with his folks. In the end, though, it might be for the best. Spending time alone with Charlotte was becoming more dangerous every time he saw her. She was a distraction he didn't need.

Having his arms around her just now overwhelmed his senses, making him burn with the desire to kiss her. He nearly had until he'd reminded himself. They were on the sidewalk in the middle of town. That hadn't stopped him from wondering how she would taste or if she would kiss him back. Or how she'd respond to him when he nipped the soft skin of her shoulder.

He'd pushed those thoughts away, then she kissed him, bringing all his fantasies rushing back. A growl escaped him. Thinking about this wasn't helping. He had to get to work.

Getting into his car, his phone vibrated with a text. It was nothing new, just Matt texting with another vague update. His boss was staying in close contact — probably afraid Adam would get another job.

Which brought him back to the problem at hand. Tossing the phone on the seat beside him, he ran his hands through his hair. He couldn't say the possibility of returning to Phoenix thrilled him, even though he liked the company and Matt was a solid boss. Shaking his head, he started the car. He'd get around to thinking about all this later. He had to get to work.

Inside the store, his mom was seated at the small table having a cup of tea. "Hi Mom," he said, planting a kiss on her head as he passed. Grabbing a cup of coffee, he came back and parked himself in the other chair. "Sorry I'm late. I ran into Charlotte. Literally."

"Where did you see her?"

"Outside of Pie," he said. "Actually, I invited her for Sunday dinner. Not tomorrow. Next Sunday." He took a sip of coffee before noticing the sharp look his mother was giving him.

She placed her teacup back on the saucer. "You invited her to Sunday dinner?"

"I did," he replied. Why was she looking at him like that? "Is that a problem?"

His mom looked at her tea for a moment before meeting his eye. "What's going on between you and Charlotte?"

His brows snapped together in a frown. It was none of her business if something was happening. He swallowed and waited a beat before answering. "Nothing's going on, Mom," he replied. "I'm sorry if I overstepped by inviting her. I'll make some excuse and cancel."

"Dinner's not the problem. I mean, it is, but I'm just wondering what it means."

"What it means?" He gritted his teeth. "Mom, just tell me what you're getting at."

"You have a job and life waiting for you in Phoenix. When you get the call, you're going to go back there, right?" Not waiting for a response, she barreled on. "I love Charlotte. She's lovely—a bright light in this town. But she's been through a lot and doesn't need more heartache, especially with what happened with that ex-boyfriend of hers."

Seeing his inquisitive look, she shook her head. "That's a story for Charlotte to tell. But I can tell you I don't want you to start something and break her heart when you leave. She deserves better."

He wanted to ask about the ex-boyfriend, but his mom's blunt words hit him square in the chest. As the words landed, he clenched his jaw as anger rolled through him. "You're so sure I'll break her heart?" he shot back.

"You know I love you, Adam," she countered. "I'm just trying to be realistic, honey."

"Well, if that's true, then let's really be in reality. Charlotte and I are not involved." He wanted to stop there but couldn't. "Even if we were, how can you be so sure it would end in heartbreak? If Charlotte and I were together, she could come with me to Phoenix." As the thought rolled off his tongue, he realized he liked that idea more than he should. It was something that finally made returning to Arizona look appealing.

"Or maybe I'm not going back to Phoenix," he spit out, cursing himself as he did so.

"You aren't going back?"

"I don't know, Mom," he sighed, the fight draining out of him. "It's just something I've been thinking about."

"Where would you go? What would you do?" she pushed.

"I don't know," he replied, massaging his now pounding head. "I really don't know."

She must have realized she'd get nothing more out of him on the Phoenix question, so she returned to Charlotte. "If you get involved with Charlotte," she said. At his pointed look, she added, "Not that you are. But if you did and it's serious, it is possible she would move to be with you." She paused and added gently, "Only Charlotte can answer that question. But knowing her as I do, it wouldn't be a simple thing. She has a community here, a family of people she's gathered around her, that she's connected to. It would surprise me to see her give that up, especially since you don't stay longer than a few years in any one place."

At his sharp gaze, she raised her hand to forestall the argument. "No judgment, just truth. You need to see it from Charlotte's point of view. She'd have to start over in Phoenix and again each time you moved. Is that what you'd want for her? I know you love your nomadic life, but will she?" She paused, then said almost to herself, "I do wonder if Abigail hadn't... if things had happened differently... how different your life would look now."

Adam's whole body locked up with rage. His first reaction was to shout at her, but he was able, just barely, to keep his mouth shut and take a breath. Granted, his mom was looking out for him, Charlotte too, but her words still ticked him off.

Mug clutched in his hand, he took a sip of coffee, admitting to himself he was being defensive. His reaction was disproportionate to the conversation. It had been years since Abigail, and he should be able to talk about it. But not today. Not right now.

Cracking his neck from side to side, he looked over at his mom, who was measuring his reaction. Catching her eye, he forced himself to smile. It wasn't great, but it was something. His mother leaned over to rest her hand on his arm, her eyes swimming with love and understanding. His anger drained as he acknowledged she had a few legitimate points he needed to think about.

"Thanks mom," he said calmly. "I hear what you're saying."

She gave his arm a squeeze. "I love you, and I just want to see you happy. You know that, right?"

He nodded. "I know you do, and I appreciate that more than you know. Speaking of happiness," he said. He couldn't talk about Abigail or Charlotte; he needed to talk about something else. "I've been looking at some of the store data, and I have a few ideas." He smiled, hoping his charm would help in changing the subject.

She laughed, and he knew he'd won. "So, you'll listen?"

"I will, but remember, your father is a little more conservative when it comes to making changes." She waved a finger at him. "You need to be patient."

"I will be, but no matter what, the business needs to change," he countered. His parents had spent decades building this business, and he respected that. He just didn't want to see it crush the life out of them. "It would be nice to see you freed up and not chained to the store as much."

The small smile on her face told him he was right. "It would be enjoyable to travel," she sighed. "I love the business, I do. But I'd also like to get out and enjoy a few things while your father and I are still young enough to take full advantage."

"I agree. Let me just outline a few ideas. You tell me which ones you think are worth pursuing. I can take those and do additional research and planning before talking with dad. Does that sound okay to you?"

"That sounds like a plan, honey."

Adam launched into a few of his more promising ideas. Not a further word was mentioned about Charlotte or Abigail, but both topics weighed heavily on his mind long after the conversation ended.

CHAPTER THIRTEEN

Charlotte

As it turned out, Charlotte and Lisa were able to relax on the deck for half an hour before Alex and Rachel arrived. Both timeout and the glass of wine, helped center her and calm the worst of her nerves. She was as prepared as she could be for the meeting.

Settling the two newcomers with glasses of wine, Charlotte couldn't help but remark, "Rachel, it's so nice of you to come. I don't know many people who would willingly jump into the deep end of family drama. I think that makes you either super crazy or a superhero!"

"Neither," Rachel laughed, though her face flushed. "I know it must be weird for a virtual stranger..."

"No longer a stranger," Alex interrupted, putting her hand on Rachel's arm. "A friend. One who *has* jumped into the deep end, and who I can't thank enough."

Rachel gripped Alex's hand, "It's my pleasure." Her expression sobered as she gazed out over the yard. "My sister Jessie got into some trouble a few years ago. I wasn't able to help, and it's kind of stayed with me. After that, I promised myself if I could help someone I would. Silly, right?"

"No. Not silly at all," Charlotte assured her. "I'm with Alex. I can't thank you enough."

They all heard the car door slam in the driveway. As much as Charlotte wanted to get more from Rachel about her sister, it looked like their time was up. Lisa was the first to stand. "Places, everyone! It's showtime!"

Half an hour later, Charlotte wondered why they couldn't

jump to the showtime part of the afternoon and skipped everything else. After introductions were made and everyone was seated, Lisa brought out the small finger sandwiches. Charlotte made sure everyone had a tall glass of sangria.

At first Aunt Jennifer seemed in a pleasant mood, but soon launched into a diatribe of issues about family and planning the wedding. It was astonishing how much Aunt Jennifer sounded like Charlotte's mother. It looked like winning her aunt's approval would be just as hard as winning her mom's.

Thinking about her mom made Charlotte's stomach drop. On a normal day, they got along—for short periods of time. But the moment her mom found out she'd designed Alex's gown, all bets were off. It wouldn't matter if the dress was a rousing success and applauded by everyone; her mom would find a reason to criticize.

Rolling her shoulders to ease the tension, she could only pray no one had told her mother of her involvement yet. Handling her aunt was one thing, handling her mother was another. This lunch was looking like a bigger mistake every moment it continued.

As Charlotte was trying to figure out how to segue into the dress conversation, Aunt Jennifer lobbed the first salvo.

"I've told Alex, and I will tell you, I don't think a dress purchased at a thrift store is appropriate for a formal wedding. I doubt it's even appropriate for a casual event, but unquestionably not for the occasion we are planning."

As an opening gamete, it was rather impressive. And Aunt Jennifer wasn't done, not by a long shot. Rather than interrupt, Charlotte remained quiet, listening to everything she had to say.

"I understand you've had this pastime for years," Aunt Jennifer went on, warming to the subject. "But this dress would need to be worn by an actual person, not adorning a mannequin. And while I'm sure you're very skilled, we have a tight timeline with no wiggle room for first-time seamstress blunders."

As her aunt continued, a funny thing happened. While Charlotte burned with humiliation, it was fleeting. Rather than ripping her apart, every negative sentiment cascading from her aunt's mouth calmed Charlotte. It was a little off-putting, actually. Certainly not her usual reaction. Aunt Jennifer's words sailed by, finding no purchase in her armor.

"I'm sure you do lovely work." Aunt Jennifer's smile was tight, as if even that was painful to admit. "But I'm sure you can understand why we'll be leaving without a dress. I have a gown on hold that is suitable for this occasion. It's the same style Alex tried on during her search. It's quite elegant, and best of all, it's available. The experienced seamstress there assures me they will complete any alterations in time for the wedding."

Her aunt sat back in her chair, letting her pronouncement hang in the air. Reaching for her wineglass, she tossed in a final comment: "Honestly, Charlotte, after what happened with your last boyfriend, I would think weddings were the last thing you'd want to involve yourself with."

As a final salvo, that one hit the mark. Her friends' echoed Charlotte's sharp intake of breath. Before she had a chance to respond, Alex jumped in.

"Mother, you promised." Alex's cheeks were flushed, although from anger or embarrassment or both, it was hard to tell.

Jennifer turned to her daughter. "I said I would come and see Alex. I will look at it, but I don't want anyone to labor under the false belief that a secondhand gown could ever raise itself to the level of sophistication required here. I speak only the truth, not to offend, but to educate."

Charlotte was fairly certain she'd meant some offense. Observing her aunt, she felt pity rather than anger. Like her mom, Aunt Jennifer was one of those people who thought her opinion was the only truth in the room. Spending all that time and energy having to be right must be exhausting.

Charlotte was shocked how peaceful she felt. Maybe it was Lisa's top-shelf sangria. Maybe what it came down to was there was nothing to lose. Knowing she had no chance of winning made her feel bold.

Taking a sip of her drink, she smiled, garnering suspicious

looks from her friends. Time to beard the lion. Squaring her shoulders, she dove in, "Obviously, you've given this a great deal of thought, and you've also put a tremendous amount of energy into finding Alex a suitable gown. That's what you do for someone you love."

Charlotte paused and reached out to grab another sandwich. She was consciously relaxing her manner and slowing her speech pattern. Aunt Jennifer had come in ready for a fight, but she wouldn't get one. At least not yet.

"Lisa, I love the cream cheese you put in this. Have you tried the sandwiches, Aunt Jennifer? Lisa is a talented cook, and we so enjoy sharing a good meal with friends. It made us so happy when Alex said you were coming for a visit." Charlotte beamed at her friends who were eyeing her.

Turning back to her aunt, she continued, "About the dress. I have to agree with you." You could have heard a pin drop as Alex, Lisa, and Rachel stared at Charlotte, jaws agape. "Asking a vintage gown to stand up to a modern, elegant event like Alex's wedding, well, that's asking for the moon on a platter," she said merrily.

"Alex has been nice enough to fill us in on the details, and I must say it's going to be a remarkable event with family and friends. What a lovely opportunity to gather all the people you care about in one room."

With Charlotte agreeing, Aunt Jennifer relaxed, taking a sip of her sangria, clearly more than happy to talk wedding plans. "I'm glad Alex has been keeping you in the loop. We've been putting a lot of effort into providing our guests an outstanding experience. As you know, family will come in from some distance, so this will be a multi-day event as we entertain out-of-state guests."

"That's very nice of you. I'm sure they will appreciate it. Entertaining family is always enjoyable. Even with all of your responsibilities, I hope you'll have a chance to visit and catch up with everyone."

"Funny you should mention that. Alex and I were just

discussing the other day, having a late afternoon tea the day before the wedding for just that reason. Since my sisters all live a little too far away for casual visits, I'm looking forward to spending some time with them." As she talked, her face took on a shine and her smile became less forced and more genuine.

Alex, Rachel, and Lisa all remained in stunned silence as Charlotte continued. "That's a smart idea. I wish more people would follow your example and make time for catching up with friends and family." Charlotte paused a moment and took another bite of the sandwich on her plate.

"That's what I've always loved about the gowns I rescue," Charlotte said after she swallowed. Aunt Jennifer looked skeptical but didn't interrupt. "When I see a gown, I always wonder about the family who owned it. Was it something passed down from mother to daughter? When the bride's mother saw her in the dress, did she cry? Did the groom cry when he saw her?

"Then I think about the ceremony and envision the bride walking down the aisle or garden path, moving toward her future. Did they dance all night under the twinkling white lights of a tent? Did the gown's fabric hold the perfume of the flowers that filled the room?" Not only was Aunt Jennifer intently listening, but her friends seemed enthralled as well.

"But mostly," she continued. "I think about all the love and prayers stored in that fabric. For me, that's the magic. Family and friends embracing the bride, wished her well. The bride's hopes and dreams for the future. All those moments become entwined in the fabric of the dress.

"When I look at a gown, the outside may be worn and outdated and maybe even stained, but that can't diminish its energy. It's a fabric woven with hundreds of thoughts and prayers. And that's what I can't walk away from or abandon. Something that precious needs to be protected and given a chance to share all that energy with the next person on its journey."

She took in a deep breath and sent a silent prayer to Gram. "I honor the past but redesign my dresses into unique and timeless creations that any bride would be proud to wear. The dress comes with a history; I put a modern spin on the story and offer it to the bride of today. So, while I agree that a secondhand gown isn't appropriate, my gowns are not secondhand. My creations are new and unique—and made with the magical fabric of hope and love."

Charlotte reached out to take a drink, hoping no one saw the slight shake of her hand. She couldn't remember ever speaking so confidently about her work. It was both terrifying and exhilarating.

When her aunt didn't fill the silence with an argument, she could have jumped for joy. Before she got overconfident, there were other things to address. She leaned on the table with her arms, tilting her head at her aunt. "You know, you're also right about the timeline. I thought Alex was crazy to consider it. The project plan has next to no wiggle room in it," she chuckled.

"But the great thing is this is the only dress I'm working on." Her aunt's eyes gleamed in appreciation. If anyone appreciated something exclusive, it would be her aunt. "Sure, it will be hard work. But just because something's difficult doesn't mean it isn't worth doing. And this is worth doing."

Looking at Alex, Charlotte raised her eyebrows. "Alex, why don't we leave your mom and Rachel to enjoy some dessert, and we'll go get the gown."

Aunt Jennifer made a move to stand. "There's no need to bring it down. I can go see it."

Alex jumped in, knowing what Charlotte had in mind. "That's okay, Mom. You sit here and enjoy the breeze. You've been so great to come, the least I can do is bring it to you while you enjoy the sunshine."

"Jennifer," Lisa chimed in. "Have you tried one of these madeleines? They have gold leaf on them. Can you imagine? What are you serving your guests at that afternoon tea?"

With that, Aunt Jennifer sat back down and seemed content to sip sangria, nibble cakes, and talk. Lisa gave Charlotte and

Alex a sharp nod. They would have to make this super quick if they were going to pull it off.

Charlotte took a few steps from the table before turning around. Clenching her hands into fists, she pressed them into her thighs, forcing herself to look her aunt in the eye. She wouldn't allow herself to leave without saying something. "Aunt Jennifer," she said, her voice raspy. Clearing her throat, she forced herself forward. "My relationship with Todd, how it ended, and how it makes me feel or not feel about weddings are not relevant to our discussion here. Although just because one relationship ended poorly doesn't mean every relationship will. I still believe in love above all. Perhaps more so now," she added. Unbidden, memories of Adam flooded her mind. Heart racing, she waited, needing to know her aunt got the message. It was all she could do to keep her feet nailed to the floor and not run. Just when she thought she would pass out from her pounding heart, her aunt gave a small nod. An apology would have been better, but she'd take the simple acknowledgement.

Her chest eased as she dipped her chin in return. She'd finally stood up for herself and hadn't died.

Running up to the workroom, Alex undressed while Charlotte went to wrangle the gown. She'd done her best to cut stray threads, but the dress was still in rough shape. The high sleeves were off, but the straps weren't fully formed. Pieces of lace were loosely attached in different areas. All in all, it looked a little worse for wear. Not an ideal way to show it, but there was nothing to be done about that.

Charlotte zipped up the dress, breathing a sigh of relief when it slid easily. Then she realized it had been too easy. The bodice of the gown hung off Alex and looked terrible. Grabbing a clamp from the desk, she had Alex turn around.

"Is that a wood clamp, Charlotte?" Alex asked, her brows furrowed.

"Yup," she chuckled. "Don't question the magic." Charlotte was having way too much fun. Now that she'd stood up for herself, she felt like she could fly.

Alex laughed but didn't comment further. "Now, some of these stitches are temporary, so go easy on the dress. No huge moves or breathing too deeply. I don't want you busting a clamp in front of your mother." Grabbing an elastic, she took Alex's hair and put it into a low ponytail near the nape of her neck.

"I wasn't sure I was going to wear my hair up," Alex interjected.

"Doesn't matter. We just want your mom to see you differently—as a sophisticated bride. Trust me." Charlotte ran back to the closet and came out with a fingertip length veil. It wasn't what she would pair with the dress, but for today, it would work. The goal was to get Aunt Jennifer to see Alex as a bride and understand the potential in the dress.

"We're kind of flying by the seat of our pants with this, but I think it will seal the deal." Alex scrunched down a little, and Charlotte set the veil in place. Standing in front of her cousin, she couldn't believe the transformation herself. With the ugly sleeves gone, the stains mostly eliminated, and the veil floating gently behind her, Alex was a vision. "Perfection! Now let's go."

Charlotte grabbed the back of the train as Alex maneuvered down the stairs and out the front door. "To the right. It will give you a better entrance, and your mom will have a great vantage point."

Alex stopped as she was crossing the driveway and turned back to Charlotte. "I can only imagine how much you and Lisa put into all this. How can I ever express my gratitude?"

"Name your first born after us?" Charlotte joked. They both had a laugh because, after all, they were running around the front yard in full bridal regalia. If you can't see the absurdity of that, you need serious help, Charlotte thought. And seeing Alex laugh was all the reward Charlotte needed.

They made their way around the garage to the backyard. "Okay, this last corner is where I leave you. Walk forward, turn the corner, and then pause. I just need a second to fluff the train, then you can walk. Good luck."

As instructed, Alex paused while Charlotte gave the train of the dress a healthy snap. One simple move and all the fabric laid out nicely. That done, Charlotte ran back around the front of the house, praying none of the neighbors were watching. They must look like loons.

Charlotte was able to round the corner of the deck and hear the collective gasp of the group as Alex came into view. The sound made her want to do a jig right there on the lawn. She wished she could live in this moment forever.

Alex looked radiant. The sunlight filtered through the trees, hitting different parts of the gown as she moved. Thankfully, the light breeze was playing with the edges of the veil, making it move and dance. She was a vision.

Aunt Jennifer came down the steps to the lawn as Charlotte walked up next to her. The closer Alex got, the darker Aunt Jennifer's expression became. Looking at Alex, Charlotte could see why. From a distance, the dress looked lovely. With each step Alex took, the missing details, rough edges, and flyaway threads came into focus. For someone seeing it for the first time up close, it looked like a hot mess. She needed to get in front of this.

"As you can see," Charlotte started, remembering to relax her voice and keep her pace slow. Sounding frantic would only stoke Aunt Jennifer's fears. "The dress is deep in the redesign process. With original sleeves removed, in their place we'll have delicate lace-covered straps. The overall visual effect of the straps will frame Alex's face and draw your eye down to the slight sweetheart neckline. The bodice will remain as is, with its lace and sequined embellishments flowing into the fitted waist and full ballgown skirt." She paused for a moment and risked a glance at her aunt. So far, she seemed to follow Charlotte's narrative. Time to bring it home.

"The design of the dress gives Alex a beautiful hourglass silhouette while the exceptional lace details elevate the look. Alex, can you turn around so your mother can see the back?"

Alex shot Charlotte a smile before complying. They both knew the lace detailing on the back was a huge selling point. While Charlotte said every prayer she knew that the dress didn't pick up any grass stains, Alex slowly turned.

Charlotte stepped forward and gave the train another snap before laying out its full length. If she hadn't been listening for it, she might have missed her aunt's sharp intake of breath. Gotcha!

"The train is cathedral length," she continued, pretending not to have heard. "As you can see the lace cutouts make a dramatic statement. I'm sure Alex mentioned we believe some of the lace is Scottish—such a fitting embellishment for the joining of two families, two traditions, two lives. As Alex walks up the aisle and stands with Jason, I can assure you every eye will be on the exquisite detailing of the gown."

Charlotte stopped. There was a point where it would just be too much. As the silence stretched, Aunt Jennifer bent to look closer at the details of the train and started walking around examining different areas.

Alex gave Charlotte a scared look. "Mom," she breathed, her hands running across the fabric of the skirt. "The other dress is okay, but it can't hold a candle to this one. Charlotte is going to make this the most incredible, one-of-a-kind gown for me." She looked down, her fingers tracing over the lace of the bodice. "Can you imagine if this is Scottish? You can't get a bigger sign from the universe. This dress was meant to be mine. And Charlotte was meant to make it."

Charlotte's eyes burned with tears she refused to let fall. This project was stressful and at times she questioned her sanity in taking it on, but hearing Alex's belief in her made every crazy, stressful moment worth it.

But still, the silence stretched. Glancing at Rachel and Lisa, they both shrugged. Aunt Jennifer was touching the veil of the dress, and Charlotte broke, blurting out the first thing she could think of. "I would recommend a lengthier veil, something even longer than the train. The lace from the dress, especially any Scottish elements, could be periodically clustered to highlight the veil edge." What am I doing? Why did I say that?

Before she could kick herself for adding such a complicated

piece to an already jam-packed project, her aunt dropped the veil and looked up, her eyes filled with unshed tears.

"It's beautiful. All these details on the dress and the veil… You were right, Alex. This dress was meant to be yours."

Charlotte blew out a breath she hadn't realized she was holding, feeling her shoulders sag in relief. This was a better outcome than she had allowed herself to dream of.

"Really, Mom?" Alex asked, her eyes widening. Seeing her mother's smiling nod, she reached over to hug her. "I'm so glad you think so."

Charlotte felt like she was floating, happiness coursing through her. This day could not have gone better. She walked over to Alex and her aunt, admiring and talking about a few different details of the fabric. After a few minutes, she ushered Alex back upstairs and out of the dress.

Before they went back outside, Alex pulled her into a fierce hug. "I can't thank you enough," she said, her voice rough with emotion. "I don't know if there are words to tell you how I feel."

Returning the hug just as tightly, Charlotte gave a delighted laugh. "You, almost speechless? I never thought I'd see the day. You're welcome."

Rejoining the group, it looked like Aunt Jennifer was leaving. Alex gave her mother another hug, stepping back to ask, "Are you sure you have to leave so soon?"

"I am," she said. Gazing at Charlotte, her smile slipped. "I was wrong. About a few things, it turns out. That gown is going to be spectacular." She gave Charlotte as fierce a hug as Alex had. "I was out of line earlier," she whispered. "And thank you," she added as she stood back, her eyes shining, "for making Alex so ecstatic."

She said her goodbyes and walked down the stairs to the lawn. Before she disappeared around the corner of the garage, her voice carried back to them. "Yes. I need to remove a hold I have on a wedding gown."

Aunt Jennifer's announcement prompted a round of hugs between the friends before they settled back at the table.

Snagging a madeleine, Charlotte took a large bite, savoring the burst of lemon flavor.

"This calls for a toast," Lisa said, raising her glass. "To Charlotte, for the best wedding gown presentation ever heard!"

"Hear! Hear!" the other girls said before clinking glasses.

Alex was vibrating she was so delighted. "Charlotte, you were brilliant. You were so masterful in walking her through what the gown will look like. Oh! The part about the Scottish lace was my favorite, especially using it to highlight the veil. I can't wait for everyone to see it! Can you picture the faces when I walk down the aisle?"

Listening to Alex made Charlotte's heart feel light. The warmth of unconditional love and support was a sensation she wanted to remember forever, but at the same time her stomach tightened with dread. She could picture all those people, especially her mother, watching the dress go down the aisle. The thought of it gave her joy and made her equally queasy.

Pressing her lips together, she kicked all the negative thoughts to the curb. This dress had to be impeccable. She could do that. Not only for Alex, but because this was her lifelong dream on the line. She wouldn't mess this up.

"You must be so proud of yourself, Charlotte." Alex's comment pulled her from her thoughts.

"I am, Alex. I am. Getting your mom's approval is quite the accomplishment. Now I just need to, you know... create the gown."

"It's going to be beautiful," Rachel added. "You'll have to send me photos."

"What do you mean, photos?" Alex asked. "You'll see it in person." Seeing the confused looks Lisa and Rachel exchanged, she pressed. "Aren't you coming to my wedding?"

Rachel and Lisa shared another look before Rachel said, "Well, I think we assumed we weren't invited. It's a day for family and close friends."

Alex's face fell. "You have to be there. It wouldn't be the same without you both. I consider you friends. None of this," she gestured at the table and backyard. "None of this would be happening without you guys. You have to be there to help me celebrate my special day. And," she added, "you have to be there to celebrate Charlotte's big debut!"

Lisa shook her head, laughing before turning to Rachel. "She has us there. So, do I get to be your date, or do you get to be mine?"

Rachel laughed. "Looks like we're going to a wedding!"

The girls toasted again, Alex grilling Lisa and Rachel on potential wedding dates. Taking out her phone, Charlotte gave in to temptation. The day had been so astonishing she needed to share it. Specifically, she wanted to share it with Adam.

Victory! AJ not only approves, but loves the dress

She wondered what Adam was doing today. He was probably still at the store. Somehow, the momentousness of the day seemed more real by telling him. His response popped up.

Congrats! Knew U would do it. Of course AJ loves it. She knows quality.

Charlotte smiled as she read his response and fell a little bit more for Adam. How could she not be drawn to a hot guy who was not only intelligent and funny, but believed in her? It was something she hadn't felt with Todd. Before she could follow her thoughts into the past, Alex pulled her into the conversation about all things wedding.

CHAPTER FOURTEEN

Charlotte

Charlotte heard the text message hit her phone, but as she was currently elbow-deep in the skirt of Alex's gown, it would have to wait. That is, if her arms didn't collapse. The week following Aunt Jennifer's approval, Charlotte had been working almost nonstop on the gown.

At least she'd made some solid progress. Meaning she'd worked her butt off, but the enormity of to-do items still loomed like Mount Everest. When she wasn't at her job or working on the dress, she was trying to get some rest, but even then, she couldn't escape. Her dreams were terrorized by images of dress failure a million different ways. By day, she worked tirelessly, fulfilling her dream of being a wedding gown designer. At night, she watched that dream disintegrate into a thousand tiny pieces.

What Charlotte lived for were those moments like this morning. When she was working with the dress, unfettered by distractions and worries, her soul soared. The feel of the fabric, the delicate swirls and patterns of the lace, all worked their magic to center her. Here in the workroom, she didn't allow the doubts that plagued her or the stress that dogged her steps to interfere with the work. In here, everything was pure.

Making the last adjustment, she retracted her arms from beneath the skirt, smoothing the layers as she went. She was pleased with the result. Replacing fabric panels from the skirt wasn't the best option for dealing with the stains, so she'd hidden the discolored fabric using lace from the sleeves. Thankfully, once the additions were in place, you wouldn't even know the stains existed at all. The only issue now was running out of lace. Since she'd promised a matching lace veil, it looked like she would need to supplement with something new.

Still examining her work, she felt around the floor for her phone. Glancing at the screen, a slow smile spread across her face. Since letting him know about her success last week, she and Adam had kept up a steady stream of texting.

She knew she should put a stop to it. Getting involved with Adam was a poor decision. At some point it would end, and she would be here in Jennings, with all the memories and the whole town knowing she'd been dumped yet again. She didn't think she could survive another round of heartbreak and humiliation. Being close to Adam was like dancing with fire. He made her feel things she'd never felt before. Her attraction to him was unfamiliar territory, and that scared her.

She told herself it didn't matter because she wasn't falling for him. Though she tried to deny it, she couldn't control the heat that filled her whenever he was around. Even their barely there kiss had turned her knees to water. Or like now, when just seeing his text filled her with happiness.

How's the land of lace and tulle?

She shot off a reply.

Brilliant! You at the store today?

Yup. Mom and Dad are out on an adventure.

Adam had mentioned his parents needed more downtime and less stress, so it was nice to see that happening.

I hope they have fun.

Me too. You still up for dinner tomorrow?

Sure thing. What can I bring?

Mom says nothing but an appetite. And the dress. If that's a pain, Mom says just an update.

Charlotte felt her stomach clench. She still wasn't sure how she felt about dinner with Adam and his parents. Of course, she didn't have a problem packing up the dress to show Mrs. Mac. She always appreciated her comments and suggestions. It was spending more time with Adam that had her on edge. She feared she'd forget all the logical reasons to protect her heart and just give in to her attraction. Well, it was too late now to back out.

Appetite and dress coming up.

Laying back on the floor, she let the phone drop from her hand. No sooner had she let it slide from her fingers, it vibrated with an incoming call. Perhaps Adam needed to talk with her about dinner. She didn't recognize the number but answered anyway.

"Hello?" she said, ready to hang up once the automated telemarketers spiel started. It startled her to hear a real person.

"Is this Charlotte?"

"Yes, this is. How can I help you?" she asked.

"Hi there," a woman cheerfully replied. "This is Mary Verselli. I'm a friend of Ethel's. You emailed me some photos concerning some lace you're working with?"

Charlotte's heart raced. Mary! Please, please, please let the lace be Scottish. There was too much hanging on this for it to be otherwise. "Mary, thank you so much for calling me. I really appreciate it."

"Oh, it's my pleasure," she replied. "Ethel talks about you so highly, I feel like I already know you."

"That's so nice of her. She's such a love," Charlotte replied, trying to keep the nervousness from her voice. What was she going to do if the lace wasn't Scottish? Not only did Alex have her heart set on the symbolism of it, but they'd sold it to Aunt Jennifer as such.

"That she is," Mary replied. "I have to say, this project you're working on is lovely. Ethel told me your plans, and I can't wait to see it finished."

"I'll be sure to send you a photo."

"I'd like that. But down to business. I'm afraid I'm going to have to agree with Ethel that the lace you sent close ups on isn't a Scottish thistle design."

Charlotte's heart dropped. "Oh, that's too bad. I was so hoping." This was going to crush Alex. What would Aunt Jennifer say? She had to think fast. "You wouldn't happen to know of any manufacturers that make a bridal lace with a

Scottish thistle pattern, would you? I would still love to add that element into the gown."

"Well," Mary responded slowly. "Nothing springs to mind. Unfortunately, I think with thistle, it's just one of those designs that doesn't translate well. I remember talking to a textile designer once and she said there are just some patterns that need color. Wouldn't a traditional thistle design just look like a pineapple if it didn't have color?"

Charlotte hadn't thought of that. It explained why her own research had turned up a lot of embroidered tablecloths with colored thistle patterns. She couldn't contain her sigh of disappointment. "That does make a lot of sense. All I've found are colored versions. I never stopped to wonder why.

"Well, it looks like I'm out of options. Thank you so much for helping me with this, Mary. It was considerate of you."

"It was my pleasure. Although I'm sorry it wasn't what you had hoped for," she said gently. "If I can ask, why is the thistle pattern so important for your project?"

"It isn't the thistle pattern itself, but more that it was a Scottish thistle. The bride is marrying into a Scottish family," she explained. "When I thought the lace on the dress was a Scottish thistle, well, it just seemed meant to be.

"I'll just have to break it to her," she lamented. "She has some other Scottish traditions in the ceremony and reception, so I'm sure in the end she won't miss it." Charlotte doubted that was true. Both she and Alex would miss that little piece of whimsy.

Just as she was ready to say goodbye, Mary said the most enchanting thing: "If the Scottish part is most important, why not add in some Scottish lace?"

Charlotte's grip on the phone tightened. Did she hear that correctly? "I'm sorry what was that?"

"If you're looking for something Scottish, why not use lace produced in Scotland?" When Charlotte didn't respond, she added, "Have I misunderstood what you're trying to accomplish?"

"Oh no, Mary," Charlotte wanted to cry she was so pleased. "I think you've hit on a perfect solution. I didn't even think that was possible."

"I'm glad," she laughed. "I hated having to give you bad news. If you need names, I'd start with a company called MYB Textiles. They're an accomplished company with some appealing designs. In fact, I think they still use traditional looms. They may be the last lace maker working with the Nottingham Lace Looms," she mused. "The machines are amazing works of art—over 100 years old. I'm not sure what they have in production, but surely using one of their designs would fit the bill."

As Mary started providing details, Charlotte rushed to her desk for pen and paper. Looking over her scribbled notes, she wanted to make sure she had it correct. "I think I have all that. MYB Textiles in Scotland. Traditional lace looms."

"Yes. MYB stands for something, but exactly what, escapes me. You'll be able to find them under MYB."

"How can I thank you, Mary?" Charlotte asked. "You've made me and the bride deliriously happy."

"Aren't you lovely," she replied. "It isn't every day I get to say I made not one, but two people deliriously happy! I'll take that as thanks enough as long as you send photos and promise to update me on the lace."

"It's a deal."

Once Charlotte hung up, she grabbed her laptop and started searching. Ethel's friend was right, finding MYB wasn't difficult. Surfing around the site, she saw several patterns she loved, like the circular design of Honey Bee or even the Catkin Madras with its delicate leaf pattern. The problem was that they were curtain panels or tablecloths.

Digging deeper, it looked like MYB did work with some bespoke designers to provide them with lace for clothing. Unfortunately, timing and price were not on her side. The lace would need to be purchased wholesale, which meant she'd need to buy a large quantity. Not only was that impractical, but it was a budget-buster. Finding a solution and then having it taken away so swiftly was frustrating.

Unwilling to let it go, she mulled the problem over a bit. Now that Mary had given her the idea, she'd just have to look around and find something produced in Scotland that she could use. Even if it was the tiniest of pieces, she could make it work. A solution was so close. She just had to get creative.

CHAPTER FIFTEEN

Charlotte

Walking into the house, Charlotte laid the flowers on the hallway table and dashed up the stairs to get ready for dinner with Adam and his parents. Bundling the dress into a gown bag, she stopped in her room to change.

Ten minutes later, looking at her third outfit attempt, she decided she was trying too hard. Going back into the closet, she put on her favorite pair of jeans, a funky pair of low top canvas sneakers she'd painted herself, and an indigo print shirt. Walking to the mirror, she examined the results. This was her; casual but tidy, with a dash of fun thrown in for good measure. She felt pretty in this outfit, and that was the most important thing to her. Grabbing a sweater just in case, she headed out, flowers and dress in hand.

When she pulled into the MacDonalds' driveway, Adam was already there, working in the garage with his dad. As she stepped out of the car, she had another flutter of nervousness, or maybe it was just the anticipation of seeing Adam again. She didn't want to contemplate either.

Walking toward the building, she heard music. She didn't know the name, but she recognized it. It was from the '50s. Stepping inside, she heard both Adam and his dad singing along with the music. It was adorable; no other way to put it. Her heart lurch a little watching them work together on an old truck. It was such an exceptional moment; she didn't want to interrupt.

As she stood watching them work in harmony, she felt someone come up next to her, brushing her shoulder. Looking over, Mrs. Mac beamed a smile and gestured to the two men.

"They are a sight, aren't they?" Seeing Charlotte's smile, she continued. "I saw you arrive through the window. I'm glad you're here for dinner."

"Oh," Charlotte said. "I'm sorry, I should have stopped at the house to say hi to before coming back here."

Mrs. Mac waved away her apology. "I was on my way out here anyway to tell these two it was time to wash up."

Just as Charlotte was going to thank Mrs. Mac for having her, Adam looked over and caught her eye. "Hi, Charlotte. Good to see you."

He smiled, obviously pleased to see her. She loved that his smile was also reflected in his eyes. As he looked at her, the intensity of his gaze made her feel warm and shaky at the same time.

"Hi, Adam. The truck looks like it's getting some well-deserved attention."

"Some routine maintenance, for sure."

"Are you almost at a stopping point?" Mrs. Mac asked. "Dinner will be out of the oven soon."

"I think we are. Just give us a few minutes to wrap up and clean up, and we'll be in."

"You have fifteen minutes," she pronounced before turning to Charlotte. "While they finish, why don't we look at the dress? You brought it, didn't you?"

"I did. I'll just go get it from the car."

As she turned to walk out, Adam called to her. "Do you need help with it?"

Charlotte turned, looked pointedly at his greasy hands and back to Adam's face. "Are you crazy? You go anywhere near that dress with those hands, and I'll hurt you."

Adam held up his hands in defeat. "Valid point. I'll make sure we scrub up completely." Looking down at his shirt and over at his dad, "We also may need to take a moment to change our shirts."

"Do what you have to do," Charlotte said. "But you're still not getting near this dress. I won't risk a stray glob of grease ruining it. Not only would I be pissed, but you'd be in the crosshairs of one furious bride. Trust me. You don't want to deal with that."

Both Mrs. Mac and Adam laughed. Mrs. Mac looked at Adam, "Believe her. I've met more than my share at the dry cleaners. They're scary."

Still laughing, Adam turned back to the truck as Charlotte and Mrs. Mac walked back toward the house.

"I just need to check on dinner," Mrs. Mac said. "I'll leave the screen door propped open so you can maneuver the dress inside."

Charlotte had the dress laid out across the whole back seat. She pulled it out and breathed a sigh of relief when she tucked it safely over her arm, the flowers in her hand. A swing of her hip closed the door, and she headed into the house.

The screen door led her into a tidy mud room, and then into the kitchen to see Mrs. Mac tasting something from a large yellow Dutch oven. If the smells were any indication, tonight's meal was going to be tasty. Walking forward a few steps, she could hear Mrs. Mac singing under her breath, making Charlotte smile. She wondered if the family was aware of the shared habit.

After depositing the pot back into the oven, Mrs. Mac turned to her. "We'll take it out in the living room where there are a lot less potentially spillable items. I don't want any angry brides after me!" Indicating the doorway on the other side of the kitchen, she said, "Just through there on the right."

"Okay." Nodding at the flowers in her hand, Charlotte said, "These are for you. Thank you for having me for dinner."

"These are beautiful, Charlotte. You didn't have to. I'll just get these in some water and be right in."

Although Charlotte had been friendly with the MacDonalds for years, she'd never had a reason to visit them. Seeing them together here just seemed right to her. They fit the house, or more accurately, the house fit them. The house was tastefully decorated, not overly fussy nor too casual. Everywhere Charlotte looked, she saw small personal touches that made the house feel homey and welcoming. Not to mention, the large front porch she saw as she drove up had a large swinging seat on one end. It just seemed like an ideal place to sit after a meal. She was sure the home had seen its share of superb meals.

In the living room, they had set up a temporary rolling rack. While she felt bad they'd gone to such trouble, she was relieved the dress could hang off something tall.

Hooking the bag onto the rack, she set about getting the dress out, mindful of the all the pins tucked in various places. Just as she was fishing out the train, Mrs. Mac came in, a kitchen towel in her hands.

Seeing Charlotte's look, she held her hands up for inspection. "Thoroughly washed and dried. Cross my heart," she finished, making the motion with her finger over her heart.

Charlotte smiled. "I trust you, Mrs. Mac. Thank you for setting up this rack. I feel bad you had to go through all that trouble."

"No trouble, dear. We have a bunch of them. Occupational hazard. Now, let's see what you have."

Charlotte took the dress train in her hands, fluffed open the fabric and laid it out on the living room floor, her stomach tightening in anticipation of Mrs. Mac's judgement of the changes.

"Oh my," Mrs. Mac gasped, "That it stunning! No matter how many times I see that train, it always takes my breath away. But looking at the whole thing, if I didn't see that train, I would have thought this was an entirely new dress. It looks so different without those sleeves. What a transformation." Taking a few steps backward, she admired the full design. "I still can't believe you found this in a second-hand store. So sad to see such workmanship end up there, but I'm happy it landed in your hands." She walked over to Charlotte and put an arm around her shoulders, giving her a squeeze. "You're giving this gown a new life."

As Mrs. Mac looked at the changes to the dress, Adam and his dad had come into the house. Mr. Mac went up the stairs to change while Adam paused in the living room doorway.

Charlotte's chest tightened. It was bad enough to show it to Mrs. Mac, but having Adam see it as well just made her nervous. When he caught her eye and said, "Wow," she felt the tension fall from her shoulders.

As Adam and his mom continued their examination, Charlotte noted the strong family resemblance between mother and son. Their hand gestures were similar, and their faces often had the same look. She wondered if Adam's children would also have the similarity. She shook her head to stop that train of thought. Adam was off-limits and thinking about his future kids was ludicrous.

Still, she had to admit it was getting harder and harder to resist the pull of her attraction. He was awesome; kind and devoted to his family and his work. Was she letting fear keep her from what could be a terrific relationship? Frankly, she was tired of finding reasons they shouldn't be together.

What if she and Adam dated? She pictured lovely evenings talking over dinner or snuggling on the couch watching a movie. They could go bowling. She loved bowling but never got to go. Did he even like bowling? Would she care if he didn't? They both liked the outdoors. They could go hiking or maybe even take a run together. Or maybe spend a Sunday afternoon by a fire. They could play cards or just read.

Lost in the picture she was painting for herself, she didn't hear Mrs. Mac leave to get dinner out of the oven. Next she knew, Adam was standing in front of her, saying her name. Looking up into his eyes, she stopped breathing.

"Charlotte," he said, his brows creasing.

He took a step toward her, inhaling deeply as his eyes darkened. Suddenly, she didn't care that she could get hurt. All she knew was that her need to kiss him again was almost painful.

He touched her face, running his finger down her jawline. Her skin erupting in a fiery trail of tingles. She thought she would melt when his thumb traced the contours of her bottom lip, his eyes following the trail. Just as he was leaning in, they both heard the rattle of his dad on the stairs. Adam looked into her eyes. Their lips were so close she could feel his breath on her face.

"Dinner's ready!" Mrs. Mac called from the kitchen.

Adam didn't move. His face still hovered maddeningly close to hers. His eyes flicked away when his mom called, but quickly came back to her, looking first at her lips and then into her eyes.

"To be continued," he whispered. "Coming, Mom," he called, standing up straight and taking a step back from her. "After you," he said, gesturing her out of the room.

Charlotte wasn't sure her feet could move just then, but she needed to get herself together. She was disappointed Adam hadn't kissed her. Thankfully, looking into his eyes, she could see her frustration mirrored there. That knowledge helped ground her and gain some perspective. As he said, to be continued.

Her lips twitched upward as she passed him going out the door, and he muttered, "I can't wait until Act II."

Walking into the kitchen, she couldn't stop her smile. "Can I help you with anything?" she asked Mrs. Mac.

"If you would just take the rolls to the table, that would be great. There's iced tea and water on the table, but if you'd like something else, please let me know."

"Iced tea would be fine," she grabbed the basket. At some point they must have done a renovation to the home. There was no way a house this age would have such an open floor plan, but Charlotte loved that they'd somehow kept the charm of the older home. Setting the rolls down, she noted with a smile that Mrs. Mac had put her flowers out on the table.

She wasn't sure where to sit, so she started looking at the photos on the wall. One frame showed the family at what must be their daughter Julie's wedding. It was not a formal portrait but a snapshot capturing them with their arms around each other, joking and smiling. Charlotte envied the obvious closeness between them. Glancing around, she could see there were more wedding photos, some older ones looked like they went back a few generations. Walking around the table, she was able to examine the gowns.

"Aren't those lovely?" Mrs. Mac said, coming up behind her. "I've tried to get photos from as many family members as possible. Adam suggested we scan them and make them available on one of those family tree websites. One of these days, I'm going to get around to doing that."

"That's a terrific idea. I'm sure other relatives would appreciate seeing them."

"Her and her to-do lists," Mr. Mac interjected, walking over with the covered Dutch oven. "One of the many reasons I fell in love with her."

Mrs. Mac shook her head at him and smiled. "Good thing, too, or you would have ended up with Betty Hanson!"

"Not a chance," he countered. "After I set eyes on you, there was no one else for me. Although Betty Hanson did end up owning her daddy's car dealership, so maybe I should have thought that through a little more." He nimbly caught the hand towel Mrs. Mac threw at his head.

"Enough of you! Go get the couscous, sir—before you stir up any more trouble." Leaning over the table, she removed the cover of the Dutch oven and Charlotte's mouth watered. "I hope you don't mind a Moroccan stew," she said to Charlotte.

"No. No. I can't say as I've had many, but I'm sure I'll love it. It smells heavenly. What's in it?"

"Well, it started as a butternut squash and carrot stew, but I've morphed it a little. It still has the butternut, but I've added chickpeas, cauliflower, and a bit of chicken to round it out."

"She's added rabbit food," Mr. Mac added, placing the couscous and salad on the table. "She's been trying all sorts of things for my new diet. I've eaten more vegetables in the past month than in the past ten years." As Mrs. Mac walked back into the kitchen, shaking her head, Mr. Mac leaned over and whispered to Charlotte, "She's made some damn tasty new food. But don't tell her I like it. It'll ruin all my fun." He smiled and gave her a wink before returning to the kitchen.

She wanted to ask Mr. Mac how he was feeling but didn't want to pry. She'd ask Adam later. Hopefully, he wouldn't think she was too nosy for asking. Charlotte turned to look at the rest of the framed wedding photos.

"See the veil here?" Mrs. Mac said, pointing to a black-and-white photo of a bride standing with her back to the camera. The veil was longer than the dress and had accents of what looked like lace periodically edging the veil. "This is the image that came to my mind when you were talking about the veil you want to do. Something as long as this one with those little details."

Moving closer, Charlotte examined the photo. It was breathtaking. "The veil is amazing. That's what I was thinking. I'll need to find just the right fabric; not standard tulle, but something that has softer movement to it. And at this rate, I'm going to require more lace. I won't have enough to cover the stains and put some on the veil.

"I'm taking another trip to see Barry. I'm sure I'll be able to find something. Thank you again for suggesting his warehouse. It really is incredible."

"You're off to Barry's warehouse?" Mr. Mac asked as he sat down at the table.

"Yes," she replied. "I need fabric for the veil and some new lace."

"Adam, you should take her. It's a boring drive and hard to find," he explained.

What's with this family and volunteering Adam as a chauffeur? Did they think she couldn't drive? A look passed between Adam and his mom, but Charlotte couldn't decipher its meaning.

"Oh, Adam's shown me where it is, Mr. Mac," she jumped in. Any more time in an enclosed space with Adam and she might spontaneously combust. "That's considerate of you to suggest, but I'm sure I can find it again." She actually wasn't sure, but she didn't want to say that out loud. "Oh, and I heard back about the Scottish lace!"

As she updated them with the good news and bad news from her talk with Mary, she sat down at the table. When they were all seated, Mrs. Mac held her hand out to Charlotte. "We always say grace," she said.

Charlotte glanced at Adam and saw his hands were now clasping his mothers on one side and his fathers on the other, so she did the same. As they bowed their heads, she caught Adam's eye, and he smiled at her.

"Lord, we ask that you bless this meal, and the people gathered here. Our thanks to you for your love and guidance. Please bless us with clear sight to see the true path and courage to take the next step. Amen."

They all gave a squeeze of their hands before letting go. Mr. Mac raised his glass and said, "To the chef!"

"To the chef!" they echoed as they toasted. After everyone had taken a sip, they focused on the delicious-smelling food. Charlotte took a spoonful of couscous and passed her plate to Mrs. Mac so she could ladle on some stew. The first forkful was an enchanting overload to her senses. It wasn't spicy, but it had a deep twinge of curry that gave it a staggering amount of depth. The various textures amazed Charlotte. The cauliflower and carrots were an outstanding balance for the chicken and chickpeas. It was as delicious as it smelled.

"Mrs. Mac, this is amazing."

"Thank you, dear! It's something I've been working on."

"If you have a recipe, I'd love to get it from you. I think Lisa would love this."

"I can write up something to give to you. And I've made so much, please take some home for her."

"That's very generous. I'm sure she'll be over the moon."

"It's a shame you can't get that Scottish lace you want," Mr. Mac said. "That's another reason you should take her, Adam. Check in with Barry and see if he can do anything about getting it."

"That's unnecessary," Charlotte tried to interject, but Mr. Mac kept going.

"If he can't get it, he should be able to find some other lace produced in Scotland. Don't worry, Charlotte," Mr. Mac grinned over at her. "Adam will make sure Barry helps you out."

Charlotte didn't know what to say without being rude. Before she could come up with an excuse, Adam chimed in.

"I can go with you, Charlotte. When were you thinking? Or should I ask when it's scheduled on your big project plan," he said with a smile.

"Um. I have the day off Thursday," she stammered. "I was going to go to the warehouse and also drop off the gown with you for cleaning. This Saturday is two weeks before the wedding, so it's time to do a full cleaning."

"Sounds like a plan," Mr. Mac interjected. "Adam can get the gown when you go to the warehouse. Save yourself a trip to the store." Mr. Mac look pleased with his solution, while Mrs. Mac looked like she had indigestion.

Adam raised his eyebrows to her as if to say, 'What are you going to do?' She could see the look in his eye and knew he was enjoying her discomfort.

"It sounds like it's all planned out," Adam said with a touch of humor. "I'll pick you up Thursday, and we'll go see Barry." He took a bite of stew, looking every bit as pleased as his dad.

Thankfully, they dropped the topic, and the rest of the evening was full of talk and laugher. Charlotte couldn't remember the last time she'd had a sit-down meal with her family. Even when she was younger, this wasn't the type of thing they did. She envied the easy rapport they seemed to share.

After the meal, Adam and Charlotte cleared the table and fought Mrs. Mac about doing the dishes. Citing the well-known rule of "she who cooks, does not clean," they won the argument, and Mr. and Mrs. Mac each took a glass of iced tea out to the porch.

"I knew your parents were great," Charlotte said, placing another dish in the dishwasher, "but they really are awesome. Thank you for inviting me."

"Hey, thank you," he said as he stood in front of the sink, washing out pots. "My parents like you a lot, and the dress update was a big hit," he added with a sly look.

"Your dad is a hoot," she said, nudging him with her shoulder. "He's so sweet. But about Barry's, you don't have to go with me, Adam. I'm certain I can find it.

Adam laughed, reaching to put another pot on the drying rack. "Oh no, I'm going. Dad's got it all planned out, right down to the gown pickup. And to think I can't get him to consider retail customer pickup, but for you he implements it in a heartbeat." He smiled. "Besides, I want to go."

His tone and the way he looked at her made butterflies erupt in her stomach. Trying to find solid footing, she asked, "Your dad mentioned a new diet. Is he okay? I know it's none of my business..."

"No, it's fine. Things are still a little unknown right now. He goes back in a few weeks for a follow-up. So far, he seems to be implementing all the doctor's orders and doing everything he can." Adam fell silent, staring out the window.

Seeing the concern on his face, Charlotte put a hand on his arm. "I'm sorry, Adam. I didn't mean to pry, but if he's following doctor's orders, I'm sure his health will improve."

"I'm sure you're right. I just wish there was a way to make him try some of my ideas," he replied with a shake of his head. "Streamlining a few things would reduce his stress."

Charlotte gave his arm a gentle squeeze before letting go. "I'm sure it will work out." She picked up another plate, unsure if she should say what she was thinking. What the heck, she decided. "At the end of the day," she said, "he is who he is, and you can't change him."

She didn't need to look at him to see he was shocked. "I'm not saying people can't change. They absolutely can," she clarified. "What I'm saying is that if someone doesn't want to change, they aren't going to. Sometimes you need to accept them as they are, not for what you want them to be," she finished, her stomach plummeting. She should have kept her mouth shut.

"I think I understand what you're saying, but it just seems a pretty negative viewpoint," he replied his expression sobered.

She thought about it for a moment before responding.

"Perhaps you're right. I learned the hard way from an ex that you can't make someone be who you want them to be. Sometimes you need to open your eyes and see them as they are." The pain of Todd's betrayal had left some serious scars. If she'd only seen who he was before he eviscerated her life.

Pushing away thoughts of Todd, she turned to Adam. "Sorry, I don't mean to imply your dad won't change. It sounds like he already has. He just may need to go at his own pace, and not yours."

"Well, that is a valid point. He's making a lot of changes in his life." He paused. "That ex must have been quite the lesson."

"Todd was a lesson in many areas," she admitted. No way was she going to unpack that nightmare. Giving him a bright smile, she changed the subject. "My dad used to tell me all the time that smart people always listened more than they talked. At first, I thought he was just trying to tell me I talked too much," she laughed. "As I got older, I realized there was a lot of wisdom in that saying." She respected that Adam didn't respond right away and seemed to consider her words.

"Listen more than you talk. That's an interesting piece of advice. I'll give that some thought."

Smiling at his praise, she felt the warmth of his regard flow through her. "My pleasure. I'm sure you'll find a way to help."

As they finished the dishes, Charlotte was disappointed the evening was ending. Perhaps that was beneficial though. A little distance to figure out what was going on between them would be an excellent idea. They went into the living room and worked together to put the gown back in its storage bag.

As they worked, she asked something she'd been thinking about. "Do you miss your old job?"

Adam looked alarmed and blinked a few times before responding. "I do, mostly. I haven't thought much about it. I've been a little preoccupied." He smiled at her as she gathered up the bag and walked toward the front door.

Following him out, she wanted to ask another question, but she needed to say goodnight to his folks. It surprised her when both Mr. and Mrs. Mac stood to give her a hug. They were such demonstrative people and an excellent couple. Their simple acceptance made her heart feel light.

As his parents went back into the house, Adam took the garment bag from her and reached out to assist her down the stairs. Excitement raced through her at his touch. Trying to rein in her emotions as they walked toward her car, she asked, "What do you miss most about your job?"

"I think I miss running a team project the most. When we're all working together looking for solutions, it's very energizing." He smiled vaguely, caught up in memories. "When you have a great team, brainstorming and problem solving are the best."

Opening the car door, he laid the dress down across the back seat. Closing it, he leaned against the car. "I guess I missed it more than I realized," he said with a sigh. "Although all that said, there are a lot of reasons to be here, as well."

His gaze fell to her lips, and she remembered the touch of his fingers caressing her. Heat flushed through her, and her knees went weak. She hadn't realized that was even a real thing, but lord help her, it was.

He pushed off the car, closing the distance between them. The tempo of her heart rate jumped as she desperately tried to remember to breathe. His cologne wound its way up through her senses, scrambling her thoughts. He reached out to touch her, his thumb caressing gentle circles on the back of her hand. So wrapped up in him, she wasn't aware of how she ended up leaning against her door, but there she was. The solid warmth of him pinning her marvelously against the car.

He released her hand, slowly running his fingers up her arm, leaving a trail of fire and chills. He caressed her face before placing both of his hands on the car surrounding her. His heated gaze sent a flash of desire through her, making her question if she could handle the intensity.

He slowly leaned down until their faces were inches apart again. His breath dancing across her skin. She knew she could stop this, but her desire won out. She didn't want to stop. She needed to know what it was like to be really kissed by him, not just the brief barely there kiss they'd shared. Her mind argued she was playing with danger, but the fire in her veins was yelling to get marshmallows because this was going to be mind-blowing.

He said one thing before he closed the distance between them. "Act II."

She closed her eyes in anticipation of his kiss, but it didn't come. Instead, she felt his breath on the side of her neck, sending chills skittering down her spine, tightening her nipples. Tilting her head to give him better access, the feeling of his breath cascading over her skin made her squirm. He hadn't even touched her, and already, she felt him everywhere.

His lips descended, kissing her neck, tormenting her. His lips rested momentarily on her pulse point, and she hissed in pleasure when he opened his lips to taste her. He continued nibbling along her neck until his hot breath tickled her ear. His slow exhale caressed her sensitive ear, making desire pool in her core.

"Adam," she gasped. She hadn't meant to say his name, but she wasn't completely in control of her responses. He hadn't even kissed her on the lips, and already her brain was scrambled, and her body overwhelmed with desire. She felt him shift back, so she opened her eyes, only to be caught by his dark green eyes that burned with the same excitement that throbbed through her.

Done waiting, she raised herself up and kissed him, rejoicing in the taste of him. He quickly dominated her soft kiss, grasping her neck and angling her face to deepen it. His fingers caressed the soft hair at her nape. She'd died and gone to heaven. Those fingers made her tremble, eliciting a small groan.

It seemed like everything stopped and nothing else existed. Their lips met in a tangle as the passion of the kiss grew. When he used his teeth to nip her bottom lip, her body responded with a jolt of electricity, and she gasped at the pleasure of it. Winding his arms around her, he pressed her body tightly to him. She could feel every resplendent inch of him. She lost herself in the feeling of him holding her, surrounding her, kissing her.

When he broke off the kiss, she couldn't contain a growl of frustration. Opening her eyes, she didn't understand why he was frowning. Had she done something wrong? He released her suddenly and took a step back. Losing his warmth was a physical pain.

"Adam?" she questioned breathlessly.

"Sorry," he said, shoving his hand through his hair looking anywhere but at her. "I got carried away."

She wasn't sure what was going on, but something had changed in the blink of an eye. It was like emotional whiplash. They'd had gotten a little carried away, but that didn't explain the chasm she felt between them now.

"Oh, sure," she offered. "You're probably right. I should go anyway." Before he could respond, she slipped into the car. As she backed out of the driveway, she glanced back. He stood in the same place, watching her. He didn't move as she drove away.

CHAPTER SIXTEEN

Adam

One moment he was worshipping Charlotte and loving every moment, the next his mother's words were reverberating in his brain.

You'll break her heart.

You love your nomadic life, but will she? Is that what you want for her?

He hadn't intended to kiss her, but so much about the night had spiraled out of control. First in the house and then again now. When it came right down to it, he couldn't walk away from this kiss again.

With her car out of sight, he walked back toward the garage. He needed a few moments before saying goodnight to his parents. Even with his mother's words haunting him, in his heart he knew he'd do it again. It scared him how much he wanted it. Wanted her. Then again, his mother's words scared him too.

Charlotte was smart, beautiful, and talented—*and a fantastic kisser*, a small voice in his head added. The problem was she represented what he didn't want. Right? She loved living in Jennings, having roots and a community of people around her. He enjoyed moving around, trying unknown places, and making new friends. Granted, these days he wasn't sure he felt the same about his roaming lifestyle, but what did that really mean?

Charlotte's universe was centered on friends and family. He appreciated an existence with fewer entanglements, or at least he used to. Now he had to go and complicate matters by kissing her, in his parents' driveway, no less. He shook his head as he walked into the garage. Was he in high school or something?

But damn, the way she breathed out his name almost undid him. He wasn't sure what had changed tonight, but he was certain the more time he spent with her, the more he came to care about her. He wasn't only talking about his parents or the business when he said there were other reasons to stay. She made him feel things he hadn't felt since Abagail.

Moving automatically, he put away tools and made sure everything was back in its rightful place. If only his own life was as easy to organize. His stay in Jennings was supposed to be about finding clarity. So far, he wasn't an iota closer to figuring out his next move, nor why he was feeling so discontented. If anything, he was more confused than ever.

Caught up in his thoughts, he didn't hear his father come into the garage.

"That Charlotte is an amusing girl," he said, walking up beside him. "It was kind of you to invite her over for dinner. Your mom always enjoys when the two of them have a visit at the store." He moved over to the tool bench, putting away the few items still left out. They worked companionably together for a few moments before he said, "I hope she'll be visiting more often."

Adam reined in his frustration. This wasn't helping the situation at all. "It's complicated, Dad," he responded.

His dad gave him a small nod. "I can see that." He walked over to the wall to move a tire out of the way.

"Dad," Adam barked. "Don't lift that. I can get it." He rushed to take the tire.

"I'm perfectly capable of lifting a tire, Adam," he said, voice tense.

Adam wrestled the tire on the top of a stack without looking back. "You need to be careful. Remember what the doctor said."

"The doctor didn't say I couldn't lift things!" he shot back.

"Dad," Adam turned to face him. "The doctor said to avoid anything that puts undue stress on your body. You're supposed to be taking it easy. Slinging tires about isn't taking it easy. You have to adjust to the new reality."

"I am adjusting to—"

"You need less stress in your life. The doctor said so. Have you even looked at the changes I proposed for the store? We need to get started on them. I've spent weeks combing over information and data. There are some solid ideas for streamlining."

His father walked away to stand in the doorway, staring out across the yard.

Adam wasn't sure what to do. He never set out to argue with his dad. They just always seemed to end up clashing rather than talking. Normally, they argued until someone got so frustrated, they left. Not a great communication plan. His father walking away without saying a word was new. It was unsettling.

"Dad?" Adam asked, filling the silence. "Listen, I'm sorry. I shouldn't have started in. It's been an unsettling night. And I'm just scared for you."

His dad turned with a small smile. Now Adam really was confused.

"I know you're scared for me, Adam. I get it. To be honest, I am too. But I am taking the doctor's orders seriously. I've made a lot of changes so far. I know there are more to come." He took a deep breath. "But we need to learn to communicate and compromise better.

"Actually," he said, his smile widening. "Perhaps you should try this deep breathing technique your mother has me doing." Seeing Adam's skeptical face, he laughed. "I know. I'm surprised too. She wanted me to try meditation, but I wasn't going for that. We compromised, and I've been learning deep breathing to better manage stress."

Adam felt like an ass. He was supposed to be helping the situation, not stressing his father out. "I'm so sorry, Dad. I shouldn't have pushed. I don't want to be part of the problem."

"No, that's okay. We should discuss your ideas. Let's just try to do it without getting all hot under the collar."

"Listen more than I talk," Adam muttered to himself.

"What was that?"

Adam smiled. "It was something Charlotte said to me tonight.

She said I should listen more than I talk."

"Smart girl. I knew I liked her."

"Yeah. Me too," he admitted.

His father walked over and put a hand on his shoulder. "I know."

Adam saw the twinkle of mischief in his dad's eye. He should have known. Before he could call him out on his matchmaking attempts, his dad proposed a compromise.

"Why don't we finish up in here and while we do that, tell me about one of your ideas. The one you're most excited about. Let me hear about that one."

He wasn't sure his dad would make any changes, nor was he sure they'd fix their communication, but it felt like a solid start. Mentally running through the list, he picked his favorite project and started talking.

As they finished up, Adam outlined what he wanted to do, backed it up with the data he had and then, as Charlotte said, he stopped talking and listened to his dad's questions and feedback.

When he finally drove home, there weren't definitive plans to implement, but that felt okay. Their conversation felt like a win.

Now all he had to do was figure out his life and what was going on with Charlotte. If they recalled him, he'd have to give them an answer within ten days, so he needed a plan. He just didn't know where to start. That kiss with Charlotte wasn't helping him think straight, either.

As he drove, he replayed the evening, examining everything that had happened. Charlotte must be so confused. When his mom's words had darted into his awareness, he'd just frozen up.

That said, his comments to his mom were still valid. If they got serious, Charlotte could come to Phoenix.

Or he could to Jennings.

That thought stopped him. Would he move back to Connecticut? It surprised him to realize it wasn't an immediate "no" in his mind. It had possibility.

The problem was, he didn't even know if what he felt for Charlotte was real. Did she feel the same? Worrying about where they'd live was putting the cart before the horse. He needed to explore his feelings and this relationship before worrying about things down the road.

As he pulled into his garage, he felt like he had a plan. He would let the relationship with Charlotte unfold. Even with deciding that, he could still feel his mom's warning flashing like a neon sign. Obviously, this wasn't going to be easy.

CHAPTER SEVENTEEN

Charlotte

Charlotte stared back out the car window. So far, this trip to the warehouse with Adam was not going well. She wasn't sure what was wrong, but things were off. He seemed standoffish from the moment he'd picked her up; it was if they'd picked back up in the same awkward moment they'd left things on Sunday. Their conversation was pleasant but lacked its usual affection and fun. All she could attribute it to was that perhaps he regretted that mind-blowing kiss on Sunday.

Since that toe-curling kiss, they'd been texting back and forth as if nothing had happened. Her entire world had tilted in those few moments, but obviously Adam had not felt the same.

She'd started to text him a million times this week, canceling their trip to the warehouse, but each time something held her back. If she was truthful, she wanted to see him again. She enjoyed being with him. Plus, there was the very practical reason she wasn't sure she could locate the warehouse again.

Between all the work for the dress and worrying over the Adam situation, she hadn't gotten a lot of sleep the past few days. What she really wanted was a fun outing and for her brain to stop worrying about every little thing. It was a tall order, but a girl could hope.

So far it didn't look like she was going to get her wish. The conversation was stilted, they'd hit traffic, and Adam seemed annoyed. The prospect of being stuck in the car even longer was not appealing. She wasn't aware she'd sighed out loud until Adam called her on it.

"That was a pretty big sigh. Sorry about the traffic. If we'd gone this morning like I hoped, we probably wouldn't have hit any, but Mom needed my help this morning."

"No problem," she replied, trying to keep her voice light. "I didn't care when we went. I'm just happy to be out of the house. Between my regular job and the wedding gown, I just needed a break. A day off where I don't think about what needs to happen with the gown, or what I need to take care of at work. Know what I mean?"

Adam glanced at her, the corner of his mouth ticking up. "I can relate to that."

He fell silent, and it looked like he was having an internal debate. Charlotte waited him out and see if he would expand on that. She didn't have to wait long.

"I'll make you a deal," he said, his tone light and playful. "For the rest of today, no overthinking, no stressing, no worrying. Just a day of fun and relaxation. What do you think? You up for that?" He shot her a look as he issued the challenge.

She didn't hesitate. "Absolutely," she fired back.

"It's a deal then!" He extended his hand for her to shake.

As her fingers touched his, she felt electricity buzz up her arm. The power of it made her breath catch. Releasing his hand, she tried to shake off the tingle of awareness that remained. She didn't even want to think about that today. She just wanted exactly what he'd described. A day of fun and relaxation with no worrying. Granted she had some decisions to make when they got to the warehouse, but being surrounded by all those amazing fabrics was never a hardship.

Thankfully, after they made the deal, Adam seemed more relaxed. They started talking about an upcoming concert and fortunately the conversation flowed easily for the rest of the ride.

When they arrived at the warehouse, Charlotte made her way back to the bridal section while Adam stopped at the front desk to talk to Barry. He wasn't gone long, but she was already in the fabric zone when he returned.

She was searching for veil fabric when she heard his muted laugh. He tried to make it sound like a cough, but she knew better. Without turning her head, she said, "What?"

"Sorry," he laughed again. "You were doing the muttering thing again."

Damn. She wasn't even aware she was doing it. Adding some sass, she shot back, "If you're not going to be helpful, then go chat with Barry."

"Well, Barry isn't here right now. The front desk will let him know we're here when he gets back. I can be helpful. What are you looking for?"

"I'm looking for fabric for the veil. I want something with the body and movement of chiffon but the sheerness of illusion tulle." When she didn't hear any response, she turned to look at Adam and laughed. He looked like she'd just asked him to name pi to a thousand places. The blank stare and scared look made it clear he wouldn't be much help. He recovered nicely, though.

"Of course, of course," he said, rubbing his hands together. "I get what you're after. Let me jump in and pull a few samples."

"Excellent," she replied, playing along. "What I would really like is the fabric used by costume designer Sandy Powell for Cinderella's wedding veil in the 2015 live action film. Can you whip that up for me?" she asked with a smile.

Adam laughed. "Man, I am in some serious trouble. You're in designer mode."

"I'm going to take that as a 'no,' then. Well, why don't we try something easier and move over to the lace?"

As they settled in, looking through samples, it became clear the lace would not be as easy as she hoped. While there was an extensive selection, nothing was catching her eye. It was disheartening because there were so many incredible and beautiful patterns. Any of them would look stunning on the gown, but none of them excited her.

"You know what the problem is?" she said after rejecting yet another pattern.

"What?"

She sighed, defeat weighing down her shoulders. "The problem is I can't get the Scottish lace out of my head. It would be the crowning glory. Why did I have to fall in love with something I can't have?"

"That's the lace you found after talking with Ethel's friend Mary?"

"Yes. It was more like I fell in love with it being produced in Scotland. I looked up the company she mentioned, and they look terrific. They use antique lace looms! I mean, come on! It's perfect!

"But I can't get it, so I shouldn't even be thinking about it. I just can't get it out of my head. I wish I had never found them."

"What's this about lace you can't get?" a voice boomed behind her.

Charlotte jumped and whirled around to see Barry looming over her. For such a big man, he moved with surprising stealth. "Hi, Barry," she said trying to slow her heart rate. "It's nothing. I was just telling Adam about some of the lace research I was doing for the gown. You have an amazing selection here. I'm sure I'll find a few options to choose from."

"What lace did you find that was perfect?" he questioned doggedly.

Barry wasn't going to let this go. Well, no harm in telling him about the Scottish lace. "It's produced in Scotland by a company called MYB Textiles. I found a few patterns like their Honey Bee or Catkin Madras that I thought would work. But really, it was about it being produced in Scotland on antique lace looms that was brilliant, more than what the pattern actually looked like."

"Hmm." Barry rubbed his chin, thinking. "I can't believe they still produce using antique looms."

"Well, I believe they're the last lace maker to use the Nottingham Lace Looms," she said, her face lighting up. "They've hooked them up to modern CAD machines. Isn't that astounding? They have thousands and thousands of antique lace patterns in their archive."

Barry was quiet for a few moments, then gave a sharp nod.

"Done. I'll get you the lace."

"Oh no, Barry," she blurted. "Thank you for offering, but you don't have to do that. Between the minimum order you'd need to place and trying to get it here in time, it's just not workable. I need a small amount. What would you do with the rest?"

"With the story you told, I can sell that lace. People appreciate craftsmanship as much as they appreciate a rich, historic origin. Traditional lacemakers using antique lace looms to craft stunning works of art? Practically sells itself.

"I'll tell you what," he continued. He took a quick look at his watch. "It's too late over there, but I'm going to check out their website and pop off an email. I'll call them tomorrow. If I can't get you the lace before the wedding, I'll let you know. You can always buy something we already have in stock."

Not waiting for a response, he started to walk away before halting and turning back. "You have photos of the lace currently on the dress?"

"Yes," she replied.

"Great! Stop back up at the office. I want to include photos of the dress in the email. If they have thousands of patterns, maybe they have something on hand that would complement the dress even more than what you found. I'll see you up front." He turned and was out of sight before Charlotte could respond.

"Force of nature strikes again," Adam chuckled.

She turned to him, eyes wide. "I can't even believe that conversation. Was he serious?"

"Oh yeah, he was." Adam shook his head. "That's Barry. That said, he's right. Lace produced on antique looms is surprising. People will take notice of the history."

Charlotte could appreciate the story of the lace; it was definitely a big draw for her. She hoped Barry wouldn't be going to too much trouble. Well, it wasn't like he'd stuck around to discuss it. Might as well let him investigate.

Looking back at the fabric, she started shifting through options with renewed energy. She didn't want to get her hopes up, but it was hard to not get excited about the possibility.

She'd pick a back-up lace pattern just in case. Quicker than she thought possible, she had the lace picked and the veil fabric as well.

After checking out and stopping in to see Barry, they were back out into the late afternoon sunshine. Charlotte felt a little shell-shocked over how the afternoon had gone. And even though she knew it was a long shot, she couldn't help but feel overjoyed with the possibility of getting the Scottish lace. One step closer to the perfect dress.

Walking to the car, Adam opened the trunk so she could put her package inside.

"So," he said, closing the trunk and looking at her. "You up for some more fun?"

"More fun than that?" She nodded at the warehouse. "That's a tall order."

"I was thinking since we won't be getting back until later, what about dinner at Manor House Inn tonight?"

Immediately, her stomach rumbled as she thought of the fantastic food there. She hadn't been there in months. Glancing down at her outfit and at Adam, she decided they looked respectable enough. The Manor wasn't too fancy, but it was a few steps above her normal fair.

Would that make this a date? Did Adam think it was a date? Before making herself crazy with supposition, she reminded herself today was a no stress, no worries day. If that was the rule, then the answer about dinner was easy.

"That sounds fantastic. I'm in!"

The drive back toward Jennings passed quickly as their conversation ranged over a host of different topics. When she could clear her mind of the stress and worry, Charlotte felt so much lighter and enjoyed herself a lot more. Adam had an excellent sense of humor, and she loved the way he told stories. They compared growing up in the same town but attending different schools. It was weird to think they probably passed each other many times as they grew up but had never met until now.

Arriving at the inn, she was happy to see that while there were a decent number of cars, it didn't look crazy busy. Grabbing her sweater, they strolled toward the stone portico entrance. Perched on top of a hill, Manor House had a magnificent vista, but was also flanked by pine forest. She'd always thought of it as a balanced location—light and airy with earth and shadows.

Taking a deep breath of the sweet air, Charlotte's shoulders relaxed. She loved this place and didn't get here often enough. She'd have to grab Lisa and get here more frequently.

Opening the door, Adam ushered her down the hallway to the restaurant. Manor House was a popular destination in Jennings Township. For years it had been a very successful B&B, run by a terrific couple, John and Martha. When their son John, who they called JJ, and his wife had their first child, they moved back to the area.

As a trained chef, JJ had worked in many well-respected kitchens, but what he really wanted was a restaurant of his own. So John and Martha decided to expand the B&B to include a restaurant and function rooms. Thankfully, they made the changes with great skill, so the interior still held all the charm and historical atmosphere of the original building.

Just thinking about her last mouthwatering visit, her stomach rumbled again. Loudly. Adam's laugh told her he'd heard it. What could she say? She was looking forward to a delicious meal.

The hostess checked them in and told them it would be a few moments before a table was ready. Rather than waiting inside, they decided to sit on the patio and enjoy the view. At the small outdoor bar, Adam got drinks, and they settled into two chairs on the edge of the patio. They spoke little, each savoring the evening and the beautiful view.

Charlotte was more and more aware of Adam's hand as it brushed against her in passing. Each small touch made her skin prickle and filled her with a heady sense of longing. Normally on a date she would panic about the silence that stretched between them. With Adam, she simply felt at peace. It was almost a shame when they were called in for their table.

Savoring the feel of Adam's hand on the small of her back, she almost didn't see Martha before the woman engulfed her in a tight embrace. "Charlotte! It's so good to see you. How have you been?"

Smiling at the women's gregarious affection, she returned the hug. "Martha. It's wonderful to see you. I hope things are well. How are John and JJ? The inn looks fantastic, as always."

"Oh, we're all terrific. And who is this handsome gentleman?" she asked.

"Pardon my manners. Martha, this is Adam MacDonald. His parents own MacDonald Cleaners. Adam, this is the ever joyful and lovely Martha. She and her husband own the inn."

"Nice to meet you, Martha," Adam said, extending his hand. "Your place is beautiful, and from what I hear, the food and hospitality are second to none."

"Lovely to meet you too, Adam. Watch out for this one, Charlotte. He's a charmer! Now sit, sit. I'll let JJ know you're here. Whatever you want, you just let your waitress know." Martha took a few steps before turning back. "Charlotte, I happen to have a lovely bottle of your wine in the fridge—all nice and cold. Would you like me to send it out?"

"Oh, I couldn't ask that of you."

"Pish! I'll send it out right away. It's the least we can do for you."

Once they were settled, the waitress came with menus and the evening's specials. As Charlotte eyed the very tempting offerings, she asked Adam what he was getting.

"I'm debating between the highland burger, the baked stuffed sole, or the Thai spiced pizza. They all sound amazing."

"Oh, the baked stuff sole is on my list, as well. Although chicken piccata is a favorite of mine. I bet JJ does an incredible job with it. I think I'll have to try that one."

"Maybe I'll give the Thai spiced pizza a go," Adam responded. "It sounds like nothing I've ever had before." He placed his menu down on the table and turned his attention to Charlotte. "It looks like you're close to the people who own the inn. I had no idea. I hope it's okay we came here."

"Oh yes. I love it here, but I'm afraid I don't get a chance to come up all that much. I met the family a few years ago. It was right after they opened the restaurant. One of the first events they held here was a wedding." Charlotte smiled at the memory.

"They renovated a few years ago adding the restaurant and function room, so they could host weddings and other events," she explained. "One of their first brides had an emergency with her dress. Or as Martha said when she called, there was 'a hysterical bride, a panicked mother, and a pack of clueless bridesmaids,'" she finished with a laugh.

"They had called Ethel looking for seamstress help. But with her arthritis, she couldn't do the work. She recommended me. Before I knew it, I had grabbed my sewing kit and was driving up here. Never let it be said I left a bride in distress."

"That was considerate of you."

"Oh, it was my pleasure. The poor woman was beside herself. Someone who remained nameless stepped on her train a few minutes after she put on the dress. Some of the lace ripped off, and one seam tore open. I was able to mend it quickly and get her back into it before any of the guests knew there was an issue."

The waitress arrived with the bottle of wine and poured Charlotte a glass. When she went to pour one for Adam, Charlotte thought she should caution him. "I hope you'll try it. It's one of my favorites, but I won't be offended if you don't like it. I don't know how your tastes run, but this is a southern sweet wine. Not many people in Connecticut run into that type."

Nodding permission to the waitress, he let her pour him a glass. "I'm not much of a wine person, but I'd love to try it. Does Martha always keep a bottle waiting for you? That seems odd for someone who says she doesn't get up here much."

"It would be odd if Martha hadn't fallen in love with this wine as well. After I sewed the bride's gown, Martha and John wanted to pay me for my time, but I wouldn't hear of it. I was just doing something nice for someone. I guess they didn't feel that was right, so they reached out to Ethel for suggestions on a thank you gift. Since you can't buy this wine in Connecticut, Ethel mentioned it. JJ ordered a bunch of bottles, thinking if I liked it that much, perhaps he should have it for the restaurant."

She laughed again, remembering the look on their faces when Martha and JJ had finally told her the whole story. "When the wine came, JJ tried it and hated it! He couldn't believe I enjoyed it. I think it offended his chef-honed wine palette. Nonetheless, they sent me a few bottles with a lovely thank-you card. JJ stuck the remaining wine in the back room. Martha got curious about it and tried it. She loved it! Much to the chagrin of her 'uptight northern son's tastebuds.'

"After she was hooked, Martha called, and we talked about the rest of the winery's offerings. I steered her into trying a few different varieties. She now has it shipped up for her own private use. To hear JJ talk about it, he has relented and allows her to store no more than two bottles in his fridge. His mom loves to tease him about it. Martha lets me know when she's ordering, so I can add in a few bottles."

"No wonder you're a hit around here," Adam said, taking a careful sip of the wine.

Charlotte watched him, wondering how he was going to feel about the sweet taste.

After a moment, he said, "I'm not sure. It's nothing I'm used to, but I can say for certain, I don't hate it. And it is properly chilled."

Charlotte practically purred. "Oh, it is. I put mine in the freezer a little before I open it. Lovely for a summer evening relaxing on the back deck."

"That sounds fantastic."

After they placed their orders, Adam glanced around the restaurant, his eyes following Martha as she wove her way through the tables, greeting people. Turning back, he said, "You're very connected to this town and the people here."

Charlotte wasn't sure why the statement made her nervous. Perhaps it was how serious he looked. Did he think that was weird or something? "I do have a strong attachment to this community, to these people," she said finally.

Adam looked thoughtful before replying, "I've never really had that. I envy you that connection."

She was surprised by his admission. She knew he moved a lot, but had he never put down roots anywhere? "I'm blessed to have so many amazing people in my life. I certainly don't take that for granted."

She took a small sip of wine, gathering her thoughts. "Growing up, I never felt like I belonged anywhere. I never fit my mom's ideas of who I should be. I didn't have a lot of close friends. I was a shy kid who liked to sew and kept mostly to herself. I just never felt like I had a place in the world.

"As I grew up and especially now that I've moved back to Jennings, I finally feel like I fit somewhere. I've found my people, and that means the world to me. It's like I'm becoming comfortable in my own skin. Or at least getting there," she offered.

Adam nodded but didn't respond. He toyed with the stem of his wineglass as if considering what he wanted to say next. "But don't you ever get bored staying in the same place year after year? Haven't you ever wanted to live somewhere else?"

She would have been offended if he didn't look so earnest. Her expression sobered. "No," she replied. Their dinners arrived, and they took the next few minutes tasting the magnificent food.

Eventually she couldn't stop herself from saying, "Picking up and hauling off to some new location isn't the answer to everything, you know." She snapped her mouth shut. She hadn't meant to say that with such snark; not surprised to see Adam's eyebrows arch in response. He must be as startled as she was with her tone.

She raised her hand before he could respond. "Sorry. Not sure why that came out snarky." She looked out over the restaurant, smiling when she spotted Martha talking animatedly to a customer. She was always an excellent source of positivity. Turning back to Adam she saw he was scrutinizing her. He hadn't deserved her snapping at him. It had been an honest question. Given how he lived his life, she could see why he would ask it. Just because he moved around didn't make him Todd.

"Well, maybe I do," she offered. "I was dating someone for a while. His name was Todd. We met at a work conference, and I was pretty taken with him right from the beginning. After we'd been dating for eight months or so, the lease on his rental was up, and he ended up moving to Jennings.

"It was fun having him in town. We spent even more time together; I showed him all my favorite places. As the months went by, our relationship became more serious. Around our one-year anniversary, we started to talk about marriage and our future. We even looked at houses together. It looked like our lives were coming together perfectly. Or at least, I thought so."

She rubbed her chest, trying to ease the pressure. Sometimes it was hard to figure out what hurt more—their actual breakup or how stupid and humiliated she felt about the whole thing. Taking another sip of her drink, she swallowed past the lump in her throat before continuing, "Christmas was just a few weeks away, and I noticed Todd was acting a strange. He seemed unsettled and preoccupied."

Her laugh was hollow and bitter. "I thought he was getting ready to propose. It seemed like the right time. We had been dating for a year and a half, and I thought he would surprise me with a ring on Christmas. I was such a fucking idiot," she said with heat. She saw Adam's eye widen. Charlotte wasn't in the habit of swearing, but sometimes regular words just didn't cut it.

She paused and took a deep breath. Now that she'd started telling Adam she couldn't stop, but that didn't make it any easier. "I should have seen it coming. Instead, I was blindsided."

"What happened?" Adam asked in a hushed tone.

"A few days before Christmas, Todd and I were supposed to get together for dinner and a movie. When I showed up at his apartment, he didn't answer the door. When I called his cell phone, he didn't answer. I feared that something had happened to him— that he was lying injured on the floor or something, hurt. I was banging on the door again when his neighbor came out of her apartment. She apologized because she was supposed to have put a note on his door but just hadn't done it yet. It was addressed to me.

"He was gone." She registered the shocked look on Adam's face. She'd seen that same look on her friends and family when she'd had to tell them. "He left. Packed up his apartment and moved out. Actually, he moved to Chicago. He had a job offer from a company out there, and he felt he shouldn't pass up on the opportunity. I didn't even know he'd been looking for a job," she whispered.

Reaching for her wineglass, her hand trembled slightly. Taking a drink, she paused for a moment before continuing. "His note said he was sorry, but this was just something he needed to do. I guess he'd been feeling trapped and wanted to focus on his career. He said he loved me but needed to explore more in life before settling down with someone. Seems he couldn't find a way to tell me any of that. Instead, he accepted the job, packed up his life and moved out of town without telling me."

Charlotte wrapped an arm across her stomach, gripping her elbow, unable to stop the familiar burn of humiliation and shame. What an idiot to not see something like that coming. She was practically planning the wedding, and he was planning his escape.

Her eyes burned as the memory of that day played out again in her mind. The pitying look of Todd's neighbor. The five short lines of handwriting that had crushed the life she thought she was living. She didn't even matter enough for him to tell her in person. He dumped her, moved hundreds of miles away, and all she rated was five lines. She wrote more than that in a thank you note to her letter carrier.

"One moment I thought we were getting married, the next I was staring at an empty apartment and learning from his neighbor that he'd left me. I felt devastated and depressed for a long time. Not to mention embarrassed. He dumped me in the most horrid and public way. For weeks, I refused to leave the house, refused to go anywhere in town. I was sure people were gossiping up a storm about the whole nasty business. I could see the pity in their eyes. Poor, pathetic Lottie." Her voice broke, and she struggled to get a hold of her emotions.

Why was she sharing all of this with him? Looking at him, she saw understanding and compassion shimmering in his eyes. She had her answer. For whatever reason, she trusted Adam. She trusted him to understand and not judge, to have compassion but not pity. She took a breath and cleared her throat before continuing.

"Perhaps the silver lining is I learned who my genuine friends were, and I realized what a caring family I'd created for myself. Ethel and your mom, even Mrs. S. at the bakery. They all took care of me in one way or another. For that, I will be forever grateful.

"The whole situation kind of messed with my head. It's been a tough road back, but I've been blessed with people here who love and support me no matter what."

"Did you ever talk to Todd again?" Adam asked.

"He called a few months after he'd moved. I answered the phone, told him to burn in hell, and was about to hang up when he said he was sorry. It wasn't the easiest conversation to have, but at least I know more about why he did what he did. I just wished it made me feel better," she sighed. She was glad she hadn't hung up on him, as it had given her a better understanding, but it hadn't given her any closure. And she hoped it hadn't given him any either. Sure, that made her a vindictive person, but screw it. He deserved to feel like crap for what he'd done.

"I don't know why I told you all that," she said, looking over at Adam. "You must think I'm crazy." She never talked about Todd and sharing it with Adam was pretty far outside her comfort zone. Although, she felt lighter now, like it had taken a weight off her shoulders. Still, not great dinner conversation, especially as they were having such an awesome day.

"I don't think you're crazy," Adam said, pulling her from her thoughts. "Why would I think that? We all experience loss. It's not easy. It's never easy. And it shouldn't be."

Charlotte wasn't sure what he meant by that last part. "It shouldn't be?"

He hesitated and then said, "It shouldn't be easy to just walk away from someone you cared about, that you loved. The pain of that is because you cared about them deeply. I understand how losing someone can mess with your head."

The waitress came and started clearing their plates. Hoping to cajole him into a better mood, she joked, "You? You're so laid back, I bet you never lost your head about anyone."

He paused a beat before responding, "My college girlfriend, Abigail, was killed in a car accident our senior year."

Charlotte barely contained her gasp.

"She was home in Colorado for Christmas break," he continued. "The roads were icy and caused a multi-car accident. Several people were injured, but Abigail was killed."

Instinctively, Charlotte reached over to grip his hand. "I'm so sorry, Adam. I didn't know. That must have been horrible for you." Here she joked that he'd never lost his head about anyone. How could she have been so callous? Could she have sounded like more of a monster?

Adam gave her a small smile. "It was. We'd been dating since sophomore year, and it was serious. We had all these plans for after college. After she was gone, I'm not sure how I finished out the semester. It's kind of a blur. After graduation, I accepted the first job offer that took me far away from anything I'd known. I thought if I wasn't near anything familiar, it wouldn't hurt as much."

"Did that work?" she asked.

"Yes and no," he said. "Being some place new and having to find my way distracted me, but no matter where I went, the grief eventually found me."

Charlotte nodded as she put together the puzzle pieces. "So that's why you move around so much? You're still trying to come to grips with losing Abigail?"

"No," he responded, but then stopped for a beat. "She passed away over a decade ago. There's still the sense of loss but nothing crippling like it was for those first few years." He stared down into his wine as if it held the answer. "I think I just got used to moving. I never felt like I wanted to put down roots anywhere." He looked up at her. "At least not until recently."

"What do you mean?" she asked, reminding herself to not read too much into what he was saying.

"I've been feeling unsettled, like something's missing. At first, I thought it was time to move on, but for the first time the thought starting over someplace new just doesn't appeal to me. Honestly, watching you here and listening to you talk about your life in Jennings has illustrated what's been missing from mine. But I'm just not sure if putting down roots is the answer for me."

Before Charlotte could reply, the waitress came over with a few plates. As she set them down, Charlotte said, "I think you have the wrong table. We didn't order dessert."

"Compliments of Martha and JJ," the waitress said with a smile. "This is our famous red velvet cake with cream cheese frosting, these are our orange raspberry cake bites, and we have chocolate-covered macaroons."

"That's a lot of dessert!" Charlotte exclaimed.

"I thought so too," the waitress said, looking around. "So, I'll bring over two take home containers," she whispered. "That way, you can split what's left."

Charlotte laughed as the waitress spun off to get containers. Grabbing a fork, she looked at Adam. "Where do you want to start first?"

"Well," he said in mock seriousness. "The red velvet cake is famous, so I'm thinking we shouldn't keep it waiting." He picked up his fork and arched his eyebrow.

"Agreed!" She dug in and tasted the first heavenly bite. "Mmmmm. This cream cheese frosting is the best."

Adam could only nod as his mouth was full of red velvet cake as well. As they polished it off and sampled the other desserts, their conversation remained light. Adam's words had given her a lot to think about, but that was for later. For now, they debated the pros and cons of various desserts. She wasn't sure if she could get past his total love of tiramisu. Well, it could have been worse; he could have said flan.

Looking at him now, his green eyes dancing with humor as he laughed, she could see herself falling for him. It felt like something had shifted in their relationship. Not just tonight, but the entire experience of today. She'd never felt so connected to someone.

As they left the restaurant with a wave goodbye to Martha, Adam had his hand on the small of her back again. The warmth radiated throughout her whole body.

As they were driving, she decided she needed to be honest, at least with herself. It wasn't a matter of falling for him—she'd already fallen. He was the real deal. He made her feel remarkable, both comfortable in her own skin but also tripping over herself with heat and desire. The question was, did Adam feel the same?

When they arrived at the house, Charlotte said, "I can get the dress and bring it down or, if you'd like, you can come see the workroom."

Adam already had the car turned off and was opening the door. "Oh, no way am I not seeing this workroom I've been hearing so much about. I want to see Charlotte Baker Designs headquarters!"

She just shook her head and walked into the house. That he took her skills and talents at face value and never doubted her was a gift that touched her deeply.

Putting her dessert box on the table by the door, she heard a noise coming from the living room. Ducking her head in, she spied Lisa, reclined on the couch, a bowl of popcorn on the coffee table. Looking over at the TV, she smiled. "Hey Lisa. British Baking night?" she asked.

"It's bread week. You know how much I love bread week. Hi, there," she said, spying Adam behind her. "You must be Adam.

Nice to meet you."

Adam smiled and replied, "Nice to meet you too, Lisa. I've heard a lot about you."

Lisa's smile grew, and she gave Charlotte a pointed look. Her friend was going to have too much fun with this. "Did you two have an enjoyable day?"

Charlotte felt the blush grace her cheeks. "The best," she replied. And it had been. The best day she could remember in a long time. She saw Lisa raise her eyebrows, but before her friend could ask questions, she ushered Adam up the stairs and into the workroom.

"Wow," he gasped, his eye wide scanning the room.

Looking around, Charlotte tried to view it as an outsider would. She could see where all the dresses and fabrics and sewing equipment could be overwhelming. "Sorry for the mess, but with trying to get the dress finished, cleaning up my space hasn't been possible."

Adam recovered quickly. "No, that's fine. It's a working space, so long as it works for you, it's perfect. It's just a lot to take in at first." His eyes trailed around the room, taking in all the gowns. "Would you mind showing me some dresses you've finished?"

"Sure thing," she laughed, even as she wrapped her arms around herself. Although she was getting better at showing her work, Adam was special. Dropping her arms and squaring her shoulders, she gestured him over to the racks and started pulling out finished works.

By the third dress, she started to relax. His attention was focused, his comments thoughtful, and he appreciated her work. His open admiration for her creativity made her want him even more.

When they wrapped up the tour, Adam looked at the mannequin that held Alex's dress. "Shall we pack this up so I can take it?" he asked.

"I should have had it ready, but I was working on it up till the last moment."

Adam walked over and stared down at the gown. Looking up

with confusion, he asked, "Where do we start?"

Walking over, she showed him where he should hold the dress. "You hold it here; I'll get the zipper down and then we can lift it off."

As they worked to free the gown, Charlotte was aware of every time their hands touched or he brushed her arm. It was like an electric pulse that radiated out from wherever their skin contacted.

Working together, they bundled the dress up in a storage bag, Charlotte tucking in a stray piece of fabric before zippering its length. Catching his gaze, she felt pinned in place. Memorized again by the small flecks of gold that shimmered in his eyes. Did that gold color change depending on what he was wearing?

Before she could follow that thought, he reached out and tucked an errant strand of hair away from her face. The feeling of his fingers on her skin set off a wave of desire. Her breath caught as his fingers resting on her cheek and throat. This was quickly becoming one of her favorite things, but there was no way he didn't feel the pulse of her rapid heartbeat beneath his fingertips. His eyes searched hers for a moment, then the back of his fingers were leaving a fiery trail across her cheek to her chin as he caressed her face. Tendrils of heat wrapped around her, pooling in her stomach.

He stepped closer, his arms drawing her in to him. Without a word, he bent his head and kissed her. It started off soft with a sweetness she could have drowned in, but within seconds, the heat erupted between them. He tightened his hold, his hands pressing her against him. As he deepened the kiss with a growl, she was thankful for his embrace. She didn't think her legs could hold her right now.

She ran her fingers through his hair, eliciting a groan from him she felt down to her toes. It was so grand, she did it again, letting her nails lightly scratch his scalp. She threw everything she had into the kiss, his passion matching her own.

"Hey, Lottie!" a jarring yell interrupted. Adam released her and stepped back, but his eyes still reflected his desire.

“Are these desserts you brought home for me?” Lisa continued to shout from downstairs.

Charlotte tried to slow her breathing and galloping heart. Looking at Adam, she could see he was also breathing heavily. At least she knew he was just as affected as she’d been. “Yeah, dig in!” she yelled back to Lisa.

Adam blew out a deep breath, a smile tugging at his lips. “Thank you for showing me your work, Charlotte,” he said. “Cynthia and my mom were right,” he paused, his gaze shifting to look out across the workroom.

When he glanced back, his eyes seemed haunted. “These gowns are beautiful. You have a good thing going here,” he said his smile fading.

Charlotte wasn’t sure what was wrong, but it felt like their conversation had just taken a right turn. A turn she didn’t understand. “Thanks Adam,” she replied automatically, her thoughts whirling to decipher what had changed. “That means a lot.”

“Well,” he murmured, taking another step away. “I better get going. I’ll just show myself out. Have an enjoyable evening.”

Before she could blink, he disappeared around the corner of the door, his footsteps echoing down the hall. Walking to the doorway, she listened until she heard him pull out of the driveway. Brushing her fingertips against her lips, they felt swollen from the intensity of their kiss. She didn’t know what had happened there at the end, but she knew she’d be reliving that kiss tonight in her dreams.

CHAPTER EIGHTEEN

Adam

As Saturday mornings went, this one was pretty agreeable considering he was still half asleep. He had a coffee in one hand and a pastry in the other, so things were looking up. He hadn't slept well, making a stop at Pie in the Sky for extra fortitude a requirement. Last night, he just couldn't shut off his brain. When he should have been sleeping, his mind kept going back to Charlotte and that kiss. Or kisses, to be exact. It was hard to sleep when his thoughts kept returning to how her body had responded to him.

Once he stopped berating himself for getting distracted, he enjoyed replaying the day. When he'd picked Charlotte up, he was annoyed his mother's warnings were still echoing in his head. He didn't want to hurt Charlotte, but he wanted to explore the relationship. Denying his attraction to her on the chance that she may not want to move to Phoenix if they got serious was crazy.

Although hearing her talk at dinner last night had lent credence to his mother's warning. Charlotte was part of the community here. He would hate to see her have to start over again in a new location, especially if that move was just the first of many. Why was his life suddenly so complicated? He finished the last bite of pastry, hoping the delectable taste would distract him from the confusing nightmare of his life.

Looking over the spreadsheet in front of him, he made a note to call the manufacturer to check the numbers. He needed to ensure his information was correct before talking to his dad. While they'd had a successful conversation about work in the garage, nothing had changed because of it. When Adam pushed the other day to either move forward with the idea or look at another suggestion, his dad had snapped at him.

It felt like every step forward he made; he took two steps back. He assumed they'd turned a corner the other night, but so far, that wasn't panning out. The only things changing around here was his frustration level. Well, he wasn't giving up yet.

Taking a sip of coffee, he looked through the list of changes he wanted to suggest to his parents. The majority centered on streamlining and tweaking some processes to make them more efficient. On the off chance his dad was interested, he'd also put together a few ideas on expanding without adding to his parents' busy schedules. Now he just had to get them to listen.

The rustle of fabric behind let him know someone was at his door even before he heard the quick knock. Turning, he saw Cynthia, and his stomach dropped. Her face was pinched, her eyes troubled.

"What is it?"

"Charlotte's dress… it's…" She twisted her hands together, her knuckles whitening with the pressure. "I'm so sorry."

"How bad?" he asked before she could say anything else.

"It's not destroyed, but some of the fabric gave way. Not in all the areas I feared." She paused, shrugging her shoulders. "But in a fair amount. It'll mean a lot of repair work."

Adam groaned and sagged back into his chair for a moment, closing his eyes. This was going to kill Charlotte. If he remembered correctly, the wedding was in two weeks. But sitting here wouldn't fix anything. Standing, he turned back to Cynthia and saw his own guilt and misery mirrored there. "This wasn't your fault, Cynthia."

"I know. It just doesn't make me feel any better."

"Well, let's go look. Then I'll get Charlotte on the phone and let her know what happened. There's got to be a way to salvage this."

A few minutes later, Adam was hard pressed to see what was recoverable. Cynthia was right. All the segments were there, but many of the lace accents and decorative pieces had either fallen off or hung by a few threads. It could be fixed but repairing it and finishing the alterations given the timeline seemed impossible.

His shoulders tense, he couldn't put off the inevitable. Dreading what was to come, he sent a text to Charlotte, asking her to call him. It did not surprise him when his phone rang moments later.

"Hi, Charlotte."

"Hi Adam. I was just going to text you to see when the dress would be ready," she greeted him. "You beat me to it. Is it already done?"

"Charlotte…" He drew in a deep breath. Best to just get it over with. "The dress didn't handle the cleaning as well as we hoped. Some of the fabric around the lace areas did give."

"Oh no. No."

"Charlotte, it can all be repaired…"

"What am I going to do?" she whispered. "The wedding is in less than two weeks."

Hearing the anguish in her voice punched him right in the gut. "Come down to the store. We'll look at it together. I'm sure we can figure a way around this."

"I don't think so, Adam, but thank you for trying." Her voice cracked. "I should never have taken this job," she said muttered. "What the hell was I thinking? There's no way I can pull this off."

"You can do this. Bring your project plan." He was grasping at anything to bolster her spirits. "You'll think of something. I'll help. Don't lose hope."

"Thanks." Her usually vibrant voice was dull and heavy with emotion. "Um, I'll come down now."

"Okay. I'll be here," he said. He didn't think she'd heard him.

◆ ◆ ◆

Charlotte hung up the phone and sat down hard on the couch, her legs giving out. This was her worst nightmare come true. It took a moment to realize Lisa was talking to her.

"Lottie?" she asked, her voice laced with concern. "Are you okay? What happened?" She came and sat down next to her.

She couldn't look at Lisa, knowing it would undo her entirely. "It's Alex's gown," she said, her body trembling. "It's destroyed."

The stark word hung in the air and seemed to echo forever in her head. She was glad when Lisa took charge and ushered her out of the house. She said nothing on the drive over to the cleaners, but Lisa's solid presence kept her from losing it.

With Lisa's arm wrapped around her shoulders, they walked into Cynthia's workroom. No one said a word as the four of them stood looking over the damaged gown arranged on Cynthia's table like a dying patient.

"I tried to be as gentle as possible," Cynthia said, her anguish clear.

Charlotte looked up and caught the other woman's eye. "This is not your fault. There wasn't anything you could have done to prevent it. I work with vintage gowns and sometimes this happens." She looked at the dress, her eyes glassy with unshed tears. "I'm the designer," she said with a bitter laugh. "I should have expected this." Reaching out, she picked up one fragment of lace, "I should have stuck with my nice little hobby," she whispered.

"Charlotte," Adam stepped close. "You are a fantastic designer." Before he could say more, his phone rang. He glanced at it before declining the call.

"Lottie," Lisa said, giving her a squeeze. "We're going to get through this. You'll see."

"She's right, Charlotte," Adam added. "It looks bad as a whole, but why don't we go through and catalog what needs to be done? Perhaps it isn't as bad as it looks." He shot a look at Cynthia.

"Adam's got a point," Cynthia chimed in. "Let's take a closer look. There's so much that is still intact." Cynthia walked closer to the top of the dress, peering at the bodice. "All your changes to the straps and bodice are solid. The embellishments in this area all look fine. It's just a few points here and there that need to be reattached."

As they crowded around the gown following Cynthia's examination, Adam's phone went off again.

"I'm so sorry," he said.

"You should answer it," Charlotte said. "Obviously, someone needs to talk to you. We'll be fine."

He looked at Cynthia, and at her sharp nod, he turned to Charlotte. "I'll just be a minute."

He walked away before connecting the call, but Charlotte could still see his screen, which was now filled with the most attractive woman Charlotte had ever seen. Her long blond hair framed her flawless and beautiful face. Charlotte hated her on sight.

"Adam!" the woman exclaimed. "It's so delightful to see you. I told Matt I would call and give you the wonderful news."

"Hi Zara. It's good to see you as well," he replied. "What's the news?"

"Well, it's official," Zara beamed, making Charlotte clench her teeth. Turning back to the dress, she tried to listen to Cynthia's comments, but couldn't force herself not to hang on every word of Adam's conversation.

"We're recalling you back to work at the end of the month! Thanks for your patience as we got this all sorted out. Sorry we had to let you go temporarily, but as we discussed, your job is here waiting for you. I can't wait for you to get back in town," she added, her voice turning flirtatious. "Life around here just isn't the same without you."

"That's nice to hear, Zara," he replied.

"When you get back in town, we'll go to that little place we love and celebrate..."

The Zara woman continued talking, but Charlotte could only hear the sound of her heart breaking into tiny pieces. Tears coursed down her face when she understood what was going on. Adam was not only leaving, but he also never intended to stay. He was only here temporarily. Worse was the realization that he and that woman were obviously involved. The woman's tone, her excitement about his return, their favorite restaurant

—it told her everything she needed to know about the life Adam would be returning to.

When Adam turned to look at her, she couldn't hide her grimace. "Phoenix?" she murmured, her throat closing.

Adam reached out for her, but she turned back to the table and started packing up the dress. She needed to get out of here. Now.

She heard Zara calling, "Adam? Adam! Are you listening to me?"

"Sorry, Zara. Thanks for letting me know. I'm in the middle of something right now. Can I call you back?"

"Certainly," she replied, her tone clipped. "I will email the recall offer to you. The company requires an official acceptance, or the offer is invalid. You can send that to my attention."

She heard Adam walk back over to the table, but she focused on placing the last pieces of the dress in the bag. Cynthia scowled at Adam before approaching her and putting a hand on her arm. "If you need anything, Lottie, please call," she said quietly.

She could see Lisa shooting death rays at Adam from across the table. She could only imagine what was running through her friend's head. Adam was lucky Lisa wasn't telling him in detail what she was thinking of him.

As she went to lift the dress bag from the table, Adam reached out and offered, "Let me help you with that, Charlotte."

She twitched the bag out of his reach, glaring at him. "I don't need anything from you," she said, her tone glacial.

"What do you mean?"

That earned him an eye roll and a scowl from Lisa before she turned to Charlotte. "I'll give you a minute. If you need me, just holler. I'll be up front waiting." As she turned to leave, she shot Adam another glare.

"Charlotte, please. Let's discuss this."

"I don't think there's anything to discuss, Adam," she said. "I heard everything. Your job is waiting for you. As you planned, you're going back to Phoenix as soon as possible. Back to your work and your life there with whatever the hell her name is." She gave a dismissive wave of her hand.

"That's not fair."

"Fair?" she shouted. "Fair! Are you being serious with me right now? You've been lying to me since we met, and you're going to stand there and say I'm not being fair?" She shook her head, her face pinched in anger but still wet from the tears falling unchecked. "Wow. You are a serious piece of work.

"I guess I should be happy that I found out now. Would you have even bothered to say goodbye, or would you have just packed up and disappeared? Oh, I get it," she shot back, seeing that he wanted to interrupt. "You have a celebratory lunch with Zara to get to," she added, her voice heavy with sarcasm.

"Charlotte, I'm not involved with Zara." At her look of disbelief, he tried again. "We're not dating. There is nothing going on between us."

"Nothing going on between you?" she stabbed back. "Well, she certainly didn't get that memo." The sarcasm was back in full swing.

"Charlotte—" he tried again.

"Enough!" she yelled, her arm slashing through the space between them. "It doesn't matter. You weren't unemployed. You were always going to leave." She dashed the tears from her face with the back of her hand. "It's my own fault. I let myself fall." Her voice broke, a sob escaping. She lifted a trembling hand to cover her mouth.

Adam stepped forward and tried to fold her into his arms. "Charlotte, please."

She spun away from him. "No." Her hand lifted to halt his steps toward her. "I'm fine. It's fine!"

"If you just let me explain," he tried again.

"I think I've heard all I need to hear or not hear," she said. "Goodbye, Adam. Best of luck in Phoenix." Clutching the gown to her chest, she beat a hasty retreat, struggling to contain the sob clawing at her throat.

CHAPTER NINETEEN

Adam

Adam leaned back in his office chair with a sigh, scrubbing his face with his hands. Who knew there were so many moving parts in arranging this damn event? The past few days had been some of the longest in his life. After the disastrous falling out with Charlotte on Saturday, he felt like he'd been hit by a truck. He reached out multiple times over the next few days to beg Charlotte to let him explain, but she ignored every attempt. Every day was like struggling through mud, leaving him wrung out.

By Tuesday, when he had heard nothing from her, he was frantic needing to know that she was okay. He wasn't proud of it, but he'd used the dry cleaner's records to run down a phone number for Lisa.

"Lisa, it's Adam," he'd said when she'd picked up. "Is she okay? Please, just let me know," he added, praying she'd take pity on him. "She isn't returning my calls or texts. I need to know."

Lisa had been quiet for so long he thought she'd hung up. Then she sighed and said, "She's fine. Well, at least as fine as she can be."

"Lisa, there's nothing going on between Zara and me. Honestly," he pleaded.

"I actually believe you," she'd replied. "But it doesn't matter what I believe. Even if Lottie believed you, your return to Phoenix devastated her. That, on top of the dress situation... she's in a lot of pain."

Adam tried to explain how his job return was complicated, but Lisa cut him off. As she'd rightly put it, it didn't matter if he convinced her. Lisa wasn't the one he had to talk to. Before letting her go, he asked how Charlotte was doing with dress repairs. Lisa's defeated sigh said it all.

"If she's not at work, she's sewing. I don't think she's slept all that much. I make sure she eats every once in a while. With a vacation all next week, she might be able to get everything ready. I just don't know at what cost to her, physically or mentally." The obvious worry in her tone ate away at him.

"Cynthia mentioned she'd be more than happy to help with sewing. That got me thinking. What about Ethel?" he asked. "Could we contact her to see if she knows someone or a few someones who could help? If we can find a few people to work on the gown, I'm sure it can get done in time.

"Obviously, the store will pay any costs associated, so that won't be a concern." There was no way Adam was going to let Charlotte shoulder this setback alone. If his parents weren't on board with paying for it, Adam would do it himself. He felt responsible for her landing in this mess.

"That's a good thought," Lisa said, "but the big problem is Lottie won't go for it. She may be new to selling her gowns, but she has firm opinions on how her dream comes to fruition. Allowing other people to help her and having someone else pick up the bill just isn't going to fly."

"Cynthia said she'd do it just as a friend helping a friend," he replied. "Do you think we could find a few other friends who might do the same?"

"Wait," Lisa drawled. "That's it! Gram's sewing circle!"

"What the hell is a sewing circle?"

"Sorry. Lottie loves to tell the story of how her grandmother's wedding gown was made. The family gathered and worked on it together. They'd all sit around in the living room working on it. Talking. Laughing. A sewing circle!"

"I'm not sure I understand it, Lisa, but do you think it'll work?" He didn't care what solution they tried, as long as it succeeded.

"I think it might," Lisa said. "But we're going to have to be sneaky. She's going to fight having help. She's the first one to step forward for someone else, but it's near impossible to get her to accept help on her own behalf."

"Just tell me what I need to do," Adam shot back, seeing a small glimmer of hope for the first time.

That's when Operation LACE was born. At least that's what Ethel named it. The first time he heard the name, he thought it was cute. The gleam in Ethel's eye told him there was more to it. Far be it from him to disappoint, so he asked what it stood for.

Her smile was as quick as her answer. "Operation Love And Care Extraordinaire." Then she'd giggled, and Adam knew he had the right person on the job. He smiled, thinking of the wonderful woman. Ethel loved Charlotte immensely and had been helpful, bossy actually, in directing him on what needed to be done.

That was Wednesday when he met with Ethel. Operation LACE had picked up steam from there. Once the discreet word had gotten out, he'd been fielding calls from people wanting to help. Martha volunteered her sewing skills, but more importantly, offered a room at the Manor House to hold the sewing circle. Mrs. S. would fortify them with food from the bakery, and his mom insisted on being included, as did Cynthia.

While Ethel's arthritis wouldn't allow her to do much work, she assured him she was bringing backup. Every time he spoke with her, she made the evening sound more and more like a black ops mission. It made him smile, which was a rare occurrence this week.

Rounding out the team was Lisa. She was running interference with Charlotte. Lisa perhaps had the hardest job of all. She had to somehow get her friend to the event, none the wiser of what was happening.

It amazed him that in a few short days they'd pulled it all together. That so many people were willing to drop all their plans on a Friday afternoon and help was a testament to how much they loved Charlotte.

He desperately wished he could witness her expression when the sewing circle was revealed. As much as he wanted that, she still wasn't talking to him. He'd thought about it a great deal, but ultimately decided that Charlotte completing the dress was too important. He knew his presence would distract her when she needed to be focused on finishing the gown, so he'd sworn everyone to secrecy. If Charlotte knew he'd had a hand in planning the event, she would reject it as easily as she rejected his calls.

Glancing at his watch, he saw there were just a few hours until Operation LACE went into full swing. Grabbing his phone, he shot off one last text to Lisa.

Everything is ready. Ethel & I will get the dress this afternoon. You sure you can get her there?

The response came back a moment later.

Count on it. If I fail, Ethel will have my head on a platter. That's very motivating.

Adam laughed. Guess he wasn't the only one Ethel was "directing" in this little endeavor. Now he just had to cross his fingers that it all went smoothly, and all the repairs got made. Charlotte needed a miracle, and it looked like they might just pull one off.

Standing up, he stretched his lower back. Between organizing the sewing circle and working on the list of changes for the store, he'd spend too many hours hunched over his desk. It would be worth it if Charlotte could finish the dress. He wasn't as positive about getting his parents to implement any of his ideas, but he wasn't ready to throw in the towel. He kept trying to find the right approach, the right data, the right words, and the right time to bring his dad around. So far, those elements had been elusive.

Leaving the office, he went downstairs to grab a coffee and check in with his mom. Once he had a steaming cup of manna, he walked out front. While it had been busy this morning, there was a lull before traffic picked up during lunch. He was glad to see his mom taking advantage of the calm. Seated at her small table, she had a tea in front of her and her nose buried in a book. Maybe this Christmas he'd get her an eReader. He was positive once she got used to it, she would love the freedom.

Settling down across from her, he watched her finish the page before looking up.

"Hey, honey," she smiled. "This murder mystery I'm reading is really gripping." She paused, examining his face; her scowl let him know she wasn't happy with what she found. "Are you okay, sweetheart?" she asked, her voice tender and filled with affection.

For a moment he thought about deflecting and saying he was fine, but the evidence was written all over him. He knew he looked as sleep deprived and haunted as he felt. Why deny it? With a sigh, he acknowledged, "I'm not doing well, Mom. In fact," he continued, his shoulders sagging, "I'm pretty crappy."

She reached over to squeeze his hand but said nothing. Her look said it all. Love, sympathy, and understanding. She gave him time to find the words.

Adam paused, but then it all tumbled out in a rush, "I've made a mess of things, Mom. And I don't know how to fix any of it."

"Charlotte?" she asked.

"Charlotte, dad, the store, my job," he listed all his failings. Each one digging a chunk out of his soul. How had he landed here? Coming home to Jennings was supposed to be about getting perspective. Getting his life back on track. How was it, he was now more confused than ever about what he wanted?

She took a moment to respond, the affection and caring in her voice almost breaking him. "I love you, honey. From the moment you came into my life, you've been a source of joy and happiness. But," she continued, "sometimes, you're an idiot."

Adam sat back in shock. That took a turn he didn't see coming. "Mom," he started before she cut him off.

"Wait. Just listen." She softened her words with a slight smile. "I would love to sit here and tell you point by point how to fix things with Charlotte, but it doesn't work like that. You need to figure that out. You need to find the answer. I'm going to bite my tongue, let you flounder, and pray you make good decisions."

Adam squirmed a little in his seat. This was not the motherly pep talk he had expected. "It's not that easy, Mom," he retorted.

"Pffft," she scoffed, waving away his words. "Do the work."

"Now," she added warming to her next topic. "About your dad and this store. Your father and I have spent pretty much our whole lives building this business. It's blood, sweat, tears, and hours that created it and how it stands today. That said, I know changes need to be made, and I'm prepared to make them mostly. More prepared than your father.

"While the suggestions you have are solid, implementing them is a little daunting, especially for your dad. You've come riding in to save him, which I love you for, but you're asking him to change a business he's worked his whole life to create. And you're asking him, sometimes demanding him, to do it in your timeframe."

She paused and looked around at the store. "You need to give him time and perhaps start smaller. Simple things to implement that aren't enormous shifts in process or approach."

Adam dragged his hand through his hair in frustration. "With his health on the line, we don't have time to wait or time to make small, ineffectual changes."

She looked like she was going to say something but stopped herself. Taking a deep breath, she said, "I know you're scared. I'm scared, too, and so is your father. We feel the pressure of the doctor's words every day. But let me ask you this. Is your approach working? Do you think pushing these major changes with huge implementations gives him less stress? Is insisting we make these sweeping modifications helping him live a more balanced and healthy life?"

Adam felt the weight of his mother's words. She was right. It seemed he was being an idiot in a lot of different areas of his life.

CHAPTER TWENTY

Charlotte

"Lisa," Charlotte said, pinching the bridge of her nose. "You missed the turnoff. What are you doing?"

"Don't worry about it, Lottie. This is just a minor detour."

"I don't have time for detours. I left work early to get back to working on the dress. One week. I only have one week," she said, her tone flat. "I need every moment."

Charlotte could see her roommate's hands tighten on the steering wheel as she replied, "I know. But please trust me for a few minutes longer. I swear it will be worth it."

"Fine," she said, biting her tongue. Honestly, she didn't want to be this person, but she just couldn't seem to help herself. Lisa didn't deserve her crappy attitude, and frankly, her roommate had been putting up with a lot the last week.

After the dress destruction and her confrontation with Adam, Charlotte had been a wreck. She'd given herself an hour that Saturday to have a good cry. Since then, she'd been working on the dress with every spare moment she had. It was already Friday, not even a week since the dress was destroyed and it felt like the blink of an eye. She had so much work left to do.

Her emotions running high, the stress of the encroaching wedding, and a serious lack of sleep had left her with the personality of a porcupine. Through it all, Lisa had been understanding and supportive. From providing food and drinks to a sympathetic ear to cheerleading, Lisa had done it all.

That didn't stop Charlotte's suspicion from rising when they took a familiar turn. "Wait, why are we turning into the Manor

House Inn?"

Lisa parked without comment and got out of the car. "Come on."

"Lisa, I'm serious. I need to get home. There's barely time for me to eat, never mind having dinner out!"

Lisa turned and walked to the door of the inn. "You coming? Or do I have to drag you?"

Storming over to the door, she stared at Lisa. "Fine. I'll see whatever it is but then we're going straight home."

Opening the door, Lisa gestured for her to proceed. "Fine."

Charlotte shot her a look as she walked past. Lisa should know better than to poke the bear. She hurried into the inn, walking toward the restaurant in the back. It took a moment to register the noise coming from one of the side rooms. Even with the pocket doors closed, she could hear the rise and fall of voices talking and laughing. Martha must be hosting an event in the inn's library.

"Well?" she sniped. Although her tone was quiet so as not to disturb the party, there was no missing the clipped delivery. Before Lisa could respond, Martha sailed out from the kitchen extending her arms to Charlotte.

"Oh, you made it!" The older woman's arms gave her a quick squeeze. Looking over Charlotte's shoulder, she addressed Lisa. "Respectable job getting her here. I'm sure it wasn't easy. Did you tell her anything?"

"Nope. Not a thing."

"Will someone please tell me what's going on here?" Charlotte demanded.

A voice came from behind her, "I believe it's called a sewing circle. Or at least that's what I've been told."

Charlotte whirled around to see Mrs. Mac standing in the library's doorway.

"Actually, from what I hear, sewing circles sort of run in your family, or perhaps it's just with the women named Lottie."

"What..." The word fell breathlessly from her lips. What was she saying?

Mrs. Mac stepped to the side, and there in the middle of the room, surrounded by chairs, was a mannequin draped with Alex's wedding gown. Each chair was filled with someone working on the fabric with needle and thread. Ethel and Cynthia were working on the train, and someone was kneeling on the floor reattaching lace to the hem.

Looking at Mrs. Mac, Martha and Lisa, Charlotte shook her head. "I don't understand. That's Alex's gown."

Lisa spoke up beside her. "Everyone's here to help." Hooking her arm through Charlotte's, she steered her into the room. "Someone had the impressive idea of getting people together to help reassemble the dress. That made me think of the story you tell about your Gram—how the family would have a sewing circle with everyone working on the wedding dress. So, here you have it," she said with a flourish. "Your own personal sewing circle."

Looking around the room, Charlotte couldn't believe what she was seeing. "Lisa," she started before Lisa cut her off.

"Don't bother complaining about how we shouldn't be doing this." Lisa's tone was just as sharp as Charlotte's had been on the drive in. "We're doing it. End of discussion."

Her eyes filled with tears as she reached over and pulled her friend into a big hug. "How can I ever thank you?" She owed Lisa so much for putting up with her and for thinking of the sewing circle. How could she put into words how much all that meant to her?

"It truly is my pleasure, Lottie," Lisa whispered. Charlotte's eyes swam with tears. Pulling back, her roommate cocked her head with a smile, "Honestly, once people heard what we were doing they all started volunteering."

"Some of us can't sew to save our lives," Mrs. S. said as she swept into the room carrying a platter of cookies. "But we can all contribute something." Rachel, who was following Mrs. S. with her own platter of goodies, gave Charlotte a wink as she whisked by.

Mrs. Mac laughed. "It's been a team effort! Obviously, Marilyn was on food detail. Martha took care of the location and setup. Lisa and I were recruitment. Ethel and—" She paused, looking over at Lisa. "Well Ethel took care of gown procurement."

"Gown procurement," Ethel laughed. "Oh, I like that. It was all so very cloak and dagger. I loved it!"

Seeing her roommate's confusion, Lisa explained, "I gave Ethel a key to the house. She went over there this afternoon to get the dress."

"Hard to have Operation LACE without the dress," Ethel quipped.

Lisa nudged her in the ribs. "You have to ask what that stands for," she whispered, jerking her chin towards Ethel.

Charlotte looked at Ethel's sly smile and knew she had to play along. She may not understand what was going on, but she understood enough not to ruin Ethel's fun. "Operation LACE? What does that stand for, if not for the lace on the dress?"

"Operation Love And Care Extraordinaire," Ethel sang, earning laughs from the rest of the crew, who had obviously heard it more than once.

Looking at all the people diligently working away, Charlotte couldn't hold back the tears any longer. These miraculous people had dropped what they were doing to help her. It was all too much, and at the same time it was everything.

This must be what it feels like when your heart explodes with love.

"You gonna cry, or are you going to sew?" Ethel shot at her.

Laughing, Charlotte wiped her tears and went to dole out hugs. When she went to thank a woman on the floor, it surprised her to realize she didn't know who it was. Ethel had a good laugh as the woman stood up.

"Charlotte, honey," Ethel chucked. "Let me introduce you to my friend Mary. You may remember talking to her about some Scottish lace."

"Mary! It's so nice to meet you in person." Charlotte didn't stop to think; she just wrapped her arms around the other woman and gave her a firm hug. "I can't believe you're here helping. How can I ever repay you? First the Scottish lace and now this."

Mary returned the hug before looking over at Ethel. "I have to say, being involved in this project of yours has been extremely interesting. I've never heard of anyone 'rescuing' wedding gowns. Ethel and I haven't seen each other in a while, so once she mentioned the sewing circle..." She laughed and glanced at Ethel. "Well, I invited myself, truth be told."

"She's pushy like that," Ethel added.

Mary laughed and turned back to Charlotte. "She's not wrong," she stage-whispered. "But don't tell her. It will go straight to her head."

Charlotte laughed and looked down at the dress. "You've already accomplished so much. I can't thank you all enough." Looking around at each of them, it struck her how truly blessed she was to have these people in her life. Wiping her tears, she grappled with the words to express how much this meant. Charlotte decided that laughter through tears might be her favorite emotion.

Gathering herself, she put her purse down by the food table and grabbed a chair. Threading a needle, she settled in and started working. It was easy to relax into the rhythm of the work. She pushed her misery about Adam out of her mind and focused on the fabric in front of her.

As they worked, they talked, told stories, shared laughs. Those that could sew, sewed. Those that couldn't were another set of hands holding fabric, pinning lace, and refreshing beverages. With each stitch Charlotte felt her shoulders relax. With all of them working, it was soon apparent the dress would be close to being done, if not complete, by the end of the evening. Realizing that, she was able to take a deep breath and know truly that it was all going to be okay.

◆ ◆ ◆

Toward the end of the evening, Charlotte was taking a break, eating some of Mrs. S.'s delicious chocolate chip cookies. Looking over the group as they continued to work tirelessly, she shook her head.

"Something wrong, Lottie?" Mary asked. She took a bite of cookie and hummed in pleasure. "I need to get down to see Ethel more often so I can get a supply of these cookies!"

Charlotte grinned. "Mrs. S.'s baking is legendary." Looking back at the group, she tried to gather her thoughts. How to best say this without sounding ungrateful. "What you've all done for me is staggering. I've always wanted to be a wedding gown designer. This dress for my cousin was my chance to prove myself. I know it must sound crazy or ungrateful, but part of me is disappointed I couldn't do it myself."

Mary was quiet a moment before asking, "Can I be honest?" At Charlotte's nod, she continued, "That's bull crap." Seeing Charlotte's confused expression, she continued, "Balderdash? Claptrap? Poppycock?" When Charlotte shook her head, she added, "Well at least you know why I'm killer at Words with Friends."

She smiled before continuing, "Thinking that this dress is less-than because you didn't 'do it yourself'? Well, that's just dumb. Ethel told me what it looked like before you started. How can you look at the lines of that bodice and not see your artwork? The way the straps and slight sweetheart neckline will frame the bride's face, is all you. There are hundreds of little touches and decisions that you've made to create it. We're just providing some stitching to help you along the way. Don't diminish your accomplishment by creating false standards."

Charlotte's eyes roamed over the dress, trying to see it as Mary did. "I never thought of it that way. You're right."

"Of course I am," she agreed. "One last thought before I stop sticking my nose where it doesn't belong. In life, the path you're meant to walk is full of learning and guidance. All of us have people who help us along the way—teachers, mentors, friends, family and sometimes even strangers. Some offer support or guidance, others challenge us to push forward."

"Mary," Ethel barked. "Are you going to stand there all night, or help me attach this piece of lace?"

Mary looked at Charlotte. "See what I mean?" They were both laughing, the moment lightened. Mary gave her a quick hug before they both returned to work.

With so many hands, reattaching the lace was quickly done. As a precaution, other areas Cynthia pointed out were reinforced. Stitch by stitch, they painstakingly reassembled the dress. At the end of the evening, they all stood to admire their combined efforts.

"Lottie," Cynthia said looking over the gown. "This design is by far your best. Your cousin is going to be a beautiful bride." The other women murmured agreement.

"You are a very talented designer," Mary added. "I look forward to seeing more of your work."

Charlotte soaked up their kind words like a sponge, storing it for those times when she was plagued with doubt and disappointment. Looking at the dress with fresh eyes, she had to agree. This was her best design, and Alex was going to look amazing.

When she left work that day, she had envisioned another stressful evening battling the panic of failure. Instead, the past few hours were spent surrounded by people who loved her, who believed in her. Her heart felt like it might burst right there. Their laughter and stories created an unbreakable connection that enveloped her, filling her with a level of happiness she'd never felt before. Although there was still work to do, she was confident she could accomplish it. Now she was looking forward to working on those final finishing details.

"There aren't words to thank you all for what you've done," Charlotte said, her voice laced with emotion. "This means the world to me."

One by one everyone started leaving and Charlotte made sure no one left without some goodies and a hug of thanks. When it was just Lisa and Charlotte left, her best friend came and slung an arm around her shoulders. They stood there a moment just gazing at the dress.

"That's quite a layer of love and well-wishing we just stitched into that gown," Lisa said. Giving Charlotte a sly smile, she continued, "I always hear you talk about the magic of the fabric storing up positive energy to pass along to the next bride. I'm not saying I believe in all that," she hastened to add. "But I have to say, I believe in it a lot more today than I did yesterday. And I hope it's true. I'd like to think that what happened tonight—the energy, the love, the laughter—won't dissipate come morning."

"Oh, I don't think it will dissipate," Charlotte said her eyes lingering on the dress. Her love life may be in the tank, but this, her work and her dream, was going strong. She felt ten feet tall and ready to tackle the world. Not wanting anything to mar this astonishing evening, she drove any thoughts of Adam from her mind. He was in the past. She needed to focus on her future. A tiny voice said she couldn't do that forever, but she ignored that too.

"I think what happened tonight will carry forward, in the gown and in me," she added. As the words left her lips, she could feel the truth resonate within her.

CHAPTER TWENTY-ONE

Charlotte

The problem with Alex's gown being in solid shape was Charlotte had too much time to think. When she was panicked and stressed, it had been easy to push thoughts of Adam to the side. With each stitch of the dress and veil, she found it harder and harder to pull herself away from the depressing vortex of the Adam situation.

This morning she'd promised herself she could sleep in, but here she was, eyes wide open. It was barely 7:30. With a sigh, she rolled over and tried to will herself to fall back asleep.

Thankfully over the weekend she'd kept her focus on the dress. The sewing circle Friday night was so uplifting, she rode that high for days.

Sunday, Alex had come for a fitting. It had gone well, though she'd practically had to nail her cousin's feet to the floor. Alex had been so cheerful, excitable, and hyper, it had been nearly impossible to get through the fitting. Seeing her so joyous about her upcoming wedding was heartwarming and heart-wrenching at the same time.

Luckily, she was distracted again when she received the package of Scottish lace. The memory of opening that box still made her smile. It felt like Christmas morning. Tentatively opening the box, fearful of damaging any lace, her eye fell to the note on top of the packaged tissue paper.

Charlotte—

Sorry for the delay in getting you the lace, but I'm sure it will be worth the wait. The Honey Bee pattern is enclosed, along with a few other options. The company sent samples, and I also placed an order.

I've enclosed a selection of all those different patterns. I wanted to give you as many possibilities as I could to ensure you find the right lace for the gown.

As the craftsmanship and quality is outstanding, I've added MYB lace to our inventory. You have a brilliant eye, and I appreciate you illuminating me on its existence.

If you need anything, please don't hesitate to contact me. I've enjoyed working with you. Please keep us in mind for all your future projects.

All the best,

Barry

It seemed impossible that anything could top the happiness she felt at Barry's kind words, but then she'd peeled back the tissue paper and was overwhelmed by the Scottish lace. To say it was stunning was an understatement, especially since she was now swimming in lace options. Deciding what to use and where had carried her for a day or two.

But it was now Wednesday and with Alex coming in for a last fitting, there weren't that many things left to do. Too awake to stay in bed, she rolled out and went to brush her teeth and wash up. Looking at the mirror, she had to agree with Lisa. She looked a bit squidgy around the edges. Her roommate had still been after her about not eating or sleeping properly. But she couldn't help it. Either she was caught up in the dress, or thoughts of Adam haunted her, chasing whatever appetite she had deep into the shadows.

Throwing on some comfortable jeans and a t-shirt, she went into the workroom. The dress took center stage, majestically draped over the mannequin. Hanging from the far wall, the long veil draped over her sewing table and across the floor. The highlights of Scottish lace dotting the edges were the perfect finishing touch.

She thought about finishing the seam on the bodice of the dress, but that should be left for after the fitting today. She had no worries that the dress wouldn't fit, but best not to jinx it. Restless, she moved about the room looking for something to keep her occupied and out of her head.

Maybe she should get out of the house. Away from this. Then it just popped right into her head. Today was the day to grab Lisa and go out for breakfast. Problem: this was Lisa's first day of vacation. Since it was no longer busy season, she'd taken some time off before the wedding, most likely to make sure Charlotte didn't collapse trying to finish the gown. It would be wrong to wake Lisa up early on a vacation day. Very wrong. Bordering on evil.

But that didn't stop her from picturing a leisurely meal, not thinking about a certain someone, not obsessing about the dress. She could almost taste the French toast at the Blueberry Muffin Café already. Her stomach let out a loud growl, letting her know it was on board. It felt like she hadn't eaten in a week. Okay, so maybe she hadn't, but she was now feeling every skipped meal.

The need to get away from the dress and her thoughts of Adam drove her to circle the workroom again, looking for a distraction. She shouldn't drag Lisa out of bed just so she could run away from the obsessive thoughts haunting her. Walking back into her bedroom, she grabbed a book and tried to get lost among the pages. Her body's demand to be in motion was too much, and she was soon back on her feet pacing the room.

Maybe Lisa was up. Fat chance, her mind said, but Charlotte was deep into justification and ignored it. She should just go see. Walking down to Lisa's room she listened for any sounds of movement. Nothing. Knocking softly, she poked her head in. "Lisa?" Walking into the room, she thought she heard a vague grunt emanate from the bed. "What do you say we go to the Blueberry Muffin for breakfast?"

"Hmmm."

Okay, that was louder. She was sure Lisa was up. "Maybe some waffles? Or eggs benedict? First day of vacation breakfast feast?" She paused to see if Lisa was going to say something. Nothing. Time to make the hard pitch. "I heard Jake was working on a few new specials. Maybe he'll have some new ones today."

Lisa had a thing for the chef who worked at the Blueberry Muffin. She wouldn't admit it, but Charlotte could tell. She could also tell that Jake had a thing for her roommate. In fact, she wouldn't be surprised if Jake's new recipes just incorporated some of Lisa's favorite foods.

Time for the closing argument. "But it does get busy. We wouldn't want to wait in line to get in." She was stretching the truth hoping Lisa was too asleep to notice. While the Blueberry Muffin didn't have a lot of tables, they wouldn't have to wait in line on a Wednesday morning. The weekend was another story. Maybe she could trick Lisa into thinking it was Sunday.

"If you wanted to go, we really should get going now." She paused looking for signs of life. Time to poke the bear. "But maybe we should pass. We can always stay here and have cold cereal."

Lisa sat up in her bed. "Okay, okay. I'm in. Give me ten minutes."

"Yes!" Charlotte knew it would be closer to twenty, but that was okay. Since she was already dressed, she went downstairs and made a pot of coffee. While The Muffin's coffee would be far superior, she knew getting Lisa out the door without a cup in her system would be next to impossible. Preparing one, she ran it upstairs, pleased to see Lisa farther along than expected.

Twenty-five minutes later they were out the door and on their way. Although outside of downtown, The Blueberry Muffin had a constant flow of traffic, located as it was in a strip mall with the town's grocery store and movie theater. That, combined with fantastic food at reasonable prices, made it a popular location. A few years ago, the restaurant had renovated and expanded, taking over an adjacent store. They added more seats and increased the kitchen size to handle their popularity and growing takeout business. Many a night, the girls would call in an order before they left work and pick it up on their way home.

As predicted, there weren't many people, so they snagged an out-of-the-way booth toward the back. Charlotte really didn't feel like running in to anyone. She wasn't in the right frame of mind.

After ordering coffees, they settled in to examine the menu and daily specials. Lisa soon tossed down her menu, her choice made. Charlotte was right, the crab eggs benedict and flannel hash offered on the specials was totally Lisa's jam.

Debating the peanut butter waffles against the breakfast burrito special, Charlotte was alarmed to suddenly hear his voice. Startled, she turned and scanned the restaurant. He was there. Adam. Standing at the front counter, putting in a takeout order.

Her head whipped back, and she slid deeper into the booth. Lisa was staring at her with confusion. Before her friend could ask, the waitress came by with their coffees. Once she left, Lisa looked around the restaurant, her face turning to one of sympathy.

"Lottie," she whispered.

"Shhhh," she hissed, even though she knew there was no way Adam could hear her. "Please just scooch down so he doesn't recognize you." When it looked like Lisa would argue, she added a heartfelt plea. "Please." There was no way she could see Adam right now.

Lisa gave her a long look before sliding deeper into the booth and putting her head down, her hand covering part of her face. It was unlikely he would recognize her now.

Her hands trembling, Charlotte went about preparing her coffee, a thankfully involved process. It gave her something to do and her mind something to think about. In college, Lisa had given her a sign that read 'I like my cream and sugar with a touch of coffee.' Never was that truer today. It was a full coffee creamer day for sure. The first heavenly sip fortified her, so she whispered, "Is he gone?"

Lisa leaned out and took a quick glance. "The coast is clear. He's gone," she replied before taking a sip of her own coffee. "What are you doing?" she asked gently.

Before she could answer, the waitress returned, and they placed their orders. If today didn't scream over-the-top peanut butter waffles, what did?

"I don't want to talk to him," she whispered, trying to keep her emotions under wraps.

"Have you spoken to him at all since the day at the dry cleaners?"

"You mean since I found out he had a girlfriend and was packed up to return to Phoenix?" she shot back with sarcasm.

"Lottie," Lisa said in warning.

"No," Charlotte sighed, her anger dissolving. "No, I haven't talked to him. I can't."

"Why not?"

"Why not?" Charlotte replied, rubbing her hands on her thighs. "Why not? I can't... I mean it isn't like..." she ground to a halt. Why couldn't she talk to him? The answer was quick to surface. She couldn't talk to him because he would see right through her. He'd see she'd fallen in love with him, and now he was leaving. She couldn't face that. It was too raw. Too painful.

"Deep down, you know he wasn't seeing that woman on the phone." Lisa held up a hand to forestall Charlotte's argument. "Sure, she sounded totally into him, but that doesn't mean he's dating her. He said he wasn't." She paused for a beat then continued, "And I believe him."

Charlotte's jaw dropped. Lisa rarely gave guys the benefit of the doubt, especially guys she barely knew. Before she could question her on it, she continued.

"Here's what I think." Lisa leaned forward, her eyes boring into Charlotte. "You're choosing to believe the girlfriend hypothesis because it's a convenient excuse. You've fallen for him and that scares you. So, you tell yourself that he lied, that he has a girlfriend, so you don't have to face the fact that you're in love with him. You're so afraid of getting hurt again that you're hiding instead. Adam is not Todd. And how you feel about Adam is so much more than what you felt about Todd. I can see it in your face and how you've talked about him."

Charlotte wasn't sure when the tears started to fall, but once they'd started, she couldn't seem to stop. Lisa was poking all her bruised and bleeding places.

"Don't argue with me and say you don't love Adam, because I live with you. After your trip to the fabric warehouse and dinner at the inn, you came back glowing. I don't think I've ever seen you so filled with joy." She looked out over the restaurant, seeming to struggle with what she wanted to say. "You weren't even that happy when you thought Todd was going to propose."

As observations went, that one hit Charlotte deeply. She wanted to argue back. She wanted to stop Lisa and claim that she wasn't in love with Adam, but the words wouldn't come. Only tears.

"And I've been with you since you and Adam split up. Sure, some of this is stress about the dress, but that's only a small portion of it. You're devastated because you think you've lost him."

"It doesn't matter, Lisa," Charlotte said her voice husky with emotion. She turned her face away. "Sure. Okay. Fine. I love him." She took a shuttered breath before looking at Lisa again. "I love the way he looks at me. I love the way he makes me feel safe and cherished, and like I can conquer the world. I love how he supports me. How he makes me laugh. And lord knows I love how he kisses me," her voice faltered.

Wiping the tears away with her napkin, she took a deep breath. "It doesn't matter because he's going back to Phoenix. Sure, maybe he's not dating Zara. But you heard that phone call. He wasn't unemployed. Well, he was, but he wasn't. It was just temporary, and the company is more than ready for him to return. He never told me he would be moving back to Phoenix."

"You're making him pay for what Todd did," Lisa replied. "He's not Todd, but the fear of that pain is blinding you to the actual situation now."

Before Charlotte could answer, the waitress returned with their meals. She turned her face away to hide the fact she was an emotional wreck. Drying her face, she tried to pull herself together.

As all the assorted plates were being brought, Lisa continued in a lighter tone. "Now where have I heard that before?" She was silent for a moment and then snapped her fingers. "Got it! Will Smith. That song he did with his son. 'One day some girl's gonna break your heart. And ooh ain't no pain like from the opposite sex. Gonna hurt bad, but don't take it out on the next, son.'"

"Are... are you serious right now?" Charlotte stammered. "Did you just rap at me about my emotional state?"

"Well, in my defense, you do play a lot of Will Smith around the house," Lisa responded with a shrug.

It was just the right amount of humor at just the right time to give Charlotte a little breathing room to collect herself.

Once they were alone, Lisa sighed. "Ultimately, it's not my business, but you have a chance at something terrific, and you're giving up without a fight. No one is perfect, no relationship is smooth. You of all people should understand that. You look at old, tattered, ugly wedding gowns and see the possibilities. You don't give up. You fight to give them a second chance.

"Given how you feel about Adam, don't you think you owe it to yourself to fight just as hard for the person you love? Don't you think you both deserve a second chance?"

Charlotte sat in stunned silence. Lisa's words were hard to hear, but when she absorbed them, they rang true. Part of her still wanted to argue that fighting for a second chance wasn't worth it, but she knew Lisa was right.

"Listen, we don't have to discuss this now," Lisa said. "We can put it aside and enjoy our breakfast. Before we do, I just want to say one more thing." Lisa looked down, playing with her coffee cup. "I'm not supposed to tell you this."

Charlotte tensed her shoulders. Nothing good came after someone confessed that.

"I promised Adam I wouldn't, in fact. We all promised him."

Adam? Why was Adam asking Lisa not to tell her things? And who was we?

"Adam was the one who put together the whole sewing circle evening." Seeing Charlotte's disbelief, she explained. "He called me at work because he was trying to think of ways to help. He wanted to know if Ethel had the name of someone who could come in and assist you in repairing the gown. He said the store would pay for it."

Seeing Charlotte's scowl, she added quickly, "I know. I know. I told him you wouldn't go for it. But he was just trying to help. Anyway, his suggestion made me think of your family sewing circles. When I mentioned it to him, all he said was to tell him what needed to happen to make it a reality.

"He took it from there. Meeting with Ethel to get her guidance, he coordinated everything and communicated the plan to everyone involved. He even helped Ethel get the dress over to the inn. Without him, I don't think we could have pulled it off. Definitely not as quickly as he did."

Charlotte was so confused. Her mind was swirling with everything Lisa told her. "Why didn't he want you to tell me?"

"I asked him that. Argued with him, really. He said it would be too distracting, and the most important thing was you being able to finish the dress. He didn't want to pull your focus from the job you had to do."

Charlotte didn't respond right away, too caught up in her thoughts. Lisa waited for a moment, but then started eating, giving Charlotte space to think.

"I don't know what to say," she offered a few minutes later.

"You don't have to say anything. That's a lot to take in. Not to mention it's probably the first time you've admitted out loud that you love him." Lisa smiled. "Let it all percolate in the back of your mind for a while. For now, take a break. Eat your breakfast before it's cold."

Charlotte took a few bites but was no longer hungry. Lisa tried to distract her and eventually the conversation turned to other things. Yet in the back of her mind, everything Lisa had said bounced around looking for purchase.

Could she have been wrong about Adam? Was she using their argument as an excuse to distance herself because she was afraid of getting hurt again? Her conversation with Lisa had raised a lot of questions. Unfortunately, she couldn't find the answers.

The headache blooming behind her eyes promised to be a doozy. She'd need aspirin to make it through the rest of today.

***

Later that afternoon, when Alex whirled into the house like a typhoon riding a tornado, Charlotte wondered if the aspirin would be enough. She had expected her cousin to be in high spirits, but even for Alex this was off the chart. She'd been in the house for fifteen minutes and Charlotte was fairly certain she had yet to take a breath.

As Alex paced the kitchen rattling on about the wedding, to-do lists, preparations, Charlotte tried to take her own wildly erratic emotions and push them to the side. She shouldn't ruin Alex's day with her depressing thoughts. Giving herself a stern mental shake, she turned her attention back to Alex. And almost immediately wished she hadn't.

"I'm so nervous," Alex was saying as her pacing continued. "I mean I knew we were having a lot of people at the wedding, but now that it's here and so real I can't believe so many people are coming. It's freaking me out thinking of everyone staring at me."

Whirling back to Charlotte, her brows furrowed. "You must be so nervous too! I don't know how you can sit there so calmly."

Charlotte laughed. "Why would I be nervous, Alex? I'm not the one getting married."

"Everyone will be looking at the dress you created," Alex quickly replied and looked at her as if she were an idiot. "It's the first public unveiling of one of your designed gowns! I swear, the whole family is coming." Not seeing the smile slip off Charlotte's face, she continued, "They'll all be there to see it. And your mom will be front and center. So, if I'm freaking out about all those people staring at me, judging me, I can only imagine how much worse it is for you!"

Charlotte's stomach did a slow flip. Thankfully, she'd only eaten a small amount at breakfast. Any more than that and she would have been sick. With everything else going on, she hadn't given any thought to what was actually going to happen on Saturday. Alex was going to walk down the aisle in front of a whole lot of people wearing a gown designed by Charlotte. The thought of her mother's reaction made her chest tight.

Taking shallow breaths, she tried to dismiss Alex's concerns. "I'm sure no one will be judging anyone or anything." Even she didn't believe that but saying it out loud made her feel better.

"You've met our family, right?"

Shaking her head, Charlotte stood up from the kitchen table. Grabbing Alex's hands, she stared into her eyes. "This isn't doing either of us any good. Let's get you upstairs and in the dress. One last fitting so I can make sure it's ready. Okay?"

In the workroom Alex went behind the screen to put on the gown, while Charlotte tried to live by her own words. No thinking about Adam. No obsessing over family seeing the gown. And especially no anticipating her mother's reaction. Be present. She'd use that as a mantra to get through all of this.

Right here and right now, things were fine. Sure, the Adam thing was horrible, but the dress was in good shape. And based on the noises Alex was making, she was over the moon about the design.

The rustle of fabric warned her Alex was coming out. Turning, she was overcome with emotion. Not only because Alex looked breathtaking, but the tears swimming in her cousin's eyes, made her own tear up as well.

"Lottie," Alex murmured, her hands smoothing over the fabric of the skirt. "I know there hasn't been a vast change since the last time I had this on, but somehow it feels different. This is the dress I'm going to get married in!"

Charlotte stepped forward and pulled Alex into a quick hug, wiping the few tears that escaped. "You are stunning," she whispered. Standing back, she took another look at the gown. "Jason is the luckiest guy in the world."

"Yeah, he is," Alex said with her usual sass.

Rolling her eyes, Charlotte walked behind Alex to make sure the bodice was fully zipped. Looking at it, she was right. No changes to be made. She could just finish up sewing and the fit would be perfect.

Positioning Alex in front of the mirror, Charlotte laid out the dress and train for the full effect. She'd debated if she should keep the Scottish lace a secret for the wedding day or tell Alex now. Last they'd spoken about it, Alex knew the original lace wasn't a thistle pattern. Not wanting to raise her hopes, Charlotte had never explained about the new lace. But telling her now ensured she could fully appreciate it, rather than on her hectic wedding day.

Catching Alex's eye in the mirror, she said, "There have been a few important changes on the dress, additions really." Delighting in Alex's confusion, she ran her hands over a section of the skirt. "Do you see this lace pattern? It has a kind of circular feel with leaves." Seeing Alex nod, she continued. "That lace is called Honey Bee. It's created by a Scottish lace maker called MYB Textiles. They've existed since the 1900s and to this day still use 100-year-old Nottingham Lace Looms."

She moved back and adjusted the train and veil so Alex could see them in the mirror. "The Honey Bee pattern is repeated on the train. On the veil, besides Honey Bee, I added MYB's Oriental Blossom. That's this piece here." She tapped it with her finger.

Dropping the veil, she stepped toward Alex, taking her shoulders, and angling her cousin. She touched the back of the gown where the strap met the body of the dress. "It might be hard to see, but I also added Oriental Blossom lace here. The delicate little flowers are a simple touch but another tie between the dress and the veil.

"While the original lace wasn't a Scottish thistle, what you have now is expertly crafted lace created by Ayrshire County artists located in southwest Scotland. It's unfortunate the original lace didn't pan out, but in the end, I think what you have here is so much better."

Charlotte's stomach was in knots. Alex hadn't reacted at all while she'd explained the lace. She was looking in the mirror, twisting this way and that. She picked up the veil, running her hands over it until she reached the new lace. Tracing the pattern with her finger, she looked at Charlotte.

"It's so much more than I could ever ask for. When you said the dress didn't have that Scottish thistle pattern, I thought that was the end of it. But what you've done..." Alex sighed looking down at the dress.

"What you've done for me," she continued her voice thick with emotion. "It's so thoughtful and beautiful. I know I'll never be able to express how much this means to me and to Jason. I can't wait to tell his family, especially his grandparents."

Alex stood for a minute looking into the mirror but then suddenly laughed, startling Charlotte. It was a right turn of emotion that was hard to follow. "You okay, Alex?"

"I am," she giggled. "I was just thinking 'thank God my original dress was never ordered.'" Shaking her head, she added, "Can you believe that? Did you ever imagine I would say those words?"

Charlotte had to laugh. Leave it to her cousin. "It's been a wild ride."

"I'm excited for everyone to see it," she murmured.

Charlotte was able to push back the panic those words set off until after Alex left. Once she was alone, all of her insecurities came rushing back in. She felt like a fraud who would be denounced the moment Alex walked down the aisle. She could practically hear her mother's words about Charlotte's little hobby.

When she wasn't battling dress demons, her thoughts turned to Adam and everything Lisa had said. Was she using the situation with Adam as an excuse to push him away? If she loved him, why wasn't she willing to fight for their relationship?

But Adam had a life and a job back in Phoenix. Even if he wasn't dating that woman from the phone call, he could be dating someone else. Perhaps he failed to mention it just like he failed to mention he had a job waiting for him. Their relationship would never work. Better that she learned that now and end it before she really got hurt.

Quite simply she was a hot emotional mess. And not even finishing the last elements of the dress were enough to pull her out of her negative spiral. The problem was she'd fallen in love with Adam, and now he was leaving. Getting hurt was a forgone conclusion.

CHAPTER TWENTY-TWO

Adam

Even though he knew the reality, Adam couldn't help but open the fridge again to see if there was anything to eat. Surprisingly, food had not magically appeared in the fifteen minutes since he last looked. Another glance through the cabinets confirmed no food had appeared there either. A life lesson in how things worked: in order to have food appear, you actually had to go grocery shopping, something he hadn't done in a while.

Shopping, like so many other things in his life, just didn't seem worth doing. Looking around the condo, it was easy to see cleaning was also on that list. He wanted to justify his lack of interest and blame it on his work at the store and arranging the sewing circle for Charlotte.

Charlotte. Every time he thought of her was like a kick in the stomach. Her reaction that day in the store haunted him, to where he was reliving it in his sleep repeatedly.

He was off today and had planned to sleep in, but another dream left him wide awake and restless at 5:00. Although he'd tried to fall back asleep, it was futile. He finally gave up and took his restless mood for a long run, pushing himself hard. After he'd returned and showered, he was prowling his kitchen, famished. Not even a cracker in the damn place to munch on.

Grabbing the keys, he got in his car and headed into town. He lowered his window to breathe in the fresh air and feel the breeze on his face. He loved his VW GTI. Maybe after he ate, he'd go for a long drive. A drive usually made him feel better; perhaps it would work its magic again. Somehow, his life had become a crapfest.

Parking downtown, he decided to go to the bakery. The diner would hold too many people he knew; he wasn't in the mood to be social. He could grab something from Pie and eat at home or find a place to park and eat, somewhere away from downtown.

He read the specials board and looked through the bakery cases as he waited in line. If today wasn't a day to get something sweet, he didn't know what was. He had just about settled on a coconut macaroon when he felt a hand on his shoulder. Turning, he saw Mrs. S. beside him, and she did not look happy. She said nothing, just gestured for him to follow her into the back. She didn't turn until they were in the kitchen. When she did, she fired on all cylinders.

"Are you out of your ever-loving mind? What were you thinking?"

"Mrs. S.—" Since his life had so messy parts, he wasn't exactly sure what she was referring to. It could be many things. It was probably his dad. He knew his mom and Mrs. S. had been chatting. Most likely his mom had updated her on Adam's failure to make improvements in the business to help his dad. It didn't matter, Mrs. S. rolled right over him.

"Hush. I'm talking. You're listening. First, you don't let us tell Lottie about your part in that sewing circle—a decision I did not agree with by the way. But fine, you do your own romancing."

"Romancing!" he exclaimed. What was she talking about? He wasn't doing any romancing. He was just trying to make something right. A glare from Mrs. S. stopped him from talking further.

"Since the sewing circle, you've done nothing. Nothing! There's a timing and energy to these things, and you're missing your window."

Now that he'd recovered from his surprise, Adam would not let her comments go unaddressed. "I haven't been doing nothing. She's still not talking to me. I've called and texted, but she won't respond." He ran his hand through his hair. He didn't want to talk about this. "Thank you for being concerned, but I just needed to grab something to eat."

She crossed her arms over her chest and glared at him, "You called and texted?" She rolled her eyes in disgust. "Sit," she ordered, gesturing to the wooden stool by the large center island. She grabbed a nearby bowl and started toward the stovetop. "Chili?"

"Thanks, really, but I was going to grab something to go. Take it home to eat." The words froze in his mouth as she turned to face him. Her glare was glacial and although she was at least six to seven inches shorter than he was, she seemed ten feet tall. She made him feel like a kid who'd been caught and dragged in front of the principal.

"You had your time to make the next move. Time's up. I'm not letting another day go by watching you let the best thing that's ever happened to you slip away. And don't even get me started on what's going on with you, your dad, and the store."

Her voice softened a bit as added, "I want to hear what's going on with you. There was a time when this kitchen was a safe haven for you to bring your troubles to. Chili?" she repeated, her brisk tone back in full force.

Adam's head fell into his hands with a groan. She was never going to let him leave without saying what she wanted to say. He was too hungry to argue, and she was right. Growing up, he'd always been able to talk to Mrs. S. As his mom's best friend, she'd been a constant feature in his life and knew him better than he probably knew himself.

So, although he wasn't looking forward to it, he sat at the island and prepared himself to talk. "Chili would be great. Thank you."

In a few moments, Mrs. S. had hustled around the kitchen, grabbing them both a delectable meal of chili, cheddar scones, and iced tea. They both dug in and for a few minutes the only sound was the clink of silverware on bowls or in Adam's case, a groan as he tasted everything.

The worst of his hunger addressed, he reached for a sip of iced tea catching Mrs. S.'s eye. Her glare was gone and in its place was a look of understanding and affection. Time to come clean.

"I don't know what I'm doing here, Mrs. S. Being back in Jennings. Getting laid off from my job came at the right time. I've been..." He paused, searching for the right words. "I haven't been happy. I love what I do and the people I do it with. But now that's not enough. It's like something is missing but I don't know what.

"In the past that would mean it was time to move on from the job or the city, but the thought of doing that now leaves me cold. That's a big problem for me because that's who I am."

"What do you mean that's who you are?"

Adam broke apart another piece of scone, shifting through his feelings to understand what he meant. "I'm not a 'settle down in one place' guy. I travel and move around. It makes my life an adventure. If that's no longer true then, I'm not sure who I am anymore."

"And Charlotte just complicates matters," she snorted.

"Charlotte," he said her name as a sigh, a dream he couldn't have. "Charlotte is... amazing. I never expected to meet someone that made me feel like this." Glaring at her, he raked his fingers through his hair. "She's totally a 'settle down' type of woman. She has this fantastic community here in Jennings. She's created her own family. I can see not only her attachment to them but the importance and meaning they bring to her and her life."

Mrs. S. didn't say anything, just stared at him like he was a puzzle to figure out.

"What?" he said with a little heat. While he appreciated her listening, he didn't enjoy feeling this exposed.

She finally spoke, her eyes never leaving his face. "Is that actually how you see yourself? As someone who would never settle down and have roots, career-wise or romantically?"

"Well, yeah," he answered. "I've always felt that way. It's what makes me happy. Some people are wired to want the home and family and a job they remain at for years and years. I just wasn't born with that wiring."

Mrs. S.'s rolled her eyes, surprising him. "Bull." That was it. She gave a sharp nod of her head and fell silent again.

He met her silence with raised eyebrows. What the heck did that mean? She thought he was lying?

She took a deep breath. "You haven't always been a freewheeling, never-settle-down guy. I'd go so far as to say you aren't now either.

"When you were a kid, there was no one who loved his home and family deeper and harder than you. You loved working in the store and seeing everyone come through the door. Don't you remember? Your mom set up that little table and chairs for you. It's where you wanted to be.

"You were always greeting people, talking to them, be it in the store or when your mom took you places. I swore you knew everyone in town. Your mom and I used to joke that you'd grow up to be mayor one day." She grinned at the memory.

Adam looked down, his fingers tapping on the table. What she said did sound familiar. He had loved working at the store. He didn't remember about the table and chairs but now that she'd said it, it felt right.

"It's time for you to stop running away. You need to face your fear."

"I'm not running away," he said. "And I sure as hell am not afraid of anything."

"Adam," she said, wagging a finger at him. "You've been running since Abigail died."

The moment Abigail's name left her lips, Adam was in motion. He would not sit here and discuss any of this.

As he went to stand, Mrs. S. grabbed his arm. "Adam. Stop." Her voice was firm but filled with love. "Every time someone tries to talk to you about this, you run. You've been running since she died. You need to face this."

He threw his hands in the air. "Face what?" He remained standing, breathing hard as he wrestled with his overwhelming desire to leave. Grinding his teeth in frustration, he sat back down. "What do you think I need to face?"

"When Abigail passed, you were so young. You'd never experienced a loss like that before."

"I was almost out of college. Not young. And it was a long time ago," he interjected rolling his shoulders to loosen them. Part of him realized that his reaction alone was more telling than he felt comfortable acknowledging. Would he ever be able to think about her without being crippled with emotion? He wanted to remember all the good times they'd spent together instead of being overwhelmed by the horror of how it all ended.

"Don't let the age thing fool you. Grief has derailed many an adult, no matter their age. What I mean is that life experience comes with all sorts of loss, failure, and grief. As a parent, you hope your kids aren't saddled with a devastating loss before they've learned how to experience and move through grief, especially the sorrow that comes from losing someone you love."

Adam looked away, his chest tight as he remembered those days. The call from Abigail's parents. The days that followed as his own parents traveled with him for the funeral in Colorado. Honestly, he'd felt numb through so much of it.

The nightmares hadn't started until he'd returned to college, determined to finish out the year and graduate. Those months on campus, he had prayed for the return of the numbness. Between the lack of sleep, the nightmares haunting even his daytime hours, it had been a miracle he'd graduated. Looking back, he knew a lot of his professors had been very generous in their grading. They'd known what was going on with him even if he hadn't. He'd been raw, emotional, and if he were being truthful, frantic. Frantic to find an escape from the pain. On the outside he tried to appear calm, but on the inside, he was barely hanging on.

"Losing Abigail changed you in ways I don't think you even comprehend. Overnight, you started pulling away from everything and everyone. Perhaps if you'd come home after graduation, you would have taken the time to deal with her death," she mused.

"Instead, you ran. You took a job in a new city, where no one knew you or Abigail. I understand why. Forcing yourself into a new situation took up your time and energy. It left no room for anything else. With no one around to challenge it, you could bury the pain and the grief.

"The ensuing years set the pattern. You never let yourself get too involved with anyone or too attached to any one place. It's your way of protecting yourself. If you don't let anyone close, you don't risk experiencing that sort of pain again. You created the narrative in your mind that you weren't a 'settle down' type of guy. I don't think you did any of this consciously. What I'm saying is it's time for you to question your beliefs and decisions."

Adam fought back nausea. It was hard enough to revisit Abigail's death but thinking of the implications her accident had on him made him want to run. Again. And wasn't that her point? When confronted with this, he ran. Frankly, that ticked him off. Was he that type of guy?

He hadn't thought he was, but what Mrs. S. said felt right. Uncomfortable but right. Was it possible his whole life was about him avoiding pain? But what did it say when returning to Phoenix caused his stomach to tie itself in a knot? The company was waiting on him to provide a return date, and he hadn't been able to bring himself to make that call.

Worse yet, were his beliefs about himself based on a story he created? Did he have a skewed perception of himself? While he and Abigail weren't engaged, he'd been positive they would be sometime soon. He'd had their married life planned out where they settled some place together, eventually welcoming kids. He would have coached soccer and Abigail would be famous for her donations to the PTA bake sale. When Abigail died on that icy road in Colorado, all those dreams died with her.

Mrs. S. grabbed their bowls and worked around the kitchen, giving him space. He put his head in his hands, before looking up, his eyes tracking her automatically as she pulled trays of baked goods, boxed up items and went to refill the bakery cases in the front.

A deep sense of sorrow settled in his chest as he thought

about all the years he'd wasted. He'd not only been detached from new friends; he'd pulled away from family, past friends and even this town. How many relationships had he short-changed, walked away from?

If he'd dealt with Abigail's death differently, what would his life look like now? Would he have that wife, kids, and home? He ached for the loss of what might have been. He was a man who didn't have roots, and he'd done it all to himself.

Mrs. S. came back, putting down a tall glass of milk and a slice of pie. She left to grab herself the same and settled down beside him again, not speaking, just slowly eating her pie. Looking down Adam realized it was his favorite: peanut butter.

Looking at her, he could only think of one thing. "What have I done?"

Putting her fork down, she laid her hand on his arm and gave it a squeeze. "You've been human. You have a wonderful life, an excellent career and people who love you."

His snort echoed in the kitchen. "I've wasted years. A career I love, yes, but at what cost? What do I have to show for it? I've never stayed in one place long enough to have a deep connection to people or places. I have people who love me, but I've walked away from so many. And I haven't been there for those who've stuck by me."

"You're focusing on what you don't have," she interrupted. "When you have so much. You just don't realize it." Seeing he wasn't convinced, she continued. "Your roots are here, in Jennings. You can find that in Phoenix, too, if that's what you want. Wherever you are is home. The question is, what do you want your life to look like tomorrow, next year or five years down the road? What are you building your life toward rather than what are you running away from?"

Wherever you are is home. Her comment resonated. Was he capable of creating that in Phoenix? What did he want his life to look like? The answer that emerged was surprisingly simple. Then again, there was nothing simple about it.

He wanted Charlotte. He wanted a life with her and what they could create together. Somewhere along the way, he'd fallen in love.

He pictured her laughing at some dumb remark he'd made. Her smile as they talked over dinner. Her sparkling blue eyes before he'd kissed her. He felt alive with her. She inspired him and made him want to be a better version of himself. She made him want to be a settling down type of guy.

He took a bite of pie, savoring the remarkable taste before taking a sip of milk. As he put down the glass he muttered, "Wherever you are is home."

"What was that, Adam?"

"Wherever you are is home," he stated a little louder. That wasn't right. Looking over at Mrs. S., he said, "That's not true."

"Sure, it is. You just need to decide it is and work at it."

"No," he interjected. "Home isn't wherever I am. Home is where Charlotte is."

The smile that spread across Mrs. S.'s face was filled with joy. "Took you long enough to realize," she drawled.

"I love her," he said. He needed to hear it out loud. "I'm in love with Charlotte." He let those words sink in, savoring the happiness they produced. It felt like he was seeing things clearly for the first time in years. For the first time since Abigail. The sorrow over losing her was still there, but it no longer made his gut twist.

"It's more than that," he continued slowly, more so to himself. "It's not just Charlotte. I mean, it is. She's everything, but I want more."

"What do you mean by more?" she prompted.

"I want what she has," he replied, startling himself. He wasn't sure why he'd said that but now that he had, he needed to think about it. "I want what she has here," he puzzled out.

Looking at Mrs. S., he continued, "I want the type of life Charlotte has here in Jennings. I want us, Charlotte and me, to create that life together. You're right. I have roots here and being back has only reminded me how much I love it here.

"But that's going to take some serious problem solving. Not

only is Charlotte currently not talking to me, but my job is in Phoenix. Although perhaps I can work out a deal with my boss to work from here. I know he wants everyone to return, but maybe I could stay here and travel back to Phoenix when necessary or to wherever the client is."

Now that what he wanted was clear to him, his mind was racing with possibilities to make it happen. "If I stayed here, I could help my parents with streamlining the business."

"About that," Mrs. S. interjected. "Your mom said it hasn't been going well. You and your dad keep locking horns. More of that is not the solution."

"No, it isn't," he agreed. "I have to stop pressuring him to make a change, any change. If I'm staying here, I can partner with my parents to implement changes over time, rather than trying to get in as many improvements as possible before I have to leave."

"Your mom says he's made many changes already."

"That's true. If the store improvements take longer or don't happen, it's not a total loss. Although I'd hope he would be more open to things and perhaps expansion if I was here to assist him. Hey," he added, a smile tugging at his lips. "If I'm here maybe they can even take a vacation, travel more." His eyes lit with the possibility of his parents enjoying more time together. Not that the store was a burden to them, it would just be nice to see them take a break and relax. They'd worked hard for years to build the business. Sitting back and enjoying the fruits of their labor would be a fitting reward.

"I'm going to need to get a hold of Matt and see if the company will even entertain something like this."

"And if they won't?"

"I'll figure out something. I can always get a job in Connecticut. It might take a little longer to get everything in place, but I can do it." He fell silent, concern dampening his excitement.

"Mrs. S.," he said quietly. "Charlotte's not talking to me. How can I be sure she's on board with this if she won't listen to me?"

"What happened between you and Lottie was heartbreaking.

She's hurt and scared, just as you were. Her fear of you leaving her undermined everything. She may not listen to words, but she can't deny facts."

"I'm not sure I understand."

"You can tell her you're not leaving Jennings. But those are just words. It doesn't mean it's actually happening. You arrange your life to stay in Jennings and then go see her—in person!" she stressed. "Then it's not just you saying the words. It's a fact. Work things out before you see her so she knows you're serious. Your actions tell the story. Her damn ex-boyfriend left some deep scars on her heart. You'll need to help her overcome those."

"What if I rearrange my whole life, and she won't forgive me?"

Mrs. S. took a moment before responding, "You're going to have to take a leap of faith. Just ask yourself one question." Her eyes captured Adam's. "Is she worth fighting for?"

Adam knew the clear answer to that question.

CHAPTER TWENTY-THREE

Charlotte

Charlotte gave the fabric a final twitch before stepping back to look at the results. It had been a hard week but seeing Alex in the gown made up for a lot. Finishing the dress had taken all of her focus but hadn't stopped thoughts of Adam torturing her. It was like a loose tooth she couldn't stop herself from wiggling no matter how bad the pain was. How long would it take for her to think of him and not feel gutted?

Giving herself a mental shake, she shoved any thoughts of Adam deep down. Today was all about the bride. And what a stunning bride she was. Catching Alex's eyes in the mirror, she was quickly crying along with her cousin.

"Stop," Alex said, crying and laughing at the same time. "You're going to ruin my makeup before I even make it down the aisle!"

Rachel walked over to press a handful of tissues into Charlotte's hand. "I think we're all going to need these today." She walked over to Alex, tissue in hand, and started blotting tears before they could mar the bride's mascara.

Charlotte was so relieved that Lisa and Rachel had both agreed to come early to the wedding site. Between transporting the dress and getting Alex ready, it was all-hands-on-deck. Lisa came over and the four friends took a moment to look at the dress.

"You added more lace, Lottie," Alex said, turning in the mirror to see all of the gown. "I just saw it on Wednesday. You must have been working around the clock. You didn't need to do that."

Charlotte reached down to align the veil better on the floor. "I thought the veil needed just a bit more lace in sections. It wasn't that hard to add." The thought of it not being perfect had driven her to make the last-minute addition. It had also helped distract her from crumbling into a puddle of nerves.

Alex and Jason had found a fantastic location to hold the wedding. A grand estate house with beautiful grounds and sweeping views of the ocean, it was going to be a stunning background to their day. A chapel on-site would hold the service and followed by the reception in the main house. Arriving this morning, they'd been directed to a beautiful suite of rooms where Alex could get ready. It was one of those moments where time passed in the blink of an eye, but at a turtle's pace.

Lisa raised her champagne glass and toasted, "To the bride!"

"To the bride," they all echoed before sipping.

When the door flew open, she recognized her aunt's voice even before she was visible. "Alex, it's almost time, are you —" She came to a halt as she entered the room. Staring at her daughter, her eyes filled with tears. "Oh, Alex," she cried. "You look dazzling."

As Rachel was the closest, she leaned over and handed Aunt Jennifer a tissue. Laughing, Jennifer blotted her eyes. "Thank you, dear. Can't mess up my makeup before photos." Turning back to Alex, she beamed at her daughter. "Stunning. Simply stunning, Alex."

"Thanks, Mom. The dress is more than I could ever have hoped for. Did you see the Scottish lace Lottie put in?"

Charlotte stepped forward and walked her aunt through the distinct elements of the gown. She could hear the photographer's occasional shutter click and hoped she was capturing wonderful memories. Charlotte wouldn't forget this moment any time soon.

When she was done, Aunt Jennifer surprised her by giving her a big hug. Pulling back, she grasped Charlotte by the shoulders. "Thank you for creating such a beautiful and meaningful gown. How you've incorporated little details like the Scottish lace is what makes you such a fantastic designer," she finished, beaming at Charlotte.

Charlotte couldn't believe her ears. Such high praise from her aunt was making her want to break out in a happy dance right there. Then she heard a voice and a question that sucked the dancing vibe right out of her.

"I'm sorry," a voice said from the doorway. "I must have heard you incorrectly, Jennifer. Did I hear you say Charlotte designed this gown?"

Charlotte cringed, pivoting toward the door. Biting back a groan, she said "Hi, Mom."

Ignoring her sister's pained expression, Aunt Jennifer bustled over to her sister, looping her arm through hers. "Katherine! Oh, come look. Your daughter created the most miraculous gown for Alex."

Charlotte hid a grimace as Aunt Jennifer pulled her mom over. Not knowing what to say, she kept quiet as her aunt led her mother through the finer points. She ended by asking, "Isn't this the most beautiful gown you've ever seen, Katherine?"

Charlotte regretted the champagne and snacks she'd nibbled on while getting Alex ready. They were lead in her stomach, threatening to make her ill. In her mind she was bolting from the room, but for some reason she couldn't get her feet to follow through.

Her mother gave her a sweeping glance, her eyes piercing Charlotte's. Looking back at her sister, she gave a tense smile and said, "I hadn't heard Charlotte was making the gown."

Her mother paused, seeming to struggle with herself. She glanced over to Charlotte, but turned back to her sister before adding, "It is certainly beautiful. She did a lovely job."

From her mom, those words were the equivalent of a Nobel Prize. Did she wish her mom was more complimentary? Sure, but let's not get crazy. Before she could start writing her acceptance speech, her mom spoke and harpooned any warm fuzzy feelings that may have existed.

"It's charming to see that Charlotte's little hobby was useful."

Charlotte felt the slap of that comment but tried not to let it get under her skin. Looking back at the dress she created, she felt the resurgence of her pride. No matter what her mother thought or said, what she'd created was beautiful.

"Oh no, Aunt Katherine," Alex said turning from the mirror. "This isn't a hobby."

Looking at Charlotte, she continued, "I have a friend coming today who would like to meet you. She's looking for a wedding gown and wants to set up an appointment. Just remind me if I get all excited and lose my head. I'll introduce you two at the reception. It's the least I can do after everything you've done for me."

"Funny you should mention that," Lisa said coming up beside Charlotte. "I was telling a woman I work with about the dress, and she also wants an appointment."

Lisa's eyes were twinkling, and she was having trouble hiding her smirk. Her roommate was well acquainted with the difficulties Charlotte had with her mom, especially around her desire to design wedding gowns. Lisa was thoroughly enjoying announcing that little tidbit in front of her.

"So, Alex is right," Lisa continued. "This isn't a little hobby. Congratulations! That dress has launched your business."

Her friends cheered and started talking all at once. Charlotte wasn't sure what to say. While Rachel went around filling champagne glasses, Charlotte noticed her mother had discreetly left. She would not let that damper this moment or her joy in today. The girls were right. This dress was the start of something amazing.

With the glasses filled, Rachel lifted hers and said, "To Alex for being the most beautiful bride and to Lottie for designing the most beautiful gown. Cheers!"

Clinking glasses, Charlotte felt a pang of regret. She'd give anything to share this surprising day with Adam. Annoyed with herself for thinking about him again, she focused back on what the girls were saying.

"She could call it Bridal Reincarnation," Rachel said.

"Hmm," Lisa replied. "That sounds like wedding gowns for zombies."

Over the laughter, Charlotte asked, "What are you guys talking about?"

"We're coming up with the name of your new business," Alex offered. "I was thinking Rehab Bridal. You know, for those of us struggling with a gown addiction."

"Now that's a great tag line," Rachel giggled. "But it sounds like she'd be hosting a TV show. What about Metamorphosis Gowns?"

"Ohhhh," Alex cried. "Think of the butterflies we can put in the logo and marketing materials!"

"You guys are crazy," Charlotte laughed. They were certifiable, and she wouldn't have it any other way.

"I know what you should name it," Lisa said, gazing toward the door.

Charlotte turned to see what had captured her friend's attention.

"Adam," she whispered.

What was he doing here? The shock of seeing him took her breath away. Oh, and he looked so freakin' hot. Why did he have to look so amazing? His gray suit fit him well, making her want nothing more than to run her hands across his muscular shoulders. He looked fantastic in jeans and a t-shirt, but Adam in a suit was making her feel all tingly.

She was pulled from her visual buffet when Lisa touched her arm, "Lottie." Lisa waited until Charlotte looked at her before continuing. "You should name it Second Chance Bridal," Lisa said with a smile. And a nod toward Adam. "You always say every gown deserves a second chance."

With a last meaningful look, Lisa turned to the others and said, "Why don't we put the final touches on Alex's outfit and make sure our champagne glasses are topped off?"

Charlotte thought for a minute Lisa was going to draw everyone away to give her a private moment with Adam. She should have known better. Of course, her best friend was going to top up the drinks and get a front row seat to watch all this unfold. Well, it didn't matter. She had nothing to say to him.

She felt the burn of his betrayal fire through her once again. He'd lied about his job. He had always intended to leave her. It was the situation with Todd all over again. At least this time she'd seen it coming before he snuck out of town. It didn't make the pain any less, but she could keep a shred of her dignity. Squaring her shoulders, she turned to face him.

Adam stepped into the room and looked over at Alex. "You look lovely. Your groom is a very lucky man," he said. Facing Charlotte, he searched her eyes for a brief period. "The gown is impressive. You did a fantastic job."

She needed to get this over with quickly, or she'd forget how much she hated him and instead throw herself into his arms. "Why are you here, Adam?" she said with heat. "What do you want?"

Adam took another step toward her, his face beseeching. "I'm sorry to show up like this. I know you're busy." He paused, taking a deep breath. "You aren't answering my calls or texts, and I need to talk to you."

"I don't have time for this," she said in a clipped tone. "And we have nothing to discuss. You're returning to your life, your girlfriend and your job in Phoenix. So, you see, there's nothing we need to talk about."

"Charlotte, please." He raised his hand toward her. "Give me five minutes. That's all. Let me just say what I need to say and then,"—he paused—"then, if you want me to leave, I'll go."

Charlotte didn't need to look over at her friends to know they all were hoping she'd give in. His being here negated her ability to push away the pain and loss of losing him. The weight of which was already threatening to grind her down under its heel again. Perhaps listening to whatever he had to say before he left would give her a small measure of closure

"Say what you need to say," she replied, crossing her hands over her chest. "You have exactly five minutes, not a moment more."

If Adam was disappointed with her less than hospitable reply, he didn't show it. He looked down at his watch before spearing her with his glance. "Again, I'm sorry to barge in. I need to give my company an answer by Monday morning, and I can't give them that until I know what you'll say."

"What do you mean?"

Ignoring her question, he carried on. "Zara and I are not in a relationship." He looked down and frowned. "I know those are just words, and I have nothing to prove to you that she isn't a part of my life." He looked up. His gaze roamed her face, his eyes intense. "All I can say is that she wasn't a part of my life before and absolutely isn't now.

"When I was let go from my job, I ultimately thought it was a good thing. I haven't been"—he paused searching for a word—"I haven't been happy for a while. I just didn't realize it. Returning to Jennings was about me determining my next steps. Was I going to stay in Phoenix or find another job somewhere else?

"Then I met you. Being with you made me see what was missing from my life. A new job or a new city wouldn't fix what was wrong. What you have here in Jennings, the family and connections you've created, is everything I always wanted but didn't think I could have.

"When Abigail died," he said, his voice tense, "I convinced myself I just wasn't the type of guy who would settle down. I've been believing that lie for years. Moving around and running from any type of connection with people. I won't keep repeating that mistake.

"You challenge how I see myself," he said, letting out a harsh breath. Raking his fingers through his hair, he shook his head before gazing up at her once more. "I want my life to have more meaning."

He paused again his hands clasped into fists. "I don't know if this is making any sense."

"I'm glad you realized you want your life to be more meaningful," she intoned. "But that changes nothing between us."

"No, it does," he replied leaning toward her. "Don't you see? It has everything to do with you," he explained, his words coming faster. "I believed something about myself that wasn't true. I was too afraid to look at my actions. I mean, really look at them. And when I met you, I realized I wanted more from my life. I realized I could be different.

"Agh," he growled pacing in front of her. "I'm not explaining this very well. It sounded so much better when I practiced it."

"You practiced this?" she asked. She didn't understand the point he was trying to make, but that he'd practiced moved her.

Adam didn't acknowledge her question as he continued pacing. "But I have to let the company know. As much as I want to say it doesn't matter, what you say does matter."

He stopped and looked at her. "Just tell me, Charlotte. I need to know. If you don't love me, I won't stay in Jennings. It would be too painful to see you and love you and not have you in my life. I'll go back to Phoenix and try to make a life there, but that's hard to picture because any future I dream about includes you."

Charlotte blinked a few times. Had she heard him correctly? "You love me?" she whispered.

"Yes, I love you," he replied, almost cross that she questioned it. "I love the way you love the people in your life. I love that you rescue wedding gowns and see the beauty and possibility in them. I love that you hum and mutter to yourself when you're looking through fabric," he said with a smile. "And I love the way you look at me with those beautiful eyes of yours as if you could see all the way to my soul. I love everything about you."

It was difficult to process everything Adam was saying. Hearing him say he loved her made all her anger and pain melt. He loved her. He wanted a future with her. How could she not know that he loved her? Had she so misjudged things?

"So, you never were returning to Phoenix to be with Zara?" She hated having to ask, but she needed the words.

"Never," he said. "We weren't dating. And even if we were, that would have ended when I met you. I'm sorry I wasn't clear about my job. I wasn't trying to hide it from you. I don't want to hide anything from you. You believe me, don't you?" he begged.

"I do," she replied, her mind churning. "I'm sorry for not letting you explain. It's just..." Her voice quivered. She cleared her throat and tried again. "It's just that this felt like when Todd left. And I can't go through that again."

She inhaled deeply and continued, her voice stronger. "I love you too." She held up her hand when Adam rushed toward her. Because she loved him, she couldn't let him sacrifice himself, no matter how much she wanted him in her life.

"I love you, but I can't ask you to give up everything—your career, your lifestyle—and stay in Jennings." She shook her head vehemently stepping back when he stretched out a hand to touch her. "It may seem like the right decision now, but down the road you'll resent me for it."

Adam stepped closer and grabbed both of her hands. "I'm not giving up anything. I'm gaining so much. I get to stay here and help my parents with their business and be with you, but I also get to keep my job. I worked it all out. I can work remotely with some travel now and then. So, I'm not sacrificing anything I care about."

Charlotte wasn't sure when her tears started, but they now fell freely. What he was saying was so fantastic, it was almost too good to be true. Could she take a chance that this was all real and that it would work out? She so wanted to believe it, but she couldn't make the leap. She knew it was just fear. But that fear was clogging her throat when all she wanted to say was stay.

Shaking her hands to get her attention, Adam continued. "Listen, I've realized a lot of things recently. For years I've believed the lie that I told myself that my career was everything, and that I loved moving from place to place. What I've realized is that what I've been doing by not committing to a place or a person has just been me running out of fear.

"When Abigail died, it was so painful and overwhelming. I never wanted to feel that way again. What I didn't realize is that when we care for people or places, what we gain is so much greater than the worst we fear. I won't live my life running and afraid. I'm starting it right here, right now. With you.

"I know you're scared," he whispered. "Honestly, I am too. But there's really only one question you need to answer. Nothing else matters."

The intensity of his gaze electrified her, and she could feel his hands caressing hers. It felt like everything around them had stopped for this moment. She took a trembling breath trying to control her emotions and find balance.

"Charlotte," he said. "All I need to know is do you love me as much as I love you?"

Her heart answered immediately, but her mind kept her lips firmly shut. She loved him with all that she was. He had seen through her. Seen her fear and named it. He was right—it did just come down to one question.

Would she let fear rob her of a life with Adam? He was standing up and declaring that fear would not stop him. How could she not do the same? No way was she going to walk away from him just because she was afraid.

Reaching up, she ran her hand across his cheek. "Adam, I am crazy in love with you and don't want to picture a future without you in it." She smiled up at him, watching as her words hit him and his lips stretched into a big smile.

"You love me," he whispered, ducking his head down to hers.

Before she could respond, he captured her lips with his and the outside world ceased to exist. The kiss was raw and wild causing her heart to pound in response. Running her hands up his chest, she wrapped her arms around his neck and kissed him back with everything she had.

Wrapping his arm around her, his hand splayed across her back. A quick pull and she was pressed against every incredible inch of him. She wanted to take him somewhere and kiss every inch of his body and then start from the top again.

Eventually the noise cut through her consciousness and Charlotte noticed all the other people in the room. Most of them making comments about getting a room or steaming up the windows. Breaking off the kiss, she leaned her forehead against Adam's, both of them struggling to control their ragged breathing. When she heard Lisa call for more champagne to toast her roommate finally getting her head out of her ass, she couldn't help but laugh. Leave it to Lisa.

Her hand clasped in Adam's she turned to face her friends. "You guys are the best." She wiped the last of the tears from her face. "I'm so glad you were all here."

Alex reached out and pulled her into a tight hug. "I'm so happy for you," she whispered. Pulling back, she glared at both of them. "I love you," she said her voice playful, "but if you don't start making this day all about me, I will go all bridezilla on you!"

Charlotte laughed, her heart feeling like it would float out of her chest. How one body could contain so much happiness and joy was inconceivable. "We wouldn't dream of it, Alex!" She glanced at Adam, delighted by all the love she saw in his eyes.

He wound his arm around her waist and turned to Alex. "If I've learned anything from Charlotte, it's that the bride is always right."

A server appeared with another bottle of champagne, the event coordinator right behind him. As Lisa started topping off everyone's glass, Charlotte could see Rachel approaching the agitated woman in the doorway. Their conversation was tense but brief.

Rachel rejoined the group and silently shook her head at Charlotte's look of inquiry. With a sharp nod toward Alex, it was clear this wasn't something to discuss in front of the bride.

"To Adam and Charlotte," her cousin toasted. "Finally! And to getting this day back on track!"

No sooner had they all taken a sip than Aunt Jennifer clapped her hands for their attention. "I hate to break this up, but we have to get my little girl down the aisle!"

Everyone was in motion at once. While her aunt and Alex went to do final touches on her makeup, Rachel walked over to Charlotte and motioned for Lisa to join them.

"What was that about?" Charlotte whispered.

Looking over her shoulder to make sure Alex couldn't hear them, Rachel turned back and explained, "The event coordinator said there's a problem with the caterer. There was a glitch with part of the food order and he's saying he can't serve the meal."

"Oh no," Lisa said. "No way. Let me just go have a little chat with him."

Rachel snorted, "We want him to be cooking, not nursing a broken arm."

"Are you saying I have no tact?"

"Exactly," Charlotte added. "I'll go handle this. You guys stay with Alex."

Rachel stopped Charlotte with her hand. "I'll go. Alex needs you now. I'll use all my charm,"—she shot Lisa a look—"and smooth out any ruffled feathers to get this wedding back on schedule. Just don't let Alex know."

With that, Rachel left, and Charlotte and Lisa went over to join the bride in front of the mirror. Charlotte took a quick circle around Alex, looking over all the aspects of the dress. Adjusting small pieces here and there, she lifted the train and veil and gave them one last fluff.

As the fabric of the train floated down and settled gracefully on the floor, Charlotte stepped back, her eyes pooling with tears. She'd done it. Her design vision had come to life. More importantly, it worked. The fitted bodice accentuated Alex's curves, while the yards of delicate fabric and lace drifted around her, giving her an ethereal look. Judging by her cousin's smile as she stood looking into the mirror, she was just as happy with the results.

In just a few moments, her custom designed dress was about to make its debut down the aisle in front of family, friends, and strangers. And Charlotte didn't give a damn. She was a wedding gown designer, and no one could take that away from her, nor would she let them. Her friends were right, this wasn't a hobby. This was a business. Her business.

A stray tear made its way down her cheek, only to be stopped by Adam's thumb wiping it away. He looked into her eyes, searching. “Are those happy tears or bad tears?” he asked.

Smiling back, she said, “Happy tears. Definitely happy tears.”

Adam moved beside her, his arm wrapping around her waist. Looking over the dress, his smile grew. “It really is stunning, Charlotte. Congratulations.”

While his words effused her with warmth, his slowly caressing hand left a heat trail on her body. She’d thought she’d lost him forever, that she would never have a moment like this. But he was here, and it felt like all her dreams were coming true at once.

“Thank you for giving me another chance, Charlotte,” he said, his voice husky with emotion.

Curling into him, she placed her hand on his chest, gazing into his intense green eyes. His heart pounded beneath her fingers, and she couldn’t fathom how she thought she could walk away from him. So much had changed in the past two months, the past two minutes even. Reaching up, she grazed her fingers over his jaw, delighted to see his eyes darken with desire.

“Thank you for coming to find me and for giving us another chance,” she whispered. She had a thought that made her smile stretch further. As usual, Lisa was correct. She laughed, enjoying how right this felt.

“I am all about second chances.” She was still laughing when his mouth descended on hers.

ACKNOWLEDGEMENT

While writing is a solitary practice, bringing a book to fruition is an enormously large group effort. From friends and family who have heard tirelessly about my writing pursuits to my beta readers and all of the industry professionals who helped along the way, my eternal gratitude for your generosity and assistance.

For Stacey Donovan and her gracious support and advice. Without your thoughtful insights, I fear this book would have languished in the drawer of my desk forever.

Many thanks to Lindsay Guzzardo who changed my approach to writing forever. From editor to agent and back again, it has been a pleasure.

To the real Mrs. Mac, Mrs. S and Mrs. Albee. There are simply no words big enough.

MYB Textiles, specifically, Margo Graham, Design Director for their lace information and education and being willing to talk about Scottish thistle design embroidery with a stranger.

Many thanks to Brianna St. John for her editing skills and eternal optimism. The universe graced me with a true gift when our paths crossed. I could not ask for a better writing partner or friend.

Everyone should have a friend like Christi Spadoni. Not only for her amazing overall support, but for her culinary enthusiasm and willingness to try new recipes. She is my go-to food writing muse. From madeleines to turnovers, she's ready to brainstorm food and feed me cookies. What's better than that?

And as always, to Dianne Sullivan. Mentor, friend, inspiration, giver of gifts.

ABOUT THE AUTHOR

E R Cullen

We can neither confirm nor deny that E may have a collection of wedding gowns hidden somewhere in her house.

When not writing, she can be found searching for unique and new hiding places for her fabric, yarn, and gown stash. She lives in Connecticut with her patient and supremely awesome husband, and she is guardian to a very high maintenance cat whose love she attempts to earn daily.

Stop by and visit:
Facebook.com/ercullenauthor
Instagram.com/ercullenauthor

Made in the USA
Columbia, SC
25 June 2023

19237373R00143